Protecting his Heart

GUARDING ROYALTY 2

ELOUISE EAST

Contents

Author note

If you would like to see any potential triggers for this book and any other books I've written, please go to this link on my website: https://elouiseeast.com/triggers

1

Owen

Owen Morris stared into the night sky from where he stood by the window of the suite they were using for the New Year's Eve party. "They" being the royal family. The Sutcliffes had invited all the security staff for the evening, and most had accepted because they were all close—not just a working relationship but as friends, too. A strange dynamic that had been born of the threats against the royal family over the past few years and how closely the security staff had worked with them during it. It was hard to turn off his work mode, and his eyes kept scanning both the room and the outdoor area for new threats.

He slipped his hands into his pockets as the first firework lit the sky, smiling slightly at the thought of Amy, his little sister. She had always loved New Year's Eve fireworks, saying that there was always something different from knowing those rainbow-coloured explosions of light meant a new year had started. Owen loved that description, and even though Amy was no longer with them—it had been twenty-one years now—he remembered it fondly, despite the ache in his heart from its missing piece.

Someone came to stand beside him and nudged his shoulder with theirs. "Penny for them," Evan said, handing him a tall glass of something clear and fizzy.

"Just thinking about Amy," he murmured. "She would've loved these even more than the ones we snuck in to watch all those years ago."

Evan chuckled. "She would've. She might've been the bane of our teenage years, but she was soft on the inside."

Owen sipped his drink, coughing when he realised there was alcohol in it, too. He banged his chest with his fist. "I was expecting lemonade."

"With a little vodka added in."

"A little?" Owen smirked.

Evan winked. "A little."

Owen couldn't help staring at his best friend. The attraction had never died down—would never die down—but he wished it would. He returned his gaze to the inky map of stars above, shoving everything he felt into that locked box he kept inside him. That box he'd created seven years ago when he had pushed Evan away too hard, and Evan had left the country instead of fighting for him—for them.

He didn't blame the man. After all, who wanted to spend a blissful night with the person they'd admitted to being in love with and then be told the next morning that it was a mistake? No one, that was who. Owen had thought he was doing the right thing. He hadn't wanted to mess up their friendship and that friendship with Dominic, the third of their triangle of best friends, so he'd pretended it was for the best.

Unfortunately, the pain that had speared through Evan's eyes after Owen's words that morning had branded itself onto Owen's brain, and it had sent Evan over the edge. He'd packed and left for Italy the following week, taking Owen's heart with him.

"Is Dominic around?" Evan asked.

Owen cleared his throat. "He is somewhere. Randall is bustling around, trying to work, but His Majesty keeps scolding him, and Dominic is trying to keep Randall relaxed. Not sure how well it's working."

Evan snorted. "It's probably not. It's all well and good inviting those who work for you to a family gathering, but it's not always possible to chill when you're not used to it."

"I'm a lot more comfortable here than I used to be. The Sutcliffes certainly don't give up when they want you involved."

In the reflection of the window, Evan's lopsided grin appeared, surrounded by his barely-there beard, and Owen's stomach swooped. What he wouldn't give to feel that against his skin again.

A hand clapped on his shoulder and, judging by Evan's jump, on Evan's shoulder, too.

"Are you enjoying yourselves?" Dominic asked, sticking his head between the two of them.

Owen grinned. "You know it."

Dominic raised his eyebrows. "Sure looks like it."

Evan lifted his glass. "We have drinks. We have fireworks. We have music. What more do we need?"

Dominic opened his mouth, glanced at them in turn, and then seemed to think better of what he'd been about to say. He smiled. "We're having a nightcap in our room after we finish if you want to join us."

Owen chuckled. "I'll let you and Randall have a break from me. Have fun."

Evan nodded. "I agree. I've seen enough of your 'nightcaps' to know things get way more personal than I want them to."

Owen could attest to that. Dominic and Randall could still not keep their hands off each other, but they had only been together for a few months. They were still in the "honeymoon" period of the relationship, but they'd been through so much in such a short time that they might as well have been together for years. Someone they'd thought was on their side had targeted Dominic and kidnapped Randall, the king's personal assistant. When Dominic found him, they'd shot Dominic and left him for dead, but it seemed that bad guy was only the tip of the iceberg. Someone else was running the show, and no one knew who it was. They were all on high alert, but nothing had happened since. It was hard to keep things light when they weren't sure when the other shoe was going to drop—or bullet was going to fly.

Dominic grinned. "Can you blame me?" He looked over his shoulder in Randall's direction, and Owen knew they'd lost him.

"Oh, god. Go on. We'll see you tomorrow," Owen said, pushing Dominic in his boyfriend's direction.

He watched his best friend aim straight for the man of his dreams, slide his arms around his waist from behind and press a kiss to his temple. Randall closed his eyes and smiled. Owen sighed and turned his gaze back to the window, downing his drink despite the burning in his throat. He grimaced as it settled uneasily in his stomach. Evan nudged his shoulder again, and Owen found a fake smile to send his way.

He met Evan's gaze and couldn't look away. The green eyes shimmered whenever a firework exploded in front of them, and Evan swiped his tongue across his lips, leaving a glistening trail behind. Owen swallowed. Hard. He wanted to close the distance between them. To remind himself what it felt like to have Evan's mouth against his. To claim what was his.

The thought snapped him out of his trance, and he blinked and faced the window in time to see a starburst of colour explode. It was what his brain felt like, too.

He cleared his throat. Evan wasn't his. "What plans do you have for tomorrow?"

Evan sighed. "No plans at all."

Owen couldn't stop himself from asking, "Boxing practice?"

"You're on."

They dropped into silence again as the fireworks finished, and when Owen couldn't take it anymore, he clapped Evan on the shoulder. "I'm heading out. See you later."

"Okay."

The uncertainty in Evan's voice was apparent, but Owen couldn't stop to explain. He needed to get out of there before he did something stupid. Again. He made his goodbyes and headed home—the same place that Evan lived at the moment. Something Owen occasionally wished they could change. Seeing Evan every day was the best and worst thing in his life. Reminding him what he could've had if only he'd not been so scared of losing him. But then he'd lost him, anyway. It served him right.

Letting himself into the house he'd recently finished renovating, he closed the door and sighed, staring around him and seeing evidence of Evan. It was both a curse and a blessing to see Evan's jumper slung over the back of a chair, a book he was currently reading resting on the coffee table and his shoes by the front door. The idea that they could seamlessly fit into each other's life was like soaking in a bath and letting the warm water do its thing. Then harsh reality intruded, and the water turned ice cold.

He inhaled and blew it out, heading to the kitchen to grab a glass of water to take to his room. Closing his door gave him another small barrier between him and Evan, but it was never enough. He stripped down and slid under the covers, still in his boxers, and laid on his back, staring at the dark ceiling, the occasional firework and car lights travelling across the space. He purposefully kept his curtains a light colour so the sun would help to wake him in the morning. It was a moot point during the winter when the sun wasn't up as early as Owen usually was, but it worked, for the most part.

The front door opened, and Owen froze. His ears strained for every sound he could grasp of Evan, but the man was almost as stealthy as Owen could be; it must have been his years of entering patient's room quietly as a nurse. The pipes creaked, and the distant sound of water connected his thoughts. He closed his eyes, trying not to imagine Evan in the shower, suds sliding all over his body. His cock responded, but as always, he ignored it, unwilling to stroke himself off when Evan was mere feet away. Instead, he pulled the pillow over his head and squeezed his eyes tighter, wishing for sleep.

It must've worked because his alarm woke him the next morning. Even when he wasn't working, he made sure to get up at a reasonable time. He climbed from the bed and immediately dropped into press-ups, needing to get the blood flowing through his body before he had any kind of food or drink. It was a routine he'd perfected through the years and one he rarely changed.

When his muscles burnt from use and his head cleared, he jumped into the shower and cleaned off before dressing in joggers and a T-shirt, ready for his sparring session with Evan. He strode for the kitchen, his stomach fluttering when he found Evan already there, coffee in hand.

"Morning," he said, grabbing a mug from the cupboard and pouring himself some delicious nectar.

"Morning." Evan's voice sounded like gravel, and it lit Owen's blood, a reminder of how he'd sounded that night. He ignored it. "What time do you want to go?"

"Whenever you're ready." Neither had to work that day, which was a miracle. With Owen's shifts as Prince Frederick's bodyguard and Evan's shifts as an A&E nurse, it was often difficult to match their schedules.

"Okay. Give me five."

Evan left the kitchen, leaving Owen to brace his hands on the counter, his head lowered to stop himself from following. It was more difficult to control his impulses each time. He shook his head and focused on finishing his coffee before collecting his bag from his room. The royal family gave their bodyguards access to the training rooms at Windsor Castle whenever they wanted to, and they'd extended that invitation to Evan as well. It made things a lot easier for them all.

"Ready?" he said when Evan returned and just as the doorbell rang.

Owen opened the front door and stopped with a frown when no one was there. His gaze caught on the parcel on the top step. He grabbed it and took it to the dining table, studying the label.

"Who's it for?"

"Me," Owen said. "I can't remember ordering anything."

He grabbed a knife and sliced open the tape holding the box closed after a second of concern that it was something more than an item he'd forgotten he'd ordered. Shaking his head, he opened it. Inside was a box decorated with Christmas paper. He closed the lid again, checking the label. "No return address," he mumbled.

Pulling out the box, he checked the tag, and again, it said his name.

"Did your mum order something and forget to tell you?" Evan asked from beside him.

"No idea." He unwrapped the box, lifted the lid and smiled at the contents. He ran his hand over the soft, dark blue fabric, pulling it free. "It's a scarf."

Evan reached into the box and handed him a piece of paper. "You have a note."

Owen ignored whatever he thought he'd heard in Evan's tone and read what it said.

I thought you might like something NEW for a change.

The word new was in capitals and there was a #2 in the corner, though Owen couldn't think why, but it didn't matter. Someone had sent him a gift. A smile crept across his face.

"Who's it from?"

Owen shook his head. "No idea. There's no signature."

"Ooh, you have an admirer," Evan said, heading for the door. "Are we going or not?"

Owen glanced at his best friend and then back at the scarf. Clearing his throat, he wrapped it around his neck, grabbed his bag and followed Evan. It didn't matter what he wanted to ask Evan; it was better if he didn't know. This scarf, whoever it was from, was something for Owen to focus on instead of his unrequited love for his best friend.

When they arrived at the training room, there were already a couple of guards sparring, and he and Evan wrapped their hands before finding a space on the floor.

"Ready?" Owen asked. Instead of answering, Evan took a swipe at him, and Owen leant back in time to avoid it and grinned. "Okay, then. It's on."

Their fists punched and swiped as they ducked and parried, moving across the space, sweat streaking down their bodies. It had been a while since Evan had taken their boxing to such a high intensity, and Owen wondered if something was bothering him.

After one such blow that glanced off Owen's shoulder, he pushed Evan back. "What's got into you?"

Evan shook his hands out, bouncing on the spot. "Nothing. Just have extra energy to get rid of, that's all."

Owen didn't believe him, but he didn't argue. "Again," he said instead. Distracted as he was, after a few minutes, Evan knocked hard enough for him to slam to the floor, his ears ringing.

"Shit! Owen? Are you okay?"

Evan knelt beside him, removing his own gloves before taking Owen's padded helmet off. His hands ran over his head and neck, while Owen studied his expression.

"I'm good," he murmured.

Evan sat back and sighed, shaking his head. "I'm sorry about that. I obviously have more strength than I thought I did."

"You've always had more strength; you just never wanted to believe it." Plus, Owen had deserved the hit after what he'd done. It had been seven years in the making.

Owen pushed himself to a seated position, pulling his hands free from his gloves and beginning the unwrapping process. They sat in silence, the sounds of the other occupants of the room louder because of it.

"Owen—"

Owen stood, gathering his things and heading for his bag. "It's fine, Evan. Don't worry about it." Evan sighed behind him but said nothing else. "I'm going to hit the showers."

He didn't wait for a response, hightailing it out of there as quickly as he could. As he rested his bag on the bench in the bathroom, his fingers found the softness of the scarf, and he stared at it.

"Who are you?" he whispered.

As much as he loved Evan, he hoped he *did* have an admirer because it would help distract Owen from what he couldn't have. He just wished there had been a name or something he could use to contact them with. Even if it was to only say thank you.

"Still mooning over that scarf?" Evan chuckled, and Owen heard him drop his stuff to another bench. "Just don't use it to jack off until you know who it's from, yeah?" he said, heading for the shower.

Owen watched him go, the shorts he wore moulding to his ass and slender thighs. He wasn't misguided by Evan's looks. The man might be slender and look like he couldn't lift a child, but he had so much more strength than anyone could visually see. Owen had once felt those hidden muscles. Had brushed his lips across the skin, his fingers mapping them. Had once had those arms holding him so tightly he couldn't move even if he wanted to. Not that he'd wanted to with Evan's cock deep inside him.

He dropped the scarf back into his bag as his stomach churned and thought better of his idea of showering there, but he could hardly get out of it now. Stripping off, he grabbed a towel and headed for the shower stalls, ignoring Evan as much as he could.

"Did you say you were working tomorrow?" Evan asked.

Owen nodded, and then said, "Yeah. Prince Freddie has an appointment, but my shift finishes mid-afternoon."

Silence, and then, "I'll see you in a couple of days, then."

"Night shift?"

"Yeah, and they've called me in this afternoon. Two people are off sick."

Owen's shoulder lowered. He'd been both looking forward to and dreading spending the day with Evan, disagreeing about movies and TV shows and generally being an ass to each other and Dominic. Same old, same old.

"Rain check on movie plans, then?" Owen said.

"Definitely."

Their silences were more profound since Evan had returned from Italy. Whether that was because Evan had changed during that time or if it was because Owen had, but he wasn't used to it. Whenever they'd spoken on the phone, there had never been these pregnant pauses or uncomfortable silences. Most of the time, Owen was able to cover it up with a question about Italy or a random story about what had happened to him during that time, but recently, it had become more difficult. Despite Evan having been home for around three months, it seemed like he'd never left and that he'd been gone for decades at the same time.

Evan's shower cut off, and he walked past Owen's stall to the changing room. "I'll catch you later."

"See ya. Be safe."

Owen looked over his shoulder just as Evan did, and Evan smiled, though it didn't reach his eyes. "Always am."

He disappeared out of the showers, and Owen focused in front of him. Something had to change, but he had no idea what.

2

Evan

Evan Montgomery inhaled the coffee in the few seconds it took him to walk from the nurses' station to the cubicle he needed to enter. He paused for a second outside of the curtain, draining the dregs of caffeine that he hoped would get him through the next few hours. He threw the cup in the nearby bin and pulled the curtain aside.

"Good morning, Mr White. I'm Evan. You're up with the birds, I see. How are you doing?"

Evan checked the details on the forms he'd picked up and glanced at the monitors, recording what he saw and initialling what he wrote. He smiled at the older man, lying so calmly on the bed.

"I can't sleep in this place, Evan. Far too much bustling around."

"Understandable. I hear you had a fall?"

Mr White huffed. "If you could call it that. I missed the bottom step of my stairs, that's all."

Evan gave a small smile. "We just need to check you out, Mr White. You have a nasty bruise on your head."

"I told my wife we should've moved that radiator. No reason for it being right at the bottom of the stairs like that. Then, when she passed, I didn't see the point of getting it done. Maybe I should've."

Evan chuckled. "Hindsight is twenty-twenty, isn't it?" He fiddled with a few things on the monitors and recorded the numbers before putting the folder back. "Now, Dr Wallis will be here in a few minutes to check you over. Do you have someone coming to pick you up later?"

Mr White nodded, his eyes twitching with the movement, showing he wasn't quite as well as he proclaimed. "My son should be here soon."

"Glad to hear it. Get as much rest as you can manage, okay? I'll see you in a little bit."

Evan left the cubicle, pulling the curtain closed, and strode for the nurses' station, leaning closer to Marie. "Mr White's son should be here soon, he said. Also, he seems to have a headache, though I know he won't answer if I ask. Would you work your magic with him? Please?" He batted his eyelashes at her.

Marie rolled her eyes and sighed. "I suppose I can drop in." She grinned. "He's a lovely man."

"He truly is. I wish for many more like him instead of the shitty ones we seem to be getting tonight." He knew better than to wish for no one to be there.

"Cheers to that."

Evan grabbed the next file and wandered down the room again. One day, he was going to measure just how much he walked during a shift, though it was bound to be miles. His feet were never quite the same after eight hours, even though he'd been doing the job for over ten years. He would've thought he'd be used to it by that point.

When the last half an hour of his shift arrived, he leaned against the station and explained where things were to his replacement—his friend, Matteo. And then he was on his way home. Well, Owen's house. He doubted he would see him because Owen started work at eight in the morning most days, and Evan wouldn't be home until after that. It wasn't a bad thing in some ways because it meant he could drop into bed without worrying about small talk.

Which was exactly what he did, and when he woke, it was slowly, his mind drifting up from the depths of sleep to where the scent of coffee and Owen lived. He rolled to his back, yawned and stretched his arms and body to remove the lingering effects of slumber. Glancing at the clock, he huffed a laugh at its six o'clock offering. Three out of his six A&E shifts were night shifts, which he didn't mind because he had no social life to talk of. Owen and Dominic were understanding enough to work around his hours when they could, and the other times, they just wouldn't see each other for several days. Not much different from his time in Italy when he barely saw them.

Now he had two days off—well, one and a half now he'd slept most of his first day away—and he wanted to spend some time with his friends. If he could. He hadn't checked their plans, so had no idea if they were busy or not.

Rolling to his side, he stared at the curtained window, his mind on his ex-lover. His best friend. His one true love. He was a sappy ass, but it was true. Evan thought he'd be able to live without Owen, which was why he'd retreated to Italy after Owen had broken his heart. It hadn't been far enough, but it had also been too far. In the end, he couldn't stand being away from him even if he couldn't have him as more than a friend. So, he'd sucked it up and returned home with his figurative tail between his legs. But not before he'd had a talking to from an Italian friend.

Living with Owen hadn't been his plan. He'd wanted to get a place of his own, but when Evan saw the state of Owen's new purchase, he'd agreed to help him fix it up, staying there while he did. Once it was finished, however, he hadn't been able to contemplate moving out, and Owen hadn't asked him, so he'd stayed. A mistake, but one he couldn't find in him to regret. Yet.

He closed his eyes, remembering that night seven years ago when he and Owen had spent over eight hours learning each other's bodies. It had come as an enormous surprise that Owen was submissive. Evan didn't think even Owen had expected that, but when Evan had taken control, throwing orders at him, Owen had obeyed without question. Evan's blood had fired, and a beast had grown inside him. A beast that needed to be the dominant one in their relationship.

As the images of Owen beneath him flickered through his mind, his morning wood wept, needing attention. Evan was all for edging and delayed orgasms, but not that day. That day, he needed to let it out.

He wrapped his hand around his cock, sliding his palm over the head to collect the precome before tightening his hold and stroking to its base. His hand rose again, rotating across his sensitive frenulum, over the head, and stroking down. He repeated it several times, letting the movie of their one and only night roll, sending his arousal higher. He needed more.

Bracing the back of his hand against the mattress but still keeping it in a loose circle, he canted his hips, sliding his cock through his fist. His free hand flicked his nipples, sending shards of fire towards his groin. He panted into his pillow as he remembered the feeling of Owen clenching around his cock, pushing back against him, biting his forearm in the throes of ecstasy, and Evan increased his speed. The head of his dick rubbed against the bed as well as his hand, and within seconds, his climax washed over him, a wave he could not and did not want to deny. His groan of completion was loud.

He slumped to the bed, his hand relaxing around his cock, even as his shaft valiantly tried to release more at the brief sensation.

He was surprised he didn't have calluses from how much he had used his hand as a substitute for what he wanted.

Rolling to his back again, he sighed. He wanted Owen back, but he wasn't sure how to do it. Dominic knew nothing of their one night together, so he couldn't ask him for help, not without breaking the trust between him and Owen. They'd never mentioned keeping it a secret, but as Dominic had never mentioned it, Evan assumed Owen had said nothing.

He rose, stripping the bed and throwing the sheets in the washing basket, and then headed for the shower. After a perfunctory wash and shampoo, he dressed in jeans and a T-shirt and wandered in search of coffee. Owen often made him some, but when it was late in the day and they weren't sure who was going to be around, each of them tended to leave the coffee pot empty.

Once the coffee scent rose, Evan inhaled and sighed.

"Nothing like coffee when you wake, is there?"

Evan's heart pounded in a rapid tattoo as his stomach tried to roll out of his body. How long had Owen been home? "Definitely. Nothing like it," he rasped, trying to cool the burning that would no doubt be visible in his cheeks if he turned away from the pot.

"Did you sleep okay?" Owen stopped beside him, placing his mug on the side next to Evan's.

Evan tried to read into Owen's words. Had he heard him as he orgasmed? Had Evan been as loud as he'd seemed? He couldn't tell, but something inside him wasn't at all bothered. Not really. Let Owen listen to him. Let him remember what they had. Let him imagine what Evan was doing in his room.

"Yeah. A lot longer than I'd planned, but I feel better for it." He scratched his neck as the coffee spit out his drink.

"It's a long set of shifts for you. I'm not surprised you need sleep."

Evan sipped his coffee despite it being burning hot and closed his eyes as the taste hit him. He blinked and leaned back against the counter, curling his hands around the mug. "I thought you'd still be at work."

"Brett gave me the afternoon off because Prince Freddie was staying at Windsor today. They had enough people to cover." Owen faced him, the easy lean against the opposite counter not as easy as he tried to make it look.

"What's wrong?" Evan asked.

Owen hesitated and then shook his head. "Nothing." He pushed off the counter and left the kitchen, and Evan stared after him.

They would never get past what happened between them. It would always be a chasm they wouldn't be able to cross to get back to where they had been before. Eventually, he was sure they could narrow the gap, but it would never disappear. He glanced at the floor as he finished his drink. He had no choice but to rebuild the bridges they'd both burnt to the ground. After all, he'd promised his Italian friend he would try.

While he'd been living in Italy, he'd taken jobs as a carer, and one such job was for an elderly gentleman who was nearing the end of his life. Antonio had refused to leave his childhood home when he knew he'd never return to it, so the doctors had agreed to home care. The stubborn man had clung to life for almost a year before succumbing, but in that time, he'd become a close friend to Evan. And Evan had told him *everything*. Antonio had made him promise to return to the UK and find a way back to Owen. To find a way for them to forgive, if not forget. Evan could do it. He could forgive Owen for his harsh words and even harsher delivery, but there would always be that ember of doubt in the back of Evan's mind, and that, more than anything else, had stopped Evan's forward momentum with figuring out where they were.

He shook his head, bringing himself back from the memories of that sad time. Refusing to take on another carer role after Antonio had died, he'd instead packed his stuff and headed back to England. Right into Owen's life again. But where they went from there, he had no idea.

"Ev? Mum's asking if you want to go for dinner tomorrow night?" Owen shouted from the living room.

Evan put his mug down and leaned against the door frame, ignoring the way his body reacted when his gaze landed on his best friend. "Sure. We don't have any plans, do we?"

Owen shook his head and brought the phone back to his mouth. "Yeah, we'll be there. What time?"

As Owen finished the call with his mother, Evan grabbed the mug from Owen's hand and went back to refill them both. Sally, Owen's mother, had been his lifesaver when his parents had disowned him and thrown him out at fifteen years old. She'd allowed him to move in with them while he finished school, at which point he found a small apartment and moved out. He loved her dearly and had been fascinated with her nursing career stories, guiding him into his current role as if he'd been born for it.

"She said to be there for five o'clock, if that's okay with you?" Owen said when he returned to the living room.

He handed Owen the drink and settled in an armchair, tucking his legs beneath him and cradling the cup. "Fine by me. I'll never say no to Sally's cooking."

Owen grinned, though it didn't reach his eyes. "I doubt anyone would."

Evan inhaled through his nose, letting it out slowly before asking, "What's wrong?"

Owen looked away and drank, wincing because it was undoubtedly too hot. "Nothing's wrong."

"Yes, there is, Owen. I know you," he chided softly.

Owen sent a glare his way. "Nothing," he said again.

Evan studied him. "Okay. I'm here if you need anything." He pulled his phone free and scrolled through the different apps. From the corner of his eye, he watched Owen drain his cup, put it on the coffee table and stand.

"I'm going to nip to the supermarket to get some stuff. Do you need anything?" Owen slipped on his coat and that damn scarf.

Evan glared at the offending object, wishing he knew who had sent it, and looked away again. "No, I don't think so."

"All right. I'll see you in a bit. Message me if you think of anything."

With that, Owen left, leaving a silence that burrowed beneath Evan's skin and set his nerves on edge. He threw his phone to the coffee table, the unoffending object sliding across the surface and off the opposite edge. He had no idea how to even start bridging the gap between them. If anything, with each moment of silence, the gap widened. Would he have to be the one to reach across it and keep it from widening?

Despite picking up where they almost left off, the minute differences felt bigger, more fractured. He wasn't sure anyone could tell just by looking at and being around them, but soon, if they didn't work it out, Dominic would sense something was wrong and investigate it. He was, by nature and job, a tenacious son of a gun.

Maybe this dinner with Owen's mother would help them. He'd barely seen her since he'd returned, and it would be wonderful to sit and chat like they used to. He had no doubt she would see something between them, but he didn't think she would call them on it. Not when they were together, anyway. She might grab them individually at some point, though.

He put both feet on the floor and sat forward, scraping his fingers through his hair. If only he'd had Antonio to ask for advice. He'd seemed so worldly and wise, and Evan was floundering.

Any friends he'd had before he left—bar Owen and Dominic—had all moved on now, and although he'd made friends since he'd returned, he wasn't sure anyone could help him make sense of what was happening. He knew, without a doubt, that something needed to change. Something needed to kick their asses, even if it was to know, once and for all, whether or not they had a chance at a relationship. It was the hanging on that was destroying him.

Glancing at the clock, he saw Owen had been gone for an hour already. Evan grabbed the remote, retrieved his phone and flicked through the movie offerings. Even though it was Friday night, he wasn't expecting Owen to go out—it wasn't an impossibility, just unlikely—so he might as well find something to help ignore the silences between their sporadic conversation. Deciding on the newest release, something he remembered Owen mentioning in passing a few weeks prior, he moved to the kitchen to prepare some popcorn and chocolate raisins—Owen's favourite—and set them on the table. They didn't have any beer or anything because they rarely drank it at home. Giving Owen vodka in his lemonade at New Year's had been a risk, but he hadn't seemed too upset about it.

The door lock rattled, and Owen entered, carrying two bags full to the brim.

"Just a little light shopping, eh?" Evan said, rising and grabbing a bag from him.

Owen's mouth quirked. "Couldn't resist." He glanced at the TV. "Oh, fuck yeah. I'd lost track of time and hadn't realised that it was out already." Refocusing on Evan. "You up for a movie night?"

Evan pointed at the coffee table. "Popcorn and chocolate raisins are already waiting. Just need to decide on drinks."

Owen put his bag next to Evan's on the kitchen counter and riffled through it, producing a bottle with a "Ta-da!"

Evan raised his eyebrows. "Are you sure whiskey is a good idea?"

"Probably not, but I'm doing it, anyway."

So much for not drinking at home. Evan opened his mouth to argue but sighed and reached for his phone. "In which case..." He dialled. "Hello, can I order for delivery, please?" Owen gave him the thumbs up, and Evan ignored the spark of heat that flowed through him. He couldn't help his need to look after Owen, even if the guy didn't want to look after himself sometimes.

One day, if he could get them back on track, he would make sure Owen had everything he ever wanted.

3

Owen

The movie session the previous night had Owen feeling like things were back to the way they had been before Evan left, and it was difficult to go back to the silence again. But as they made their way through the town to his mother's house, Evan had not stopped talking.

"I'm looking forward to seeing Sally again. It feels like I've not seen her for years."

Owen chuckled. "You've definitely seen her since you've been home. Several times, in fact."

"I know. It just doesn't feel like it. I need to make more time for everyone. I don't get as much time with anyone now. These shifts are worse than before I left."

"It's because you're getting old," Owen quipped.

Evan backhanded his shoulder, making Owen laugh again. "If I'm old, so are you."

Owen frowned. "Shit." He hadn't thought about that. "Fuck that. I'm in my prime. We're obviously different ages, despite having been in the same year throughout school."

"I'm sure that's entirely possible. Not."

"Hey! Remember, Julie? She had been moved forward a year because they were smart. That could've happened." Owen glanced over at him, a smile trying to break out across his face.

"They also keep people back when they're not doing so well. Ever thought of that?" Evan grinned.

"Fucker," he muttered.

Their easy camaraderie continued until Owen parked outside his mum's house. The bungalow was smaller than the house they'd lived in when they were kids, but it was easier for his mum to manage. Fifty-eight wasn't old by any means, but she was a nurse, just like Evan, and didn't have as much time to look after the house, so buying something smaller was a good thing in her case.

Sally was already at the door when they climbed from the car, and Evan jogged around the hood and into her arms before Owen had even closed his door. He heard murmurings, but he didn't move close enough to hear until they pulled back from their embrace. His mum glanced at him with a wide smile and held open her arms.

"I'm glad you're here," she said. "I wondered if I would ever get the chance to see you."

Owen smirked. "I know. It's been soooo long since we've seen each other. Three days was soooo long ago." He stretched out the words, taking him back to when he used to complain that dinner was an hour away, which, as a child, seemed like forever.

Sally batted his chest with the back of her hand and chuckled. "It was. When you get older, time goes by so fast, three days seems like three months. Come on in. Dinner's almost ready."

Evan waved for Owen to enter the house first, and his heart raced at the gesture. Evan had always done things like that, but even more so since he'd returned from Italy. Was it something that he'd learnt over there, or was something else causing him to look after Owen in that way? It might seem like nothing, but to Owen, it was a sign of how much he cared, and he wasn't sure what to do with that. Could he truly still care about Owen after what he'd done?

He brushed the thought aside as he followed his mother, the scent of curry in the air. "Masala?" he asked.

"Try again," Sally said.

"Vindaloo?"

Evan stepped past him. "Kofta."

Sally pointed at Evan. "Correct."

"It's been far too long since I've had that," Evan said, patting his stomach. "You're spoiling me."

It was times like this that Owen wished they were together because he wanted to wrap his arms around Evan's shoulders, lean down and kiss him. He blinked, shook his head and faced his mother, who looked at him with knowledge in her eyes. *Uh-oh.* She couldn't know. No one else did.

"I'll get the cutlery." He strode for the drawer where it was kept, avoiding anyone's stares, and listened with half an ear while he set the table. He almost bumped into Evan when the man went to fill some glasses with water. "Ah, sorry."

He finished putting everything in place and asked, "Do you need me to do anything else?"

Sally stirred the pan once more, banged the spoon on the edge and set it down. "No, it's all ready. Sit down. I'll bring them over." She turned off the cooker and pulled three plates towards her. Watching her movements helped Owen get his equilibrium back, and though he could feel Evan's stare, he refused to look at him. Something was hovering by, as if ready to fall, and although he didn't know what it was, he was sure he wouldn't be able to stop it if he acknowledged it.

Sally put the plates in front of them, and they both groaned, Owen because the scent was strong and reminded him so much of home. He smiled and picked up his fork but waited until his mother had taken a seat before starting.

"Thank you for dinner," he said, meeting her gaze and seeing the love shining in her blue eyes. The same eyes he saw in the mirror every day.

"Yes, thank you," Evan said.

"You're both welcome. Anytime at all. In fact, make it more often," she chided.

Owen chuckled. "With your shifts, Evan's shifts and my own working hours, we're lucky to get tonight."

Sally nodded and spooned some curry and rice into her mouth, though her eyes still spoke—far more loudly than her voice. She knew something was up, and as any mother would, she would mine for information until she figured it out—if she hadn't already.

"Evan, how are you settling back in to English life?" Sally asked.

Evan finished his mouthful, put his fork down and picked up his glass before answering. "It's been easier than I expected, though there are a few things I've struggled with."

That was the first Owen had heard about it. "There is? What are they?"

Evan sipped his drink and placed it back on the table. "Like eating. It's a much more social experience in Italy." He waved his hand towards Sally. "Not that this isn't social and good, I mean." She smiled and rolled her eyes. "All meals there are made for socialising. Dinner could take two or three hours or more, depending on who you were with. There was never just one or two courses. It was a feast every single time."

"Sounds fattening," Owen remarked, though Sally tapped his hand in reprimand. "Intriguing, though," he added. "What else?"

"Kisses."

Owen coughed as the curry he'd just eaten tried to enter his lungs. He covered his mouth and coughed, trying to breathe. A napkin appeared in front of his watering eyes, and he used it to wipe his face. "Sorry about that," he said, clearing his throat and sipping his drink. "You were saying." He might be able to concentrate now he wasn't choking.

"Kisses. Almost everyone in Italy continually kissed others. When they meet, when they leave, in the morning, in the evening, when it's your birthday, when it's any kind of celebration. But not only that, but their physical contact completely. They had no qualms of holding hands or arms with random people in the street or inviting them to their homes for dinner, even if they didn't know your name. They stand closer to each other, too. Here, we apologise if we get closer than two metres to someone. There, you're lucky if you get half a metre of space, and no one cares. It's...freeing."

"That sounds both wonderful and scary," Sally said with a chuckle. "Maybe we need to start small. Kisses we could do, couldn't we?" She raised her eyebrows at Owen, expecting an answer, though what, he didn't know.

"Um, yeah, I guess." He didn't look at Evan. How the hell was he going to get used to kissing Evan on the cheek every damn time he saw him when all he wanted was to have the man's mouth on his every moment of the day?

His mother, thankfully, changed the subject to something about the sights in Italy, even though she'd received probably more photos than Owen had of Evan's time there. He listened, but he kept his focus on the food until there was nothing left.

"Ice cream?" Sally asked.

Owen smiled and met her gaze. "Takes me back," he murmured.

She cupped his jaw, brushing her thumb across his cheek. "Everything was better when there was ice cream."

"Still is," he said, glancing at Evan, who stared into his eyes as if he held the answers Evan needed. He didn't. He had no answers at all. Except that ice cream makes everything better.

Especially if it was cookie dough.

"I'll get it. Do you want any?" he asked them both as he gathered the plates together.

"Yes, please," Evan said.

"I'm fine, thank you, sweetie."

He put the plates on the side, intending to clean them off and put them in the dishwasher after he'd dished the ice cream, but Evan beat him to it.

"You get the ice cream; I'll do the dishes."

Owen licked his lips and nodded. "Okay."

They worked in silence, and when he returned to the table with two bowls of ice cream and a cup of tea for his mum, he tried to ignore how much he was waiting for Evan to tell him he could eat. He was a grown man, for fuck's sake.

"Eat up or it'll melt," Evan said, and Owen's entire body relaxed and then tensed again.

Why was he waiting for permission?

He dug into the ice cream, ignoring them while he ate. He wished he could figure out what was wrong with him. Yes, okay, he wanted Evan. There was no denying that, but apart from that night, when he was submissive as hell without having realised he was until that moment, he wasn't in his daily life. Why did he suddenly need Evan's approval? And why did he feel like he couldn't breathe without it?

He scraped his chair back as he finished his last mouthful of ice cream and put it in the dishwasher. Facing his mother, he swallowed hard. "I'll be…" He pointed to the door but didn't finish his sentence. Instead, he jogged to the front door and left the house, dropping to the small stool his mother always left by the front door.

Inhaling and exhaling didn't help, and he shook his hands out when he saw they were trembling. What the fuck? He threaded his fingers through his hair and closed his eyes, resting his elbows on his knees.

Knees bracketed his legs, a hand gripped his nape and another his shoulder. His head lifted, and he locked gazes with Evan.

"Breathe for me, Owen. Breathe." Owen shook his head. "Do as you're fucking told. Breathe," Evan ordered.

Owen inhaled, oxygen flooding his body, his head spinning. He wanted to close his eyes, but he couldn't look away from Evan. His eyes, mesmerising as always, tortured him with their knowledge.

"That's it." Evan's hand cupped his cheek. "Keep breathing. There we go."

Tears pricked at Owen's eyes. "I don't know…"

Evan studied Owen's expression for a moment and then leaned forward, pressing his lips to Owen's cheek, just near the corner of his mouth, and then to the other side. Owen dropped his head forward, resting their foreheads together. He closed his eyes and breathed. The scent of Evan wrapped around him, and he fell back into his memories of that night, needing the reassurance that they had, actually, experienced something amazing that Owen had ruined the next day.

He lifted his head again. "I'm sorry," he said.

"You don't need to be sorry. It was just a panic—"

Owen shook his head. "I'm sorry," he said again, swallowing hard. "I thought I was doing the right thing."

Evan stared at him, barely blinking. "And now?" he whispered. Owen's heart pounded, and his breathing became choppy again. Evan tightened his hold. "Later, okay? We'll talk later. Just breathe."

Owen followed Evan's inhales and exhales, having never experienced a panic attack himself before, although he had seen others have them. The feeling of being adrift and unable to gather his thoughts was unlike anything he'd experienced before. A sort of heightened drunkenness that was overwhelming.

"Are you okay to say goodnight to your mum? I'm sure she's worried."

Owen took a big breath and nodded. "Sorry."

"Don't be."

Evan stood, taking Owen's hands to help him stand and keeping hold of him until he was steady on his feet. Then he stepped back, and Owen immediately missed his warmth. He focused on his mum, though, and entered the house. Sally gathered him into her arms and rubbed his back.

"Are you okay?" she asked.

"I am. Just a lot going on."

She cupped his face, her gaze going behind him before returning. "He's a good man, Owen, and so are you. Despite how things have turned out, it's not impossible to go back. You can't change the past, but you can relive it the way it was supposed to happen." Her voice was low enough that he didn't think Evan could hear, but he'd been right. His mum knew everything.

"How did you know?"

She smiled. "You're my son, and he is just as much so. I know you both. I saw it happening for years. And when you both came home that morning, you looked broken. And when he left, you broke some more. I don't know what happened between you, but I know it can be saved. Talk to him. Figure it out because you belong together."

Owen closed his eyes, a lone tear trickling from the corner, which his mother wiped away. He huffed. "I'm supposed to be the strong, protective one. I'm a bodyguard, for god's sake."

She chuckled. "Only in your job. Outside of your job, you're human. Love like one. Faults and all. But talk. It's important." Her eyes took on a faraway look. "Extremely important," she murmured and then smiled again, refocusing on him.

He slid his arms around her and hugged her tightly. "I'll try." He pulled back.

Sally kissed his cheek and then the other one. "A good excuse to get close." She winked.

Owen huffed a laugh and shook his head. "I knew you were up to something."

She turned to Evan and held out her arms. "Kisses," she said.

Evan laughed and did as she asked, kissing her cheeks and hugging her. She whispered something to him that Owen couldn't hear, but Evan nodded.

"Right, get home with you. It's getting late," Sally said.

"It's not even seven o'clock yet!" Owen said.

"Exactly. My bedtime. I'm old, remember?" She crossed her eyes and stuck her tongue out, something she'd always done before sending them to bed at night.

They laughed and headed out. Owen rubbed his face as they wandered to the car.

"Do you want me to drive?"

Owen glanced at Evan and nodded. "Yes, please." Pulling the keys from his pocket, he threw them at him.

The drive was quiet, fraught with tension, but Owen couldn't bring himself to break it. He wasn't sure he was ready. Despite what he'd acknowledged to Evan and his mother, he was riding the edge of a ravine and unsure which way was the right way to go without falling off.

Evan hung the keys up on the hooks they kept beside the door, and Owen stared at the floor, his hands shoved deep into his pockets to hide their trembling. He couldn't do it. Not right then.

"I need…" He exhaled. "I need time," he whispered.

Evan sighed. "You have it. Whatever you need, whenever you need it."

Owen strode for his bedroom but froze a few steps away. Inhaling, he turned back and stopped in front of Evan. "Goodnight," he whispered, leaning forward to kiss one cheek and then the other. Then he turned and closed himself away in his room, breathing as if he'd run a marathon.

"What the hell am I doing?" he whispered.

Shaking his head, he entered his en suite and turned the water as hot as he could stand it. As the water rained down on him, he thought back to his words that morning.

We've ruined everything. This was a mistake. We can't do this again.

The words had done exactly what his mother had said—broken them both. He wasn't sure he could ever atone for the hurt he'd caused, but he could try. They were walking on eggshells around each other, and it had to stop. He wanted his best friend back in more than location.

Did he have the courage to reach for what he wanted? To heal the wounds he'd caused? To risk everything for the one person he wanted more than anything else in the world?

He wanted to say he did, but he couldn't right then. The idea of potentially losing everything was terrifying, even balanced against the idea that he could have everything he wanted if it turned out right.

The future was uncertain, and he hated it. He should be used to it, with his job being as unpredictable as it was. There was no denying he needed to talk to Evan, but he needed to shore himself up against the chances of him rejecting him. He needed to expect it because if Evan turned him down, he needed to be okay with that.

Well, he needed to be an excellent actor, at least.

4

Evan

It went against Evan's instincts to let Owen hide away when he'd cracked open the door that might help them heal, but he also knew how stubborn Owen could be. After years of being friends, he needed space to wrap his head around everything, and then he would approach Evan. But this time around, Evan would give him a day at most. More than that and Owen would retreat completely.

He headed for the kitchen, needing some caffeine, and set the pot going. Leaning back against the counter, he watched it, though his mind was really on the tentative elastic band stretched between them from Owen's earlier words. A band that could easily snap with the wrong move.

Owen had said he'd thought it was the right choice. But the right choice for who? It was a question he'd need to ask. His phone rang, and he pulled it from his pocket, smiling when Matteo's name came up.

"Hey, how're things?" he said.

Matteo sighed. "Busy, as always. I'm finally getting my dinner. We had a rush of patients when a car accident came in. Craziness doesn't cover it."

Matteo was a nurse, too. He worked slightly different shift patterns to Evan, but they'd bonded over the handover one night and become friends after Matteo had tried to tempt Evan into bed. Unfortunately for them both, neither were the other's type. Matteo wanted a Daddy, and Evan was not one.

"I can imagine. Make sure you eat properly."

Matteo scoffed. "You know I don't cook, so it's ham sandwiches and crisps for me."

Evan huffed. "Where's your Daddy when you need one?"

"Well, I quite like the idea of that Dr Wallis. He's quite the eye candy."

"Leave the doctors alone. You know you shouldn't mix pleasure and business."

"But why the hell not?" Matteo whined.

"Did you want to see the person you're supposed to be fucking? Or just imagine they're there with you?"

Matteo groaned. "Stop making sense. It's far too late in the day for that."

Evan frowned. "Hang on a minute. I thought you were on a midnight to eight shift today."

"I was supposed to be. Marie wanted to swap. So tonight I get another 1 a.m. finish. But at least I can have a lie in."

"Whereas I have to be there for eight tomorrow morning."

"Wishing you lots of sleep tonight."

Evan looked at his freshly brewed coffee. "I just made myself a coffee." He sighed, pouting.

Matteo laughed. "I wouldn't drink that if I were you. You'll feel like you worked a double if you do." A noise sounded in the background. "I have to go. Let's try to get dinner tomorrow, yeah?"

"Message me."

"Will do. Bye."

Evan put the phone back in his pocket and picked up the coffee. He couldn't drink it if he wanted to get to sleep anytime soon, but he knew someone who could. Knocking on Owen's door, he waited.

"Yeah?"

"I have coffee that'll go to waste if you don't want it."

Silence, but then footsteps, and the door opened. Owen's face was pink, undoubtedly from the burning hot showers he took—how he managed in such hot water Evan would never understand. He held out the mug.

"I forgot I was back at work tomorrow, so I can't drink it. I won't sleep otherwise."

Owen took it, their fingertips brushing. "Thanks. Are you going to bed now?"

"I'm going to stay up for another hour or so. I'm not tired enough to sleep yet. Might watch some cute dog videos to pass the time." He grinned.

Owen snorted. "You don't watch those."

Evan raised his eyebrows and grabbed his phone again. He scrolled to the videos and turned it to face Owen. "Wanna bet?"

Owen blinked and stared at him. "Seriously?"

"Wanna watch some with me?" He threw the question out there before he remembered he was supposed to be giving Owen time, but it was too late to take it back now.

Owen frowned but tilted his head, a mix of uncertainty and curiosity. "Sure." He opened his door, surprising Evan, but he wouldn't look a gift horse in the mouth—though where that phrase came from, he had no idea. When he entered, he looked around, trying to decide where to sit.

"Sit on the bed. It's fine."

Glancing at the bedside tables, he gathered Owen slept on the left, so he settled against the headboard on the right, bending his knee to rest on the bed. Owen settled beside him, sipping the coffee and shuffling close enough to see his phone screen. In hindsight, Evan should've brought his computer to make it easier, but it had been an impromptu invitation, and he was happy Owen wanted to be close to him.

Scrolling to the first video he'd saved, he set it playing, resting his elbow on his leg so his arm didn't get tired. To begin with, Evan chuckled, but Owen was more subdued. On one particularly idiotic video, though, he snorted. After that, it was like a plaster had been ripped off, and he couldn't help himself.

Evan had no idea how long they watched for, but his eyes grew tired, though he tried to fight it. The next thing he knew, he was being shaken awake.

"Hey, sorry to wake you, but I need to pee. Just roll over to the side and go back to sleep," Owen said.

Evan moved from where his head rested on Owen's thigh and rubbed a hand over his face. When had he fallen asleep? He rose to sitting and yawned. He should go back to his own bed and let Owen sleep.

Owen returned and stopped in front of Evan. He stared down at him and tilted his head. "Sleep, Evan." He reached for the cover, pulling it back, and gestured for Evan to lie down.

"Are you sure?" His heart skipped a beat when Owen nodded. He licked his lips. "Can I take my jeans off?"

Owen swallowed hard but nodded again. Evan stood, making Owen move back a step, and took off his trousers. Then, staring at Owen, he climbed into the bed, settling against the pillows. Owen pulled the covers over him and rounded the bed, sliding in beside him. Evan wasn't sure what to expect, but it wasn't for Owen to roll towards him and rest his head on Evan's pillow so they were close enough for Evan to count Owen's eyelashes.

"Sleep. We'll talk after your shift tomorrow. I promise," Owen whispered.

Evan reached for Owen's hand, interlacing their fingers, and closed his eyes. He tried not to read into his best friend's actions, but it was hard not to. Instead, he focused on Owen's scent and the feel of his hand, and he fell asleep.

When his phone alarm went off, he groaned and reached for it, surprised to feel a warm body sprawled across him. He wiped the sleep from his eyes and shut off the alarm before looking down at Owen. His head rested on Evan's chest, his arm thrown over his stomach and his leg tangled with Evan's. It was the closest they'd been for a long time, and Evan was hesitant to move. He wanted to stay like that and who cared if he missed work, but he couldn't let his colleagues down. He pressed his lips to Owen's head and rubbed his hand over Owen's arm, trying to wake him enough so he could move without jolting the man.

Owen nuzzled his cheek against his chest, and then he froze. His eyes shot open, his chin lifting to look into Evan's eyes. "Sorry," he said, moving away, but Evan tightened his hold.

"Tonight, right?" he asked.

"Tonight," Owen agreed.

Evan wanted to kiss him, but he didn't push. Instead, he let him go and slid from the bed. "I'll see you later, then."

He grabbed his jeans from the floor and headed for the door, but Owen's voice stopped him.

"Be safe."

"Always am," he replied.

By the time he'd showered, dressed and aimed for the hospital, his mind was awash with possibilities. But he couldn't let himself hope too much. He'd done the same that night, and Owen had broken his heart the following morning. He wasn't sure he'd survive if it happened again.

"Marie! My favourite nurse!" he exclaimed as he stopped at the nurses' station when he was ready to start.

Marie, an older nurse who'd been doing the job for more years than Evan had been alive, smiled and shook her head. "You, my dear boy, are a menace. That smile would get you anything and everything you wanted, and you know it."

Evan put his chin in his palm and rested his elbow on the desk, batting his eyelashes at her. "I know." He sighed dreamily and then laughed. "How has everything been?"

"I'm not saying anything," she stated.

Evan knew that meant it had been suspiciously quiet and she didn't want to jinx it. "Okay, then. What do we have?"

She handed him four folders. "A fourteen-year-old girl in room six. Her mother insisted she have a room of her own." Marie rolled her eyes. "She's suffering stomach pains, which we're treating as potentially appendicitis, but we're uncertain. Her mother has now gone home. Thankfully." Marie pursed her lips and pointed to another folder. "A five-year-old boy who fell off his new bike and broke his wrist. Says he no longer wants his bike. He's in bay one." She pointed to the next folder. "A regular drug user is in bay five. We have him hooked up to fluids. And finally, a forty-year-old woman whose drink had been spiked and is in bay three. Her friend brought her in because she wasn't sure what to do about it."

"Did anything else happen to her?" Evan asked, flipping through her folder.

"Her friend said no because they'd been together all the time, but I'm tempted to ask her for a rape kit, anyway."

"It'll have to be her choice, but I'd ask the question. Maybe phrase it as a 'don't you want to be certain' type of thing."

Marie nodded and took back the woman's folder. "You introduce yourself to the others, and when you're finished, we'll visit her together."

Evan grabbed what he needed and headed for the boy's room first. The little guy was holding a tablet with one arm and staring furiously at it. His broken arm rested on the bed.

"Hello, there, Richie. I'm Evan. How are you feeling?"

"I'm fine." His tone was not fine.

Evan took notes of the monitors and jotted down the numbers. "I broke my arm when I fell off my bike when I was younger, too. It's not nice, especially just after getting your bike. What colour is it?" He glanced at the adult, who he assumed was the father, and saw gratitude in his eyes.

He didn't think the boy was going to answer, but then he said, "Green. It's got orange flames down the side."

"That sounds amazing. Mine was just a plain blue one." He tucked the folder under his arm. "Did the bike get scraped?"

The boy's eyes widened, and his gaze snapped to his father's. "Dad, is the bike broken?"

The man shook his head. "It's all in good condition. And if you see anything wrong with it when we get back, we can always patch it up with the same colours. It'll look brand new."

The boy nodded and bit his lip, staring at Evan from the corner of his eye. "Do you have a picture to show him?" he asked his father, who dug his phone from his pocket and pressed a few things before handing it to the boy.

"Look!" He held it up.

Evan leaned closer. "Oh, wow. That is a fantastic bike. I bet you can't wait to get back on it again. It looks like it would go so fast."

"It does! I think the flames make it faster."

"I agree. So many flames. Well, when your arm has healed, you'll be able to jump right back on it and see how fast it goes." The boy's eyes lit up. "I'll be back in a little while to sort out sending him for the cast," he said to the father.

The man stood and held out his hand. "Thank you."

Evan saw the meaning behind the words, and it had nothing to do with him explaining the plans. He nodded. "No problem at all." Sometimes people just needed to remember how much they enjoyed something before the bad thing happened to make them excited about it again.

He headed for bay five, sliding the curtain back, but no one was on the bed waiting, though the fluids still hung there. Glancing around the department, he couldn't see anyone, so he decided to visit the girl first and come back to the guy.

Knocking on the door of room six, he entered, smiling at the girl sitting on the bed. She was a little pale, and her lips looked extremely red against her skin, as if she'd been biting them.

"Hello, Emily. I'm—"

He dropped the folders he'd been holding when someone shoved him forward and the door slammed and locked behind him. He stumbled over to the other side of the room before catching himself on a chair and spinning around. A guy with straggly blond hair and wide eyes stood beside the girl's bed, squeezing her arm and holding something to her neck. Evan swallowed. In the dim light, he couldn't see what was against her neck, but he was certain it was something he didn't want to move.

He held out his hands to who he assumed was the drug user missing from bay five. "Okay. I'm here now. What's the plan?"

"You need to get me some drugs. I don't need that fluid shit. I don't want it flushed from my system. I want more of it. I want to forget everything!"

"Okay. Any particular drug you want?"

The guy leaned closer to the girl. "You know what type will work! You're a doctor!"

Evan didn't feel the need to correct his mistake, so he nodded. "That's okay. Am I to go and get it?"

"No!" the guy shouted, startling the girl, and she winced. A drop of blood slid down her neck, but the guy didn't see. Evan did, though, and he needed to get him away from her.

"I can call a nurse to bring it in."

The guy's eyes darted around the room. "Yes. Do that. But you take it from them at the door. They can't come in."

"I can do that." He gestured to his pocket. "Can I get my phone out? I'll send them a message to bring it to me."

"Don't you have a walkie-talkie or something?"

Evan shook his head. "Usually, we fetch what we need ourselves, but in an emergency, we text or call someone else." It wasn't strictly true, but he didn't know that. "I can show you what I'm saying and who I'm messaging, if that helps?"

"Yes." He wrapped his arm around the girl's shoulders, holding the knife, or whatever it was, to her neck again. "Come here, but don't try anything funny."

Evan stepped closer and reached into his pocket for his phone. He brought up a message to Marie and stopped beside the guy. Not close enough for him to see clearly, but enough that he would have to lean away from Emily a little.

"Look, I'm messaging Marie. Do you remember her from when you came in? She's the head nurse here."

The guy nodded, stretching his neck to watch Evan. Evan purposefully turned the phone a little further away so he had to move closer to see it. The moment he saw the knife—scalpel—drop away from the girl, he slammed the hands holding his phone down on the guy's arm, swiped his foot behind his ankle and shoved him back, hissing in pain. The guy thudded to the floor, and Evan turned him over, locking his hands behind his back. He glanced over his shoulder.

"Are you okay, Emily? Do you hurt anywhere else?"

Emily shook her head, tears running down her cheeks. "Just my stomach and my neck a little."

"Good. Could you please push that big red button above your bed?" Evan gestured to it with his head while dropping to sit over the guy's thighs, the squirming rat that he was. He glanced at his arm and cursed, unable to do anything about it right then.

The moment Emly pressed the button, alarms rang out and people came running. The door flew open, and Marie stopped, mouth gaping. "What in the world...?"

Evan grunted at a particularly vicious motion from the man beneath him and smiled. "We need the police, and Emily needs to have her neck looked at."

Two officers entered the room shortly after, taking custody of the guy. "Nice job," one of them said.

"Thanks." Evan gripped his forearm, blood seeping through his fingers.

"Evan!" Marie said, guiding him from the room and into an empty bay. One officer followed with Evan's phone, which he put on the table. "What happened?"

He told them the details, leaving nothing out. "As we went down, the scalpel must've sliced down my arm." He looked down at it. Owen was going to be pissed.

"I think that's all we need for the report. We might need you to come down to the station, but we'll be in contact if we do," the officer said.

"Thanks." He left, and Evan asked, "Is Emily okay?"

Marie nodded. "Just a small nick, but she's being taken up for surgery now. It's definitely appendicitis."

"Poor girl. Traumatised before surgery. Not the best thing to happen."

"They'll look after her." Marie worked steadily, closing the long cut with small, precise stitches. "Do you need anything for the pain?"

"Nah, I'm good. No heavy lifting for me for a while. Owen'll be pissed I can't spar with him."

"Nope. You'll be resting for the next week at least."

Evan shook his head. "I can still work. I just need someone to help with transferring patients and stuff."

Marie glared at him. "You know that's not how this works. Seven days, at the very least."

Evan sighed. He'd barely made it two hours into his shift. "Shit. I'm going to have to call Owen."

"Uh-huh," Marie said, not even attempting to hide her glee. "It's about time I met him."

Evan huffed, grabbed his phone and dialled one-handed. That was going to get tedious. He inhaled and put it to his ear.

5

Owen

"Hey," Owen said cautiously. "You don't normally call during your shift. Everything okay?"

"Um, I need you to come and collect me, please," Evan said. "I'm okay, but there was an incident. I have stitches and can't drive, and my car is here."

Owen shot up from the sofa, squeezing the phone to his ear. "Incident? Stitches? What the fuck, Evan?"

Evan sighed. "I'm okay, Owen. Just a little scratch on my arm. I'm fine. I just can't drive. And Marie is being a witch and won't let me work."

"Goddamn right, she won't. I'll be there soon. Don't move." He hung up, shoved his feet into his shoes, grabbed his keys and raced from the house. Then he stopped. "Fuck!" He pulled up the taxi service he occasionally used and, luckily, one was close by. He wasn't sure what he would've done if there wasn't. Probably ran there.

His heart pounded as he waited. Was Evan hurt more than he was letting on? Stitches sounded bad, but they'd all had them over the years. Evan had, more than once, stitched them when they'd been hurt. But this was Evan. What the hell had happened? Maybe he should've called back to find out while he waited for the taxi, but he couldn't stay still. He paced the path in front of his house until the taxi pulled up. He climbed in and stared out of the window as they worked through the streets towards the hospital.

Owen's mind went around and around in circles until he felt dizzy with it. His breathing was uncoordinated and rough, and when he finally climbed out of the taxi, he wasn't sure his legs would hold him up. But he fought through it and entered A&E. His eyes darted around the area, trying to find someone who could help him find Evan.

"Owen!"

His gaze snapped to the right, where Evan stood behind a desk. He stalked towards it. "What are you doing working? You should be resting!"

Evan came from behind the desk and rested a hand on his arm. "I wasn't working. I was sitting watching Marie work." He glanced to the side. "Marie, this is Owen. Owen, this is head nurse extraordinaire, Marie."

Owen took a breath and held out his hand, trying for a smile. "Nice to meet you, Marie. I hear a lot about you."

"And I you. His words don't do you justice." She winked, and Owen froze, swallowing hard.

Evan had talked about him? That was something to think about later. He finally took in Evan's condition, seeing the long bandage covering his entire forearm.

"Jesus, Evan! Just a scratch!?"

Evan sighed and rubbed his head. "Can we talk about this at home?"

Owen inhaled again, trying to calm down. He needed to get them home in one piece, after all. And once they were, Evan was getting a talking to.

"It was nice meeting you, Marie. Maybe we can do it again under better circumstances," he said, smiling a little easier now than he'd seen Evan.

"I agree."

Evan led the way from A&E and to where he'd parked his car. Owen took the keys from him and held the door, closing it when he was settled. The drive home didn't take long, and they were silent during it, but once the front door closed behind them, Evan said, "Okay, let's hear it."

Owen pointed a finger at him. "Sit your ass down. I'll get us a drink and you can tell me what happened." His voice was way calmer than he expected, and he strode to the kitchen, setting the coffee going and giving them both time to breathe before they had the conversation. He had no idea how Evan had got the cut, but all the possibilities swirled in his head. But he was fine. He was home. Owen could take care of him now.

When the coffees were ready, he carried them back to the living room and handed one to Evan. He sat on the opposite side of the sofa and waited. After several sips of his drink, Evan explained, and Owen's blood boiled and heated—two very similar responses to two very different stimuli. Boiled because that asshole was in big fucking trouble. Heated because Evan being a hero was fucking hot. Even if it put him in danger.

"Aren't you going to say anything?" Evan said when he finished.

"How is the girl doing?"

Evan stared at him long enough for Owen to feel the need to shift, but he didn't. "Not what I was expecting you to say. She was still in surgery when I left. I've asked Marie to let me know later."

Owen nodded. "As much as I want to rail at you for being a stupid ass for risking your life, I can't because you saved her life, and possibly your own, even as you risked it, too. I know you're more than capable of looking after yourself, but it's…" He shook his head. "It's different when I'm not there as backup. At least then I know someone has your back. When you're alone…" He didn't finish, unable to form the words he needed to explain.

"It's no different when you go to work, you know," Evan said softly, staring at his coffee.

Owen frowned. "What do you mean?"

"You guard royalty. Not only that, but the heir to the British throne. You put yourself in danger every time you walk out of that door." Evan jabbed his fingers towards the front of the house. "Yes, you have other guards with you. But not me. I couldn't do your job because I don't have the experience. But it's still not me at your back, making sure you survive the day. It's me working through the hours, hoping you will not be the one rolled through the doors of A&E, needing my expertise. And that fucking sucks."

Owen's heart thumped painfully, and his throat closed. He needed to talk about what happened that night, and there was no better time. "I thought we would lose everything if we stayed together," he murmured, unable to look at him. "I thought we'd lose our friends, our family." He swallowed. "Ourselves. I was so fucking scared of losing you I did the one thing that lost you, anyway. And I am so sorry." He closed his eyes, trying not to let the tears escape. He had no right to them. He had caused the pain. He should carry it.

Hands cupped his jaw, startling him into opening his eyes, the tears hovering on the edges of his eyelashes. Evan's green gaze was wet but bright.

"Do you want me? Do you want us? Ignoring everything else, do you want this?" Evan asked.

Owen licked his lips. "Yes," he whispered.

Evan's smile had the tears losing the battle and falling down his cheeks. "Good."

Then Evan's mouth met his, and he was lost. Just like that night. The moment Evan touched him, Owen bowed down to him, doing whatever he asked, whether it was words or actions, he followed where Evan led. He gave over every ounce of his control to Evan's safe keeping.

And as Evan's tongue swiped across his lower lip, Owen let himself fall under his spell. He had no idea if they could make this work, but he wasn't letting go again. He couldn't. He didn't have the strength to cut their ties a second time.

Evan pulled back, and Owen chased him, joining their lips again. "Hold on, Owen," Evan said, gently stopping his onslaught. "We're taking this slowly, okay? We need to work through whatever issues you had with us being together the first time. Yes, we've grown older, but those fears won't go away unless we deal with them."

Owen nodded. "I know. I guess the first thing we should do is talk to Dominic."

"I agree. While he doesn't have the ability to stop us from doing this, if we still want to do it, we'd be wise to listen to what he says. Randall, too."

Owen dropped his forehead onto Evan's shoulder. "How is your arm?"

"Tender, but it'll be fine in a few days."

"It didn't do any permanent damage?"

Evan shook his head. "A couple of places were deeper than others, but there's no nerve damage or anything like that. I'll be good to go once the wound itself has healed."

Owen was quiet for a moment, thinking back on Evan's words from earlier. "I can't stop my job," he said finally.

Evan manoeuvred Owen to face him again, his hands resting on either side of his head. "I would never ask it. Ever. I know it's dangerous, and I know you can take care of yourself. But when I'm not there, I have to trust other people to have your back, and it sucks. But I trust you, and I trust them. It's everyone else I don't." He rested their foreheads together. "But I will never, ever ask you to stop doing what you love."

Owen lifted his head. "Do you want to rest for today or speak to Dominic now?"

Evan chuckled. "You're far too impatient."

"No. I want to mend what I broke by sending you away."

"You broke nothing. You did what you thought was right, and I can't ask for more. Yes, it hurt. Yes, I needed to leave for a while to figure things out, but you're my home, Owen. You always have been."

"I need—"

"I know what you need," Evan said, and he dragged Owen closer for another kiss, wrapping his hand around his throat and keeping him in place.

There was nothing soft about this one. No need to reaffirm anything. They just needed. Hands grappled to hold on, fingers skimmed skin, lips took and tongues tasted. It was completely new and not new all at the same time. The feeling of being adrift that he'd felt since Evan left disappeared, and Owen found that thread and held on, not willing to let it go ever again.

When they separated, Owen said, "I'm sorry for what I said and did."

Evan smiled. "And I'm sorry for leaving and not fighting for us."

Forgiveness was complete, but they would never forget, but that was something each of them would have to deal with, both individually and together. That tiny glimmer of doubt which would probably crop up in random places would need to be monitored, but Owen believed they could do it. He believed they could live happily ever after.

"Let's visit Dominic. Is he working today?" Evan asked.

"He should be at home."

"Call him to double-check."

Owen complied, always happy to do what Evan told him to. Maybe if Evan had ordered Owen not to be so stupid seven years ago, they would've been together all this time. But it wasn't Evan's fault. Not even a little.

"Hey, Dom. Are you up for visitors today?" Owen asked.

"Hey. Hang on, let me check with Randall." His voice went quieter, words distorted and mumbled, but then he came back. "Yes, sure. We'd love to have you over. Do you want to stay for dinner?"

Owen mouthed to Evan, who nodded. "Yeah, we'd love to."

"All right. See you whenever you get here."

Evan stood. "I'm going to get changed before we go. As much as I *love* scrubs, I'd like some jeans instead."

"Need any help?" Owen asked, smirking.

Evan sent a lopsided grin his way and winked. "Not this time, but maybe later." He disappeared into his bedroom.

Owen flopped back on the sofa, staring at the ceiling. He traced his fingers over his neck, closing his eyes and remembering the feel of Evan holding him. It had been the same that night. Being manhandled and ordered to do things had made Owen so fucking hot. He'd never felt that with anyone else, never even realised it was something he wanted. It was only when Evan had slammed him back against the door, hand around his throat, lips on his, that something clicked inside him. He had no inclination to disobey Evan. Ever.

That might have been something else that had tipped him over the edge all those years ago. He hadn't wanted that in his daily life, only in the bedroom. Maybe he'd thought he had to change. He didn't know, but there was no point trying to figure it out now. It was water under the bridge and all that.

Fingers covered his own that were still around his neck, and he opened his eyes to meet Evan's gaze.

"You really do like that?"

"Yes." Evan raised an eyebrow, and Owen licked his lips and swallowed. "Yes, Sir." He couldn't help but add, "But only in the bedroom."

Evan's mouth quirked. "Not in the living room? Or the kitchen? Or the garden?"

Owen's blood heated, and he shivered. "Maybe," he whispered.

"Good to know." Evan released him. "Let's go."

Owen exhaled shakily and stood, following Evan to the door. Evan opened it, but Owen didn't immediately exit. "What are we? Lovers? Boyfriends? What do we tell Dom?"

Evan brushed a finger down Owen's cheek. "I'd like to be a boyfriend at least, but we can figure out tags later if you'd prefer."

Heat bloomed in Owen's chest. "Boyfriends sounds good," he murmured.

Evan smiled and nodded. They headed for Dominic and Randall's house, stopping to grab some beer and wine in case they decided they needed it. Randall greeted them at the door, hugging them before leading them to the kitchen.

"Sorry for intruding on your Sunday," Evan said, placing the wine on the counter.

Dominic chuckled. "You know you're welcome anytime."

Randall kissed his cheek and took the spoon from his hand. "Go chat. I'll finish these and bring them in."

They headed for the living room, settling onto the two sofas: Dominic on one and Evan and Owen on the other. Owen wasn't sure how to act, so he sat on the edge with his arm on his knees.

"You both look serious. What's up?" Dominic asked.

Evan sighed. "We have something we want to run by you."

Randall came in with their drinks, passing them out. "I'll be in the back room if you need me."

"You can stay," Evan said.

Randall waved them away. "No, it's okay. You talk. Call me if you need anything." He disappeared.

"He truly could've stayed," Evan said.

"He knows. I can call him back if you'd prefer?"

Owen's stomach was in knots. Were they about to make a mistake? He glanced at Evan, who was still talking to Dominic.

"It's fine either way." Evan looked at him and raised his eyebrows. Owen swallowed and nodded. "Owen and I are trying a relationship."

Blunt and to the point. Owen closed his eyes, waiting for Dominic's reaction. What he hadn't expected was for him to hoot and holler for Randall. His boyfriend came rushing in, looking flustered.

"What?"

"Owen and Evan are together! I told you!"

Randall grinned and clapped his hands. "Oh, that's so wonderful! I'm so happy for you." He settled next to Dominic. "How did it happen? When did it happen?"

Evan cleared his throat. "Seven years ago."

Owen winced and bit his lip. "Kind of," he added.

Dominic looked confused. "What do you mean, seven years ago?"

Owen licked his lips, not wanting Evan to take the weight of the conversation. "We first got together seven years ago. The week before Evan left for Italy. Afterwards... I made the wrong choice. I told him it was a mistake." Evan's hand rested on his nape.

"I was a little upset, so I took the time for a breather. I never expected to stay gone for so long."

"How come I never knew?" Dominic said.

"It wasn't intentional," Evan said and squeezed Owen's nape. "But I couldn't stay away. I made a promise to someone to see if I could fix what was fractured. I've been struggling to find a way, but then, earlier today..."

Owen found his voice. "He decided to be a fucking hero." He reached for Evan's arm, gently pulling up the long sleeve he'd worn. "He got slashed at the hospital and has stitches. It's why he's not at work."

Dominic shifted forward. "Oh, hell. I hadn't even realised you were supposed to be at work. What happened?"

Evan went through the story again, and still Owen's anger rose. The outcome could've been so much different. He swallowed down a growl that wanted to escape. No one hurt what was his. No one. Only two positives had come from the event: the girl being okay, and that it helped them to clear the air. It might've taken them months before that happened otherwise.

"And I'm assuming Owen went all caveman?" Dominic said, receiving a backhanded slap on the chest from Randall.

Evan laughed. "A little. But it led us to have the talk we should've had all those years ago, and we seem to be on the same page now." He glanced at Owen, who nodded, and his hand released Owen's neck, sliding down his back.

"So, you're now seeing each other?" Dominic asked.

"Yes. Evan is my boyfriend," he said with a grin.

6

Evan

E van's chest expanded with Owen's words. It was something he hadn't ever believed they could get to, and though they had a lot of work ahead of them, it was great to hear it.

"This should be a celebration, then," Randall said. "I'm glad you brought drinks." He rose, shuffling out of the room.

Dominic stared at them, his mouth curving upwards. "I knew something was going on, but I hadn't realised it already had." He chuckled. "I can't believe you both kept that from me."

Evan winced. "I didn't intentionally keep it from you. I just couldn't talk about it in the beginning, and then as time passed, it seemed too little too late."

"Same here," Owen said.

"Will you tell me what happened?"

Evan glanced at Owen and shook his head. "It doesn't matter. It's forgiven."

"In that case, where are those drinks?" Dominic said, clapping his hands.

When Randall came back and handed out beers to everyone but Evan, who got a glass of iced water because of his pain medication, he put on some background music, and Owen and Evan dished all the news out to him about Dominic's and their bad behaviours as kids. They would never run out of stories, Evan didn't think, so the hours passed, and before he knew it, Randall disappeared to finish dinner.

As they settled around the table with plates of steaming roast dinner, Evan recognised what he wanted from his life. He wanted a home like this, where he could come through the door and have people ready to greet him, or vice versa. Where he could stand side by side with someone to cook their dinner. Where he could sit on the sofa and chat about anything and everything. It was perfect. He glanced at Owen. Hopefully, it would be what they eventually had.

Owen's hand rested on his thigh beneath the table. "Are you okay?" he murmured.

Evan smiled at him, though his arm was aching viciously. "I am."

"We'll go home after this. You're tired." Owen raised his eyebrows pointedly.

Evan huffed a laugh. "I am. I need more paracetamol, too."

"Oh, shit. I forgot." Owen glanced at Dominic. "Do you have some paracetamol?"

Dominic rose and rounded the island separating the kitchen and dining room, riffling through a drawer. "Here you go." He handed the packet to Evan. "I should've thought to ask."

Evan shook his head. "I should've thought to bring some with me. I usually do." He took out two and rinsed them down with some water. "It should kick in soon."

"Do you want anything else to eat?" Randall said. "There's plenty left."

He held up his hand. "I'm good, thanks."

"Owen?" Randall asked.

"Nah, I better behave, or I'll need to work it off. It's hard enough keeping this up." He patted his stomach, and everyone laughed. "Are you working tomorrow?" he asked Dominic.

"Yes. Andrew, Kean and Kendal—it's so much easier saying their names when I'm not in their presence—have an event at the local hospital."

Evan perked up. "Oh, I remember that. They had requested a visit to A&E, but we said it wasn't a good idea. They'll probably end up getting their own way, though."

Dominic laughed. "I don't doubt it, but I'll see if I can dissuade them. If I tell them what happened to you, they might give it a miss." He glanced at Owen. "Freddie's out and about, too, isn't he?"

Owen nodded, sipping his drink. He'd switched to water after his one and only beer as he was driving home. "We're heading into London. Locke is back after her Christmas holiday, so the team is back!"

Evan shook his head, resting his chin in his hand, his elbow on the table. "I don't know how Prince Freddie puts up with you two."

Owen leaned closer, resting his head on Evan's shoulder and peering up at him. "Because we're the best in the business, babe." His straight face lasted all of two seconds before he burst out laughing, ruining his words.

"For that, I'm telling Brett. You know what'll happen," Dominic said.

Owen's face dropped. "No! You're not telling him a thing! What happened to the best friend code?"

"Your ego needs a raincheck," Dominic said, his mouth twitching. "I'm sure Brett will love whooping your ass in the ring."

"Fuck, man." Owen sighed and slumped back. "I suppose I need the extra training as my wingman isn't up for it yet." He winked at Evan, and Evan's chest warmed, even as his eyes grew heavy.

"Well, now that you've upset me, I'm going and taking this man with me." Owen stood.

Evan cleared his throat, trying to keep his eyes open. He was so tired suddenly. "Do you want some help to clear up?"

Randall waved him away. "You get some rest. I remember what it was like after such a high-adrenaline event. Sleep is your best friend for the next few days. We can manage just fine."

Owen raked his fingers through Evan's hair, and his eyelids fluttered. "Come on. Let's get you home." Owen grabbed his hands and pulled him to his feet. Evan rubbed a hand over his face, trying to wipe away the tiredness.

"Thank you for dinner," he said. At least he hoped he did. It sounded vaguely muffled.

Owen said something to Dominic and Randall, but Evan was concentrating too hard on walking. They made it to the car, and Owen clicked Evan's seatbelt in place. Seconds later, Owen woke him because they'd reached home.

"Our home," he murmured.

"Yes, sweetheart. Our home," Owen agreed, taking most of Evan's weight as they shuffled to the door and onwards to the bedroom. *Owen's* bedroom, Evan was awake enough to realise. He sat on the bed, barely keeping himself upright as Owen removed his shoes, socks and jeans, and then he gently pushed Evan to lie down, covering him. "I'll be right back, sweetheart. Sleep. I'm here."

"Want..." Evan started, but sleep pulled him under.

Overly heated and thirsty, Evan woke slowly, trying to wet his cotton mouth. He shoved at the covers that were level with his forehead, hissing when his arm screamed at him. Resting it back on the bed, he rolled to his back and inhaled the cooler air now he wasn't submerged in a duvet. He glanced to the side, but the bed was empty, and when he squinted at the clock on the bedside table, he knew why. When was the last time he'd slept until ten in the morning when he hadn't been working nights or lates?

He rubbed the sleep from his eyes and swung his legs over the edge of the bed. His gaze snagged on a glass of water, tablets and a note. He started with the water and tablets, swallowing them whole and then read the note.

I didn't want to wake you. You need rest. Hydrate, medicate and veg out in front of the TV. I'll be home for six o'clock if all goes well. I'll bring dinner. And yes, it'll be pizza. Don't do too much. Think of this as a holiday. Oh, and if you're up before eleven, the coffee should still be warm enough for the first cup of the day. X

Owen knew him too well. If he had his way, he would find something to keep him occupied, which would undoubtedly mean he wouldn't rest, but when Owen made a point of it... Evan sighed. Could he sit and do nothing? Time would tell.

He rose gingerly, not wanting to move too fast after sleeping so long, visited the toilet and headed for the kitchen. The coffee was indeed lukewarm, but it would tide him over while he made another pot. Which he did while he waited for his toast. Both were ready about the same time, so he picked them up and settled on the sofa with the remote. The first thing he did was check the news reports—nothing interesting. Then he checked social media—same. He double-checked his messages and emails to make sure he hadn't forgotten to reply and then cursed and fumbled to call Matteo.

"Well, if it isn't Mr I'm-too-busy-to-call-my-friend," Matteo said as a greeting.

"I have a valid excuse," Evan promised.

"Which is?"

"I got sent home from work yesterday because of an incident and then I fell asleep early." It was half true. He'd tell Matteo that he spent the evening with his other friends, eventually.

"What happened? I've not heard about anything."

For probably the fourth or fifth time, he went through the events of the previous day, and Matteo cursed. "I'm coming over."

"No, you don't—" The silence on the other end of the line advertised that he'd hung up without Evan needing to check. He huffed. At least he wouldn't be bored. And Matteo had the entire day off, so maybe he could keep him occupied until Owen got home. Besides, he had news to share. Matteo didn't know about the past rockiness with Owen, but he would by the end of the day. Not their dynamic in the bedroom, but everything else. Although Evan was seeing a new side to Owen he hadn't expected—a possessive caretaker role outside of the bedroom. It seemed they swapped roles depending on their situation, which was eye-opening.

Matteo wore a completely different look when he wasn't working, and when Evan opened the door to him, he couldn't help but smile. His bleached light grey hair was designed to be messy, and his thick-rimmed glasses stood out against his pale skin tone, making the artfully done makeup look like he was ready for the catwalk. He wore skinny black jeans, so tightly fitted that Evan had no idea how he could move. A dark purple shirt with collar jeweller and a skinny black jacket with the sleeves of both were rolled up to the middle of his forearms, and his shoes had at least a three-inch heel. He looked absolutely stunning, and Evan—not for the first time—wondered how he had the energy to do it. Evan could barely throw on jeans and a shirt if he wanted to look decent.

"I can see I need to do something about your look again," Matteo said, brushing past Evan and making himself at home.

Evan snorted and closed the door. "Coffee?"

"Of course." Matteo sat on the sofa and pulled out his phone. "I'll make a note of what a disaster you are while you make it."

Evan smiled and headed for the kitchen, making the coffee just like Matteo liked it—a lot creamier than Evan and Owen did. When it was ready, he handed it to the man, who cradled it like a newborn baby.

"Looks worse than you said it did," Matteo said, nodding at Evan's arm.

He lifted it and rotated it a little. "It's a long cut, but it's not deep. A couple of places were deeper than others, hence the stitches, but it's fine. It'll heal in no time."

"Sometimes, I wonder about our job." Matteo's frown deepened.

"Are you thinking of leaving?" Evan wasn't sure what to think about that if he was.

Matteo shook his head, though it didn't seem like he was sure. "No. I just...it's a lot, isn't it? The hours, the shifts, the patients." He sighed. "It's not the easiest job to do."

Evan chuckled. "Not even remotely, but with every job, there are pitfalls. I try to remember the good things instead of the bad."

"Like Italy?"

Evan's heart thumped painfully as his thoughts drifted to Antonio. "Yeah," he breathed. "Antonio was a wonderful man, and it's a shame he was taken from the world so soon, but he touched people for the time he was here. Myself included."

"Are you ever going to tell me what made you leave Italy?" Matteo asked. "I know something did, but you never expanded on it whenever I asked."

Evan sipped his coffee, staring into the cup when he rested it on his thigh. He sighed. "To explain that, I need to go back to before I left for Italy."

"I have all day," Matteo said, kicking off his heels and tucking his feet beneath him.

Evan had never told his story to anyone except Antonio, but he told Matteo everything. What happened between him and Owen that night, his choice to flee the country to get away, but also not going as far as he could've because he didn't truly want to leave. How he spent his time working as an in-home carer for people and was given the position at Antonio's side, where he spent the final year of his time.

"Antonio wormed his way into my life, and I ended up telling him everything, just like I am to you. Little by little, he got more out of me until I had nothing left to tell him. Before he died, he made me promise to come home and fix things with Owen." He chuckled, though the humour was missing. "I kept the promise."

"You've fixed things with him?" Matteo asked.

"We went back to the way things were before but with strained silences between us. I wasn't sure we were ever going to properly get back to where we had been." Evan couldn't keep the smile from his face. "But then yesterday..."

Matteo leaned forward, and Evan dragged it out. His friend grabbed a cushion and hit him with it. "Tell me!"

Evan laughed, holding his cup away from the attack. "All right! I had to call Owen to pick me up from the hospital because I couldn't drive. When we got home, we talked. About everything. I found out why he pushed me away, and we made up." He peered at Matteo. "We're trying a relationship now."

Matteo squealed, almost spilling his coffee. "Yes! Oh, my god. I'm so happy for you." He grabbed his phone. "This deserves a treat." He pressed some buttons, smiling, and Evan couldn't want for a better friend. He'd have to get him, Owen and Dominic together properly. He was sure they'd get on well. "There we go. They will deliver lunch soon."

They spent the next hour catching up with Matteo's life, which was in his own words "as exciting as it ever was." When the doorbell rang, Matteo waved Evan down and fetched the food, depositing it on the coffee table. The scent of spices filled the air.

"I went with spicy pasta dishes because I know how you like them."

Evan hummed and reached for his plate. "Smells delicious. Not as good as pizza but still delicious. Thanks."

"No worries." They ate for a few minutes before Matteo said, "Are you worried about your relationship with Owen?"

Evan inhaled, letting it out slowly. "Mostly, no, but there is that lingering doubt at the back of my mind. I know he's sorry. I know why he did what he did, and although I have forgiven him for it, I doubt I will ever forget. I need to trust him, and I do, but..."

Matteo nodded. "You'll have to work through that because you don't want it to fester and make things a thousand times worse. If you don't trust him, you may as well end it now."

The man was right, and Evan would talk to Owen about it at some point. He didn't want to unbalance their relationship straight away, but it was something he would need to discuss with him, and soon.

"Anyone you have your sights on lately?" he said instead.

Matteo's cheeks flushed a little. "Yes, but he's straight, so it's just a crush."

"Who?"

Matteo ducked his head, uncharacteristically shy. "Dr Wallis."

Evan raised his eyebrows. "Seriously? Even after our last conversation?"

Picking at his food, Matteo shrugged. "He's a genuinely nice guy, which doesn't happen as often as the movies and books imply. I know he's straight because he has an ex-wife and a daughter, and I've heard the gossip from the mill, but I can't help it. I'm attracted to nice people." He chuckled and shook his head. "I'm still wanting my fairy tale ending."

"You'll get it. I know you will because you're tenacious. You won't stop until you do. Besides, who wouldn't want what you have to offer?"

Matteo's cheeks flushed again, and Evan smiled, making a note to give his friend more compliments. He deserved them because he was one of those nice guys he'd mentioned. Their conversation moved to general things as if they needed to break from the heaviness of their topics, and he couldn't believe it when he checked the clock, and it was almost dinnertime.

"Do you want to stay and see Owen?" he asked. "He should be home in half an hour or so."

Matteo shook his head. "Another time. You, my friend, need to talk to him. I know you. I know you want to put it off, but time is of the essence here."

Evan sighed. "I don't want to ruin things when we've only just started."

"But isn't it better to get things sorted from the beginning? Before you get deeper in and get hurt a lot more." Matteo stood, gathering his things.

Evan's stomach churned. He'd see what mood Owen was in when he returned and go from there, though he didn't tell Matteo that. Matteo hugged him and left, leaving the house a lot quieter, and Evan stared around the room. He would go stir-crazy looking at these walls for a week. He'd have to find something to do while he was off work. Maybe he could bother Sally for a few hours.

He settled back on the sofa, staring at the TV though not seeing it, and thought about what he wanted to do. Could he let Owen go if he realised he couldn't deal with doubting him? He hoped he could work through it, but he wasn't sure how. Maybe it was just something that would rectify itself with time.

He knew one thing for certain; he didn't want to lose Owen. Not now they'd found their way back to each other again.

7

Owen

"Edinburgh and Delta are two minutes out," Owen said into his earpiece, alerting the other guards at the event that Prince Freddie and Prince Damon were about to pull up in the car. Owen was in the car in front of the princes, while Locke was in the car with them. They usually changed who stayed with them so anyone trying to find a pattern couldn't. To be honest, though, it didn't matter. If someone wanted to try for the princes, they would, regardless of who guarded them.

"Pulling up now," he said, climbing out of the car before it had even stopped. His gaze scanned the area, studying the weak areas they'd identified during their planning session. Nothing stood out to him, and he headed for the passenger door of the princes' car, Locke joining him.

"All clear," he heard through his earpiece, so he opened the door, putting his body between them as much as was humanly possible—which wasn't much.

"Heading inside," Locke said.

When they entered the building, Locke and Owen dropped back a little, still scanning the space for potential threats, even as Freddie and Damon greeted the hosts. They were visiting a charity that helped LGBT+ people to find homes when they'd been thrown out. They also helped them to find jobs, clothing and anything else they needed to ensure they landed on their feet. Owen had looked into the charity and was highly supportive of their cause, not only because of what had happened to Evan, though that was a big part. If Owen's mother hadn't agreed to let Evan stay with them for the last six months of his school time, he wasn't sure what would've happened to him.

He tuned out the conversation, instead keeping his concentration on where they were. From the corner of his eye, he saw something. "Back wall, by the stairs," he murmured to Locke. "I'm going to take a look."

Making it look natural, he changed course, moving closer to where he'd seen a movement that shouldn't have been there. His hand was ready to grab his gun, but he wasn't reaching for it yet. When he got within three steps, the head poked around the corner again, gasping at Owen.

Owen relaxed marginally when he saw the teenager, but children, unfortunately, could still be used to hurt or kill people. He moved closer, the kid unable to go anywhere except up the stairs, and he stopped beside him.

"Hello," he said.

"Um, hey," the boy said. He pressed back against the wall, making himself as small as he could.

"Are you supposed to be down here?" Owen asked, aware of the open channel between him and Locke. The boy shook his head. "Are you here to hurt them?" he murmured.

The boy's eyes widened. "No! I promise! I...I just wanted to see them! I... They're so...nice!"

Owen's heart settled a little because he didn't think the boy was that good of an actor—though it wasn't impossible. "Would you like to meet them?"

"Owen…" Locke said in his ear, but Owen ignored her.

"Can I?" The boy's shock came across audibly.

"What's your name?"

"Riley."

Owen held up a finger to the boy. "Locke, can you ask our hosts if they know Riley, please?" He waited for an answer, not removing his gaze from the boy, waiting to see if there was anything that crossed his expression to advertise nefarious actions. But nothing showed except surprise.

"They say he's a lodger here. His parents tossed him out six months ago. His Highness has asked for you to bring him over." He could hear the disapproval in Locke's voice, but she hadn't met the boy, so he expected the uneasiness.

"You've not got any weapons on you, have you?" Riley shook his head, patting his hands down his body. "Come on," Owen said, gesturing to him. He rested his hand on Riley's shoulders, the move giving him some control of the situation. He could keep Riley in place if he tried anything.

They stopped beside the princes, who were both smiling at the boy. "Your Highnesses, this is Riley."

Freddie reached a hand out to shake Riley's, surprising the boy. "Nice to meet you, Riley. How are you finding things here?"

"G-Good, thanks. I-It's a lot better than at h-home."

Freddie's smile wavered, but he nodded. "I can imagine. What do you want to do when you finish school, Riley?"

"I w-want to be an accountant. I love numbers and figuring stuff out." His voice became stronger the more they talked.

"That's a fantastic career," Damon said. "I enjoy numbers, too. I do a lot of auditing and examining figures to make sure everything is as it should be."

Riley's eyes widened again. "That sounds great. I want to go to college, but I'm not sure if I can. I'm trying to find a job at the moment so I can pay for what I need."

Freddie and Damon shared a look, and Owen's mouth twitched. He knew exactly what they were thinking.

"Keep up the good work at school, and you never know what'll happen," Freddie said. "School is very important."

Riley nodded. "It is. I enjoy it. Today is a teacher training day, so we're not at school, but I never miss a day." He frowned. "Except once," he whispered.

They didn't ask when that was, though Owen assumed it was the day his parents threw him out. They chatted for a little longer before the hosts gently encouraged Riley to head back to his room so they could continue with their visit. As they followed the two princes through the building, Locke murmured in his ear, "That was not part of the plan."

Owen grinned. "Of course it wasn't. Plans never go to plan."

The rest of the visit was unremarkable in that nothing else happened, but the charity itself seemed to be a good one. Owen would have to look into it further when he got home—or ask Freddie and Damon about it. He always supported what LGBT+ charities he could. The only thing that had happened was the reappearance of Malachi Sanders, reporter extraordinaire. After a few words for his magazine, they were home free. Owen did wonder if Malachi would write what they said or spin it into something else, but that was the life of people in the public eye.

When they were on their way home, his thoughts turned to Evan, as they always did when he had some downtime. As much as he wanted to believe in them and their chances of their relationship working, there was this knot inside him that wanted to make it up to Evan for what he'd done. Despite Evan forgiving him, he didn't think he could forgive himself. They'd wasted so much time, and it was all his fault.

Once they were back at Windsor, Locke headed off to debrief Brett, their boss, and Owen settled outside Freddie and Damon's suite. They didn't often have guards staying outside their rooms, except for the king's office, but since the events of a few months ago, when someone infiltrated their home and tried to kidnap Dominic's sister, King Andrew had requested a slight increase in guards around the property. It was usually just Freddie who had the extra guards, but they no longer believed Windsor Castle to be infallible, which was a good and a bad thing.

Owen spent his time scrolling on his phone. He considered messaging Evan but didn't want to disturb him, especially as it wasn't something they'd done before. Usually when they were at work, they didn't message and only caught up when they got home. Maybe that would change once they found their new normal, but for now, he didn't want to upset their balance.

Locke came to relieve him an hour before his shift finished. "Don't forget to check in with Brett before you go home," she said.

Owen rolled his eyes. "When have I ever forgotten?"

They hadn't had the chance to talk about anything personal that day, and he didn't want to tarry right then, so he'd catch her up with his love life another day.

"See you tomorrow," he said.

Locke nodded and settled on the chair, and Owen headed for the security room, which Dominic had renamed "Sec HQ," and everyone had started using it. He knocked and entered, seeing the room half empty, which was usual during the day.

"Boss," he said, sitting in a chair opposite Brett.

"I hear there was an unplanned visitor."

Owen sighed. "Unplanned but unarmed."

Brett stared at him for a long second and then nodded. "Don't make it a regular occurrence."

"I won't."

"Tell me about it."

Owen went through the visit from the moment they left Windsor to the moment they returned, Brett taking notes as needed. His boss always debriefed guards separately and then compared the statements because he said it highlighted areas that either needed work, occasionally when paired guards weren't working together well, and sometimes when guards weren't happy. Owen could understand it, and he was in awe of Brett's ability to lead the security team as well as do his job as Prince Christian's guard. He wasn't sure the man could keep up the workload, but so far, everything was working well, though Brett seemed to have darker circles under his eyes than Owen had noticed before.

"Okay, head home. I'll see you tomorrow," Brett said, closing his folder.

"Thanks." He handed in his earpiece and radio, as they all did at the end of their shifts. He kept his gun, though. He had a permit for it, after all.

Owen bypassed his locker, not needing anything he didn't have on him, and headed for the exit. He walked to the pizza place down the road from his house, ordered two large pizzas and carried them home.

Juggling the pizza boxes, he unlocked the front door, surprised when they didn't end up on the floor. "I'm home! Come get your food!" He smiled when he saw Evan on the sofa. "I hope you've been there all day."

Evan grinned, standing to grab the boxes from his hands. "Actually, I have mostly. Matteo came over once he'd heard what happened and we had lunch here and spent the afternoon talking. It was nice."

Owen pushed down the possessiveness he felt at someone else getting Evan's time—it was something he would need to get used to. "I'm glad. We'll have to invite him over so I can get to know him better." Owen took off his coat and shoes before settling beside Evan on the sofa.

"I've already decided to do that. Invite Dominic and Randall, too."

Owen stared at Evan, wanting to lean forward and kiss him, but still a little unsure about their dynamic. Evan chuckled, wrapped a hand around Owen's nape and dragged him forward, fusing their lips. Owen sighed into his mouth and then wished he'd kept his air because Evan didn't let up until Owen was lightheaded and gasping for air when they broke apart.

"Wow," Owen said. "I need to leave and come back more often."

Evan's eyes darkened. "No, you don't. You get that anytime you or I want it."

"Every second?"

"Whenever and wherever."

Owen's heart skipped a beat. "Every second it is, then," he whispered. Much to his disappointment, though, Evan reached for the pizza instead of more of him, and Owen breathed to rein himself in before doing the same.

"How was work?" Evan asked after they'd each demolished one slice.

Owen finished his mouthful. "Informative." At Evan's raised eyebrows, he explained about the kid and then described the charity itself. "I had a look into it when we got back to Windsor, and it looks good. I want to do a bit more research, but if it all pans out—as I'm sure it will; otherwise, Freddie and Damon wouldn't be interested—I'll consider donating to them."

Evan smiled at him. "You have such a big heart."

Owen flushed, not used to the compliments. "I'm small fry compared to some."

"But every bit helps them, doesn't it?" Evan said. "If they're really that good, count me in, too."

They finished their pizza, and Owen tidied it away. When he entered the living room again, Evan was hiding a yawn behind his hand. "I bet you got no extra sleep, did you?"

"I didn't get up until ten o'clock."

Owen put his hands on his hips. "That's not what I meant."

Evan chuckled. "Matteo was here, and I wasn't tired."

"Come on." He held out his hand. "Paracetamol and bed."

Evan's eyes darkened. "I like the sound of the second one. Are you joining me?"

"If it will get you to stay there, yes."

Evan rose, stalking Owen, and Owen stepped backwards as the new look in Evan's eyes registered. "In the bedroom. Now."

Owen turned and almost ran. He wasn't sure what it was about Evan's tone, but whenever he spoke like that, Owen could do nothing else but comply. He waited beside the bed, not knowing what else Evan wanted. The man couldn't do much, healing as he was, but when Evan entered the room, Owen sucked in a breath.

"Strip me," Evan ordered.

Owen did, being careful of his arm, and asked, "Did you take paracetamol?"

Evan nodded but said nothing. Owen continued removing his clothes until Evan was down to his boxers.

"Everything," he said.

Owen dropped to his knees, guiding the boxers over the rapidly lengthening shaft. He inhaled, wanting so much to taste him but not being able to because Evan hadn't said he could. When Evan stepped out of the fabric, Owen peered up at him. Evan's mouth quirked as he stepped away, moving to the bed. Owen tried not to feel upset about it. He turned his head to the side, watching Evan get comfortable on his back on the bed.

"Now strip yourself and make it slow."

Owen's stomach fluttered as his hands trembled at the thought of putting on a show for him. He stood, facing Evan, and his hands lifted to the buttons of his shirt, and he slowly unfastened them, one finger extended to slide across his skin as it appeared. He undid the cuffs and shrugged his shoulders, letting the material fall to the floor. Fingering the fastening of his trousers, he flicked it open, slowly lowering the zip, switching between watching Evan's face and his cock's reaction to his show. When the trousers fell to the floor, he kicked them away, removing his socks before standing there and teasing Evan with his fingers in the waistband of his boxers.

"Remove them," Evan ordered.

Owen couldn't get them off fast enough, and when he was fully naked, his cock strained towards his stomach.

"Come here." Evan crooked a finger. Owen stepped closer. "Straddle me."

Owen's throat dried up. "But your arm..."

Evan's mouth quirked. "That's why you're going to do all the work."

Owen hesitated a second, considering the position and the pressure it might put on Evan's arm, but it was inevitable he would give in. He climbed onto the bed beside Evan before lifting one leg over his thighs, sitting back on them, with their cocks between them.

Evan reached for him, and Owen leaned forward, making it easier for him. "I know you're worried, but I'll keep my arm to the side. That way, you don't need to be concerned about hurting me, okay?"

Owen exhaled a shaky breath. "Thank you. I would hate it if I made things worse."

Evan smiled. "You could only make things better, especially when I get my cock in your ass again."

Owen licked his dry lips. "Yeah?" he whispered, extremely glad they weren't waiting to get back to the sexy stuff.

Evan didn't reply, joining their lips in a kiss so filthy Owen couldn't think about anything at all. Evan's hand circled Owen's neck, tightening his hold as he pulled away. "Now get yourself ready while I stroke my dick and watch."

Owen's blood heated, and he lost the ability to think for a moment, but then he reached for the bedside table and grabbed the lube. Squirting some on his fingers, he reached behind him to finger his ass, spreading the lube over his pucker before sinking a finger as deep as he could. It burnt. It had been far too long since he'd had someone in there, but he didn't think about that. He stretched himself as quickly as he could, not wanting to waste any time.

By the time he could take three of his fingers without pain, he was trembling so hard he was struggling to stay upright.

"That's it. Fuck those fingers for me." Evan stroked his cock leisurely, grimacing up at Owen, but Owen could see it wasn't because of his arm. He was on the edge, just like Owen was.

"Please, Sir," Owen said, using the honorific because it was how he felt about Evan. He was his sir in this situation. "Please fill me."

"Such good manners. Get me ready."

Owen pulled his fingers free and reached for more lube, ecstatic to get his hands on Evan's cock again. There was more lube than he needed, so he wiped it on the bed sheets.

"Put me where you want me," Evan growled.

Shifting forward a bit, he reached behind him again to hold Evan's shaft at his entrance. His breath left him as he worked the dick inside him, needing to feel everything. The burn was back, but he didn't care. He wanted it all. He needed everything Evan could give him.

"That's it. Take what you need." Evan echoed Owen's thoughts. "There we go. Get that cock in your tight ass."

Owen's body trembled, and he lifted and dropped, fully encasing Evan's dick. "Oh, fuck," he breathed, closing his eyes.

He circled his hips, not lifting away, letting himself get used to it again but needing to feel Evan inside him, that connection.

Evan's fingers tightened at Owen's hips, and he distantly noted it was only one side and hoped that meant his other arm was securely out of the way.

"Move," Evan ordered, and Owen hissed as heat slid down his spine.

8

Evan

T he circling of Owen's hips was as much taunting as it was sensuous, but Evan needed more. He wanted to take Owen to the edge and hold him over it for as long as he could, ordering him to stop and start as he saw fit. And he would, too.

Owen lifted, and cool air surrounded Evan's cock, but then warmth encased him again. His stomach clenched with the need to succumb, grip Owen's hips and drive himself home again and again, but it would feel so much better if he waited. Owen's groans and moans were music to his ears, and he allowed Owen to set the pace. For now.

Precome leaked from Owen's cock, sliding down with every movement to pool on Evan's stomach. He swiped a finger through it and brought it to his mouth, licking the flavour from it.

"Fuck," Owen whispered, eyes locked onto his hand and mouth.

Evan swiped his finger through it again but, this time lifted it to Owen's mouth. His boyfriend sucked the finger in, his tongue swiping over the digit repeatedly until Evan pulled it free when he felt his orgasm building.

"Stop," he ordered, gritting his teeth against his instincts. Owen stopped but whined, his legs tightening around Evan's hips. He slipped his hand around Owen's cock, slowly gliding his hand up and down. Owen hissed and bucked, and Evan released him until he sat still before resuming again. Every time Owen moved, Evan stopped. Owen's body was a trembling mess of limbs, but Evan's wasn't much better. "Move."

Owen cursed and started an intense rhythm. It wouldn't take them long to get there again, and the moment they did, Evan said, "Stop."

"Fuck, fuck, fuck, fuck," Owen breathed but stopped.

"Well done. How much more can you take, do you think?"

Owen licked his lips, meeting his gaze. "As much as you'll give me, Sir."

Evan's heart expanded, and his cock pulsed, which Owen must've felt because his eyes widened, and his mouth fell open.

"Good answer. Circle your hips."

Owen did, biting his lips to a ruby-red shine as Evan's cock undoubtedly grazed his prostate each time. Then Evan canted his hips and said, "Ride me."

Owen lifted and fell, head dropping back as his body gave an all-encompassing shiver. "Oh, my god. Fuck, fuck. Oh, damn it." The words falling from Owen's mouth were music to Evan's ears, knowing he was hitting him in the right spot.

"That's it. Let my cock fill you. Let me spill inside you, leaving my come dripping from your ass. You're so fucking tight, but you won't be by the time I'm finished with you. You'll be gaping. So loose I'll have to shove something else up there with my cock."

Owen shivered again, and Evan glanced at Owen's cock as it jerked before pulsing with his release, sending streaks of come over Evan's stomach and chest. "Fucking hell," Owen whined, his nails biting into Evan's skin.

Evan gritted his teeth, holding onto his climax by his fingertips. When Owen gasped and his head fell forward, Evan cupped his cheek, lifting his head. "Again," he ordered, and Owen's eyes widened as he shook his head.

"I can't—"

"*Again.*"

Owen swallowed. "Yes, Sir." He lifted and fell, eyes locked with Evan's.

Evan let go of his cheek and encircled his cock, stroking with a twist beneath the head, a spot he knew would take Owen to the edge quickly. But the sensitivity of his shaft would hurt a little before he got there. Owen's speed increased until the slap of their skin together and their ragged breathing were the only sounds Evan could hear.

"I can't..." Owen gasped.

Evan tightened his hold on his dick. "Imagine sticking this into *me*. Would I be on my knees and you behind me? Would I be facing you, like we are now, me riding your dick? Would we be wrapped in each other's arms as we made love? What would be the position that would take you over the edge just from having your dick in my ass?

Owen moaned, his hips frantically trying to reach for that second release. Evan pushed himself to sit upright with his good hand, stilling Owen's movements for a moment. His hand rested against Owen's lower back, encouraging him into the motion he wanted, and Owen slid his arms around Evan's neck, Owen's cock between their bodies.

He bit Owen's earlobe. "Would you want your cock in my tight ass? My virgin hole? Or would you prefer me to wreck yours for anyone else? To make sure no one else could give you what I can? Is that what it would take?" He bit him again, and Owen buried his face in Evan's neck as his ass clenched around him again, his orgasm barrelling through his sensitive body.

Then Evan followed him, the contractions too beautiful for him to ignore this time. He tightened his hold on Owen, his teeth finding purchase on his neck, and let himself go.

They both trembled, and Evan's head spun. Without letting go of Owen, he dropped to his back, being careful his injured arm was out of the way, and shivered when tremors flowed through him.

"Holy fuck," Owen breathed.

Evan chuckled. "You took my words."

His cock slid free of Owen's body, and he groaned, but he rolled Owen to the side, and slid off the bed. "On your stomach." Owen obeyed without question, though his movements were sluggish. "Bend your knees to the sides."

He studied Owen's pucker, watching the come leaking from it, and he lapped it with his tongue, stuffing it back in again. Owen writhed and moaned but didn't stop him although he must've been sore.

"Next time, I'm tying you up and seeing how much more you can take before you have no choice but to disobey me."

Owen's hole clenched, and Evan shoved his tongue inside him one more time before slapping his ass and standing. He grabbed a cloth from the bathroom and wet it, cleaning Owen's body, even as he wanted to keep it all inside him.

"Hmm, I'm also going to get a plug. You'll be able to keep my come in your ass all day," he growled.

"Fucking hell," Owen groaned. "You're going to destroy me."

Evan slid up the bed, resting beside him. "And put you back together again. Each and every time," he promised.

Owen slammed their mouths together, their tongues tangling until Evan softened it. Their lips sipped at each other, and then Evan pulled back. "Time for bed."

They turned out the light and rearranged themselves on the pillows, Owen's head on Evan's chest, their arms holding tightly, though Evan kept his bandaged one to the side. Evan listened to Owen's breathing, knowing he wasn't falling asleep.

"What's wrong?" he asked.

Owen said nothing for the moment. "I'm scared."

"Of what?"

"That I'm not enough for you. That what happened will come between us again."

Evan exhaled heavily. "I know. I'm scared of that, too. But the only answer I have is that we need to take it one day at a time. Talk to each other if there are problems. Stay on the same page as much as possible."

"Okay."

Evan stayed awake for a long time after that, even after Owen had fallen asleep, wondering if their relationship—and by extension of that, their friendship—would survive. He had to take his own advice. Communication was key.

But four days later, he was gritting his teeth as Owen opened another parcel from his *admirer*. The calendar had been wrapped in gold paper with a blue bow on top and had, yet again, been left on the doorstep. Owen's smile was radiant because it was a coffee calendar, though why he was so excited about pictures of coffee, Evan didn't understand. Drinking it was so much better. The note was weird:

With your love of coffee, I thought you might like something to brighten your day. A picture of coffee for every month of the YEAR. Enjoy.

Evan frowned at it. "Why is the word capitalised at the end of a sentence? And what's with this number two?"

Owen shrugged, flipping through the calendar. "Don't know. This is awesome, though. It also tells you how to make certain drinks. I might have to try some of them."

Evan grumbled and headed for the kitchen, needing more coffee. "Don't take too long admiring it, you'll be late for work," he called.

Arms slid around his waist, making him jump. "Don't be grumpy. It's just a gift. I won't be leaving you for someone else. When they eventually tell me who they are, I'll turn them down with a thank you but no thank you. You're all I need."

Slightly mollified by those words, he turned in the circle of his arms and cupped Owen's jaw. "I'm glad because I don't think I could be without you again."

Owen's eyes glistened. "Me either."

"Me *neither*," Evan corrected.

"Does it matter?"

Evan huffed a laugh. "No."

"Exactly."

Owen kissed him, swiping his tongue across the bottom of Evan's lower lip, seeking entry. Evan obliged, deepening the kiss until his head spun. It wasn't to wipe away all thoughts of who sent the calendar. Not at all. But when they finally came up for air, he couldn't remember the day of the week, let alone anything else.

"See you later?" Owen asked.

"I'll be here." Because where else would he be when he couldn't use his arm? It was better than it had been, but twisting it wrong made it hurt all over again, and he still couldn't drive.

When the door closed behind his boyfriend, he stayed where he was, finishing his coffee. If only he could do something useful. His gaze settled on the note, and he straightened. Would Brett help him if he asked, or would he go squealing to Owen? Only one way of finding out.

He pulled out his phone and dialled. He'd been given Brett's number in case he needed to contact him about Owen, and he hoped he wouldn't mind him using it for a different reason.

"Evan? Everything okay?"

"Yes. Owen's just left, but please don't tell him I called. I…I have something to ask. A favour, really."

Brett was silent for a minute. "Go ahead."

He explained about the gifts and notes, feeling more stupid as he talked. "It's probably nothing, and I'm probably overreacting to it, but it just seems weird. Owen doesn't seem to think anything's wrong."

"Do you still have them? The notes and the calendar?"

"Yeah."

"Owen will be going out around eleven o'clock. Bring them over then. We can take a look."

Evan sighed. "Thanks. I appreciate it."

Brett snorted. "I'm sure Owen won't, but we always do strange things for the ones we love. See you soon."

Evan stared at the phone, Brett's words echoing in his head. *The ones we love.* He wasn't wrong. He did love Owen, and he was worried. It wasn't an excuse to have things checked. He truly believed this could be some weird stalker thing or something, and if it was, the danger wasn't just to Owen. It could bleed over into the royal family, too.

He settled in to watch TV for a while but ended up watching the clock instead. Who knew there were so many minutes between eight o'clock and eleven o'clock?

When the time finally came, he walked the distance to Windsor Castle, where the guards waved him through. He didn't need escorting, he was told, so he found his own way to the security room. He knocked but didn't enter. After hearing what happened when someone unexpectedly opened the door—they received several guns pointed towards them—he wouldn't ever do that.

The door opened, and Felix smiled at him. "Hey, come on in."

Evan entered, feeling weird being in Owen's space without him. "Morning," he said to Brett.

"Take a seat and tell us what's going on."

He'd already explained it to Brett on the phone, but if he wanted to hear it again, who was Evan to argue? Especially as he was asking a huge favour. So, he did, pointing out the items as he went.

"I have no idea why the words are capitalised and what the number means." Evan shrugged. "I'm probably overreacting."

Brett nodded. "Maybe, but we can try to get some prints off them. You're going to have to come up with an excuse why there is fingerprint powder over them when Owen comes home."

Evan exhaled. "Forgiveness is easier than permission?" he said tentatively.

Brett snorted, glancing at Felix. "I'm sure for most people." He rubbed a hand over his mouth. "Give us an hour. Owen won't be back until three at the earliest."

"Thanks." He stood. "I guess I'll go home and come back again."

He headed to the door but was stopped by Felix's voice. "Why not visit Randall? I'm sure he has something to keep you distracted instead of staring at the walls of your house."

Evan glanced at Brett, who had a small smile on his face but didn't contradict Felix's words. "Okay. I'll do that. Thanks."

He headed to Randall's office, getting a smile from Nick, another guard, who sat outside.

"Dominic is inside, but hopefully, they're decent," he joked.

"Wouldn't be the first time I've seen more than I should, though I always hope never to again."

Nick laughed and waved him in. "Good luck."

Evan knocked and entered, finding Dominic in his proper seat, by the king's office door, and Randall behind his desk. Neither looked flushed nor embarrassed, so he hoped he'd caught them on a good day.

"Hey, what are you doing here?" Dominic asked, standing for a hug.

Evan exhaled. "I'm doing something stupid but need to wait an hour before I get the results."

Dominic raised his eyebrows, waiting for more explanation, but Randall bustled in. "What do you need from us?"

Evan shrugged. "I was told you might have something for me to do to wile away the time?"

Randall beamed. "Oh wow! Yes. I'm sure I have something you can do." He looked around. "How are you with data entry?"

Evan chuckled. "I get by."

"Awesome. Have a seat, and I'll get you working."

Evan could see Dominic angling for more information, but until he had some himself, he didn't want to say anything. He spent the time entering events and tasks into the calendar for Randall, something Evan knew Randall could do himself, in probably half the time, but he was grateful for the distraction. When Felix called to say they'd finished, he almost raced back to the security room. Thankfully, after saying thank you to Randall.

Felix opened the door for him again, and Evan sat down. "Did you find anything?"

"Yes and no," Felix said. "There were definitely fingerprints on all of them, and they matched, but we didn't get a match on our database."

Evan frowned. "What did they match with them?"

"Each other. So the prints on note one matched with the print on note two and the calendar. Which means they all came from the same person."

"But a person we can't identify?"

Felix nodded. "Correct."

Evan sighed. "I don't know if that helps me or not."

Felix gave a small smile. "I do have some other things I'm going to check, but I can't guarantee results from that either. But I'll let you know if I do. In the meantime, I wouldn't worry too much.

I bet it's just someone interested in him. You never know, they might end up together."

"Over my dead body," Evan growled.

"Felix, Felix, Felix. Don't you know anything?" Brett said. "Did you both finally get your heads out of your asses and reconcile?"

Evan stared at him, mouth wide, though Brett didn't look at him. "Um, kind of. Yes."

"Good. Maybe he'll stop wandering around the place like a kicked puppy."

"How did I miss that?" Felix asked.

"Because you weren't looking," Brett said. "I see everything."

Felix nodded, and Evan chuckled. "On that note, I'll say goodbye. Sorry to waste your time."

Brett and Felix both waved him away, and Evan chuckled again at their joint actions. He headed home, bracing himself for questions when Owen returned.

Instead of waiting to see if he noticed, Evan charged in, headfirst. When Owen came through the door, but after he'd greeted him properly with a game of tonsil hockey, he said, "I did something stupid."

Owen frowned. "What?"

"You might hate me."

"What did you do?"

Evan sighed. "I took the notes and calendar to Brett for fingerprints."

Owen stared at home for a long moment and then burst out laughing. "You are so jealous you're turning green," he said between laughs.

"Are you mad?"

Owen shook his head. "Not even a little." He kissed him. "Did they find anything?"

"Nope. I don't know if I feel better or worse about that, though."

Owen smiled. "It'll be fine. I promise. It's just an admirer. No one we need to worry about." He pulled away. "Shall we get some dinner? I'm starving."

And just like that, Owen let it slide that Evan was a possessive asshole who went behind his back. How he ever deserved this man was something he'd never understand.

9

Owen

Owen couldn't contain his glee at Evan's possessiveness, and he reminded the man of it every chance he got. Neither of them had heard anything from Brett or Felix about the fingerprints, and he didn't expect to. Whoever it was would show up eventually, and if Owen got gifts in the process... Well, why not?

Evan went back to the hospital a week after the incident to get his stitches removed and get everything checked. Evan wasn't worried; he was, after all, a nurse and tended to the changing of the bandages throughout the week, but Owen didn't want him overexerting and hurting himself further. It wasn't his choice, though. He did, however, put his foot down a little about the man who did it. Evan was ready to let it go and not press charges, but Owen wasn't happy with that. They'd compromised with getting the guy into rehab instead of getting him arrested. Owen wasn't sure how much it would help, but it was better than nothing. People couldn't go around doing things like that and expecting no consequences. The police were still interviewing him on his more lucid days about the event, but from what they'd told them so far, it was just a guy who wanted drugs. A freak accident, so to speak. And Owen hated it. It wasn't that he wanted there to be a nefarious reason for the incident, but it would make him feel better that it wasn't just a "he was there" thing.

As much as he loved the Sutcliffes and downtime, he also hated the downtime. Taking turns to sit in the corridors of Windsor wasn't his favourite pastime, but it was his job, and he wouldn't want to change it. One thing he enjoyed most was the closeness of the family. When he'd first started working for the royal family, there had been a few who left something to be desired, but most were kind souls. Then, with the incidents from the past few years, where members of the royal family had turned on the LGBT+ people in their own family with attempted assassinations and kidnapping, those bad eggs were slowly killed, imprisoned or disowned. It made for a more settled time, and that closeness of the remaining family members was a joy to behold.

Owen had enjoyed what some people might call a normal childhood, though he hated that word. He started school with a mum and a dad, and he'd found friends immediately in Dominic and Evan. Then things had declined into chaos. His parents divorced—to this day he didn't know the real reason, though he assumed it was because of what happened to Amy—and life became a balance of when his father would see him, until his father decided he'd had enough and disappeared. Never to be heard from again.

His mother had been amazing through it all, but he'd found himself visiting Dominic's house more often, wanting the normalcy back. After he'd grown up a bit more, he realised he'd feared his mother leaving, rejecting him like his father had. But she'd stayed, and when Evan's parents had thrown him out, she hadn't hesitated to take him in and give him a home, even if it was for only a few months.

With the job he was in now, he could easily have found his father, but he didn't want to. If he wasn't good enough for the man as a child, he wasn't going to find out he wasn't good enough as an adult.

But those experiences had moulded him into the person he was, and he couldn't say he was a bad person. Even with what happened with Evan, it was more that he didn't want to lose their friendship and get "rejected" again when he didn't have to.

Owen glanced up and down the corridor before shaking his head. He was feeling melancholy that day, apparently. This was what downtime did to him.

His phone chimed, and he checked the messages, smiling when he saw Evan's name. Apparently, they were the kind of people who messaged through the day, after all.

EVAN: *I'm fine. Stop worrying. I know you'll pretend you're not, but you are. I'll see you at home later. I'm in a mood. X*

Owen cleared his throat, his dick already interested in what "mood" his boyfriend was in, but even if it meant being woken up at one o'clock in the morning, he wasn't going to complain. Especially if it involved their cocks touching.

They'd not had intercourse since their second "first" time, but they'd fooled around, and Owen had cherished every second. He'd never thought he would get the chance to have Evan in his arms or his bed again, so to be able to kiss and hold him whenever he wanted was...exquisite.

OWEN: *Looking forward to it. Do I need to 'prepare?' X*
EVAN: *Yes. X*

Owen's mouth went dry. Okay, then.

"Owen!" His gaze darted up at his name.

"What's up, Nick?"

"Nothing. Just thought I'd stop the boredom from setting in for you. Have you decided what you're doing for your birthday yet?" The other bodyguard slumped into a chair on the opposite side of the door but faced him.

Owen rolled his eyes. "I'm too old for birthday plans. It's not like it's a milestone or anything."

"Birthdays are always times to celebrate. Oscar just had his birthday party, and that was bloody awesome, even if I do say so myself. A dinosaur party? Hell to the yes."

Owen chuckled. "You're just a big kid. And yes, that looked fantastic from the pictures I saw. But no, I've no plans."

"Okay, so let's think then. You're too boring for a nightclub. What about a pint at the pub? We can get the others to join us and make a night of it. Conversation, music, alcohol? What do you think?"

Despite not usually celebrating his birthday, especially since Evan moved to Italy, he liked the idea of something low-key. He nodded. "All right. You choose the pub, tell everyone the time, and I'll be there. But make sure you tell people not to bring presents. I don't need anything."

Nick fist-pumped the air. "Yes! Plans are afoot."

Owen's stomach churned. "You do know I'll return the favour for your birthday, right? Whatever you do to me will get done to you tenfold," Owen warned.

Nick cocked his head. "That's not the deterrent you think it is."

Owen tutted. "Trust you."

"I'll be good, I promise." Owen raised his eyebrows, and Nick held up his hands. "I promise!"

Owen couldn't do anything about it now. He'd already given Nick carte blanche to do whatever. He sighed, already regretting it. They caught up for a few more minutes. With Nick guarding the king, they didn't get a huge amount of time to talk without their jobs getting in the way. Sometimes, they worked together if King Andrew and Prince Freddie were at the same event, but it didn't happen as often as it used to. Not since the problems they'd had. Security had tightened drastically since then.

"Right. I'll be in touch about your birthday. Not long to go." Nick winked, and Owen groaned as the man wandered off.

"What the hell have I done?"

"Should I be worried?" Owen stood and shoved his phone back in his pocket as Damon exited the suite.

Owen cleared his throat. "No, not at all. Nick and his plans." He shrugged.

Damon chuckled. "He does seem to like his plans."

"He does." Owen glanced around. "Do you need escorting or...?"

"No, thanks. I'm just heading to see George. Freddie's still in there working. I thought I'd give him a breather."

"Okay, well, holler if you need anything, and one of us will be there."

Damon nodded. "Will do."

Owen settled back into his seat and watched Damon disappear down the corridor. If he thought about it, Owen and Evan's relationship wasn't much different from Freddie and Damon's. They were both best friends before they started a relationship and had to work their way through the minefield before coming out the other side.

By the time Owen finished work, he was exhausted from inactivity, and because there were far too many hours between that point and when Evan got home, he headed to the training room. He planned to use the punch bag to alleviate some of his extra energy, not wanting to jump Evan the moment he got back.

As luck would have it, Dominic was there. "Wasn't expecting to see you," Dominic said.

Owen huffed. "Evan's at work."

"Ah, that explains it. Empty house syndrome."

They settled in to work out side-by-side, the rhythmic punch, punch easing any tension that Owen had inside him. It was only recently that Dominic had started any kind of training related to boxing, and Owen tried to help him rediscover his love for it. An hour later, showered and dressed, he sat on the bench waiting for Dominic to finish.

"What's your plan now?" Dominic asked as he pulled his jumper over his head.

"Haven't really got one. I'm trying not to stress too much over Nick planning a birthday for me."

Dominic's eyes widened. "What the heck? Why did you agree to that?"

Owen shrugged. "No idea. But he was so happy. And I threatened to throw it back at him tenfold if he did anything bad."

"That's not a bad thing for him."

Owen chuckled. "That's exactly what he said." He shook his head. "Whatever. He's thinking of drinks at a pub, so we'll see what happens."

"Did he state which pub?"

"No." A shiver went down his spine. "Should I have asked?"

Dominic stared at him. "I don't know. Should you?"

He dropped his head into his hands. "I knew I should've stuck to my guns and said no to it."

Dominic clapped his hand on his shoulder. "Good luck with that. Do you want me to come over for a bit? Keep you company?"

Owen stood and glared at him. "I'm a grown man. I don't need coddling. I've been on my own for long enough. I don't need someone to keep me company because Evan's not there." Dominic raised his eyebrows, and Owen's shoulders lowered. "Sorry."

"It's okay. It's also okay to be out of sorts while you're figuring out your relationship. Remember how I was with Randall? Adding someone into your life is not all chocolates and roses."

Owen frowned. "That's not the right phrase, is it?"

Dominic shrugged. "No idea, but you understood what I meant, anyway."

"Yeah, yeah. It feels like it should be easy because we were friends before anything else. But sometimes, it seems harder."

"You're finding a new normal. Unbalanced emotions are to be expected."

Owen backhanded his shoulder. "Unbalanced? That's the word you went with. Asshole." He grabbed his bag and headed for the door, hiding the smile spreading across his face.

Dominic chuckled. "You know what I mean!"

Owen walked home despite the cooler temperature. There was no point driving to work when he could walk it in less time. Letting himself into the house, he smiled at the flowers sitting in a green crystal vase he didn't recognise in the middle of the coffee table. He hung up his coat and put his bag on the floor beside the sofa and reached for the note propped up against the vase.

Owen,

I know you're worried. But if we stopped doing things because we were worried about it, nobody would ever leave their beds. (Yes, I'm sure you would be okay with that, but that's not the point.) I had to go back. Not only because it's my job and I enjoy it a lot, but because if I didn't, there would be that slight chance I wouldn't be able to cross the hospital threshold ever again.

I love my job despite the unsocial hours. I love the patients despite their attitudes being less than desired because of their pain. I love my colleagues despite it being gossip-central. I love doing what I do...despite it taking me away from you.

I've left you a present in your bedroom. Don't have too much fun without me. I'll see you in the very early morning. Be prepared. I'm going to need you.

Evan x

Owen smiled at Evan's curling scrawl, so much like a doctor's it was almost unreadable, but Owen had learnt Evan's scratches as they'd grown. It was like reading his own writing now—instinctive. It said nothing about the flowers, though. He flipped over the note, checking to see if he'd written anything else, and yes, there it was.

I know you secretly love flowers, so I got you these. Feel free to pretend they're for someone else if you don't want to claim them.

Owen laughed. No chance was anyone else getting these. They were his. The white and purple carnations were beautiful, and he didn't care who knew he loved them. Not anymore.

Leaving them where they were, he entered the bedroom and saw a box. Opening it, he grinned at the plug. *Be prepared, eh?*

He grabbed his bag and the washing baskets from his and Evan's rooms, and shoved a load in the washing machine, setting it going before he made himself some dinner. He decided to waste some more time by cooking some batch meals. Might as well stock the freezer while he had time, and despite what everyone joked, he wasn't a terrible cook, he just preferred not to do it most days—hence the batch cooking he did.

Checking the fridge to see what meat they had, he decided on chicken meals and brought them all out. He scrolled through his phone to find a decent playlist and set it playing while he washed his hands and began preparing. The 90s music few people knew he loved cranked through the kitchen as he diced and sliced the chicken and vegetables to the requirements he needed. His hips swayed, his head bobbed, and he sang along—badly—to some tunes.

Before long, savoury and spicy scents filled the house, and he smiled. How could life get any better than it was? He'd figured things out with Evan, they were planning to be in it for the long haul, and he was happy. Nothing could take it from him.

Two hours later, he had enough meals for forty portions of the various recipes, including a chicken balti, chicken enchiladas and Hunter's chicken. He portioned them out into various containers and left them to cool, snagging one of the chicken balti concoctions for his dinner.

Settling on the sofa, he turned on the TV and ate while catching up with the news. He found several other odd jobs that needed completing—and had done for a while—to distract himself further, and when the food had cooled, he placed some in the fridge and some in the freezer.

By the time the clock said ten-thirty, he was still wired, but he needed to sleep. Having never forgotten Evan's order to be prepared, he had a shower, cleaned himself out and, once he was back in bed, he stretched and lubed himself, a process which turned him on far more than he wanted it to when there was no end to the arousal in sight.

He lubed the plug, inserted it with a grimace as his dick pulsed and leaked, and breathed out slowly, trying to calm himself. Putting away the supplies and washing his hands, he settled into bed, exhaling through every twinge and lick of fire.

He hadn't expected to sleep, but warm hands lulled him from slumber, and he blinked to clear the bleariness. "Mmhmm," he moaned as Evan's hands skimmed across his skin, goosebumps following the charge.

"I love that you're wearing this for me," Evan murmured, biting his earlobe and pressing against the base of the plug. "But go back to sleep. I'll take care of you."

Owen inhaled shakily, eyes closing as he let Evan have free rein of his body. As he floated, he felt his body let go of the plug, the emptiness dragging a whimper from his throat. But then it was replaced with something larger, and that emptiness disappeared. Heat warmed his back and legs, with more heat banding across his stomach and chest. He sighed and relaxed fully as the gentle rocking lulled him.

Soft words reached his ears, and he stretched for them. "I love you."

Another gentle caress, wrapping around his cock this time, and a slow burn licked through his body, sending him into the softest orgasm he ever remembered having. A gasp sounded in his ear, and he smiled even as he fell back to sleep, safe in knowing Evan was with him.

10

Evan

E van had never thought he was into somnophilia, but the idea of taking care of Owen's needs while he was unaware was surprisingly arousing. He loved it best when the man was awake and interacting with him, but this was a pleasant change, though he wouldn't do it all the time. After he'd cleaned them both up, he settled into bed beside Owen, listening to him sleep. He'd had a shit shift, losing two of their patients, and it weighed on him, as it always did. Losing himself in Owen was the best way to ease those memories, but he'd never forget.

Despite being home around one-thirty in the morning, he still woke at six o'clock when Owen's alarm went off.

"Sorry, sweetheart. Go back to sleep," Owen whispered, brushing his lips across Evan's cheek.

The next thing he knew, his own alarm woke him up. He reached for it, yawning, and looked, bleary-eyed, at the screen to cancel it. He dropped his hand back to the pillow, taking the phone with it, and let his eyes fall closed again. He wouldn't sleep again, even though he'd only had six hours sleep, but he could wake up gently. He'd have another nap later in the day because his last shift started at midnight, and it was the only way he'd survive it.

He rolled to his back, staring up at the ceiling, knowing he needed to get moving but not wanting to. Wanting to bask in the remembered glow of being in Owen's arms. It wasn't as good as the real thing, but it was all he had while they were apart. That and the nagging need to ignore how his thoughts sometimes couldn't trust that Owen wouldn't back out of what they had. That took him more effort than he wanted to admit aloud. He believed Owen when he said he wasn't going to push Evan away, but he couldn't help the wayward snatches of thought, even though he tried his hardest.

Refusing to dwell on them again that morning, he pushed the covers aside and got up, going through his morning routine to waste some time before heading out of the house for Book Drunk, the local coffee shop slash bookshop all the royal family used because it belonged to one of their own, Oscar, Prince Christian's fiancé.

Entering the warm building, he rubbed his hands together to get the feeling back into them and aimed for the counter. He'd only met Oscar twice, and they hadn't interacted much, but Evan was good with faces and names and knew who he was. He wasn't sure about the other people who worked there yet. He unzipped his coat and unwrapped his scarf as he waited.

"Good morning. What can I get you?" The staff member had a name tag that said Chloe.

"Morning. A cappuccino, an iced water and a cheese and ham toastie, please," he said, pulling his wallet from his trousers pocket.

"Not a problem." She rang them up just as Oscar came through a door in the back, presumably the kitchen.

Oscar glanced at him and smiled. "Evan! Nice to see you again. How're things?"

Chloe glanced at him, and Oscar nodded at her before refocusing on Evan and sliding a tray onto the counter next to Chloe.

"I'm good, thank you. Just trying to blow off some cobwebs from an early morning finish."

Oscar frowned, and then his expression cleared. "You're a nurse, aren't you?"

Evan nodded. "Well remembered. Yes, I finished at 1 a.m. this morning and have the night shift tonight. Not the best changeover, but it is what it is."

"Ouch, yeah. That sucks."

"I have two days off from tomorrow, though, so I can't complain too much."

Oscar smiled. "Make sure you drag Owen in."

Evan chuckled. "I'm sure I won't have to drag him in, but yes, I will." He glanced at Chloe, knowing he was holding up the line. "How much do I owe you?"

"Four pounds fifty," she said.

He raised his eyebrows. "Are you sure you've included everything?" It was too cheap for what he'd ordered.

"You get the family rate," Oscar said, picking up the tray again, and winked. "See you soon."

"But—"

He didn't get the chance to argue anymore because Oscar disappeared again. Facing Chloe, he sighed. "I'm not going to be able to change that, am I?"

Chloe chuckled. "Not a chance."

He sighed and paid, leaving a large tip in the jar next to the till. He studied the tables and chose on next to the start of the book shop part of the place and settled down, draping his coat on the back of the chair. Not planning to read, he still couldn't help dragging his gaze across the nearby books and smiling at the variety he saw. He usually took a book with him to the hospital for when he had a break, but he spent most of his time chatting with his colleagues instead.

Chloe brought over his drinks and food, and he checked the messages and emails on his phone while he drank and ate. Matteo had messaged asking for them to meet up during their days off that week, and Evan added it to his calendar—he didn't want to forget like he had last time. Owen had messaged, telling him to rest up and that he'd made enchiladas for their dinner that night, which Evan had already seen in the fridge. He'd reply later about him bringing dessert home. Owen would have to wait and see what dessert he meant.

The last message was from Felix, which had him sitting straighter. His finger hovered over the button to open it, and why he hesitated, he didn't know. Pressing it, he read it.

FELIX: *Tests came back negative. We have no information about who the fingerprints relate to. Yet. We're still looking into it. I'll keep you posted.*

Evan sighed and stared at the words. It had been over a week since he'd given the prints to them, and he'd hoped for more. Maybe he was overthinking things, and the jealous beast inside him was hoping it was something more than just someone who liked Owen. Almost as if it was easier to deal with a bad guy than it was a stalker or crush.

He replied to Felix, thanking him, and put his phone down. Crossing his legs, he stared around the cafe, cupping the last of his cappuccino and inhaling the scent. His gaze lazily slipped over the customers, seeing if there was anyone he knew, when his heart began to race. He backtracked a couple of people and froze on one person's face. Stomach souring, he jumped to his feet, knocking the table and sending his plate and knife crashing to the floor. He cursed and crouched, picking up the shards, when Oscar came rushing over.

"Mind your fingers on those. I can sweep them up."

"I'm sorry. I wasn't paying attention," he babbled, trying to ignore the feeling of being watched.

"It's fine. It happens. Don't worry about it." Oscar crouched beside him, lowering his voice. "Everything okay? You look spooked."

"Yeah..." He exhaled. "Not really, but it will be."

"Do you need me to do anything?"

Evan shook his head. "I'll leave in a minute, and it'll be fine."

"Go," Oscar said. "I can clear this up."

"No, let me—"

"Go. I understand the need to flee, so go. It's fine. I promise."

Evan stared at him before nodding. He squeezed his hand and rose, grabbing his coat and phone and heading for the door.

"Evan!"

He ignored the call from one of the people he never wanted to see again and dragged his coat on as he strode down the street. Wrapping himself up as tightly as he could, he walked.

What the hell had they been doing there? He hadn't seen them for years and thought they'd moved away. Had they come back again? His stomach rolled, and he breathed through the nausea.

Evan's stomach churned as he settled into a chair at the dinner table. He'd been working up to this conversation for weeks, and he'd finally told himself to get it over with. He knew it wouldn't be easy, but there was no way his parents wouldn't support him in the end. They knew Dominic was gay, and they didn't have a problem with Evan still being around him.

He watched his mother dish up the plates of shepherd's pie—his father's favourite—and wrung his hands in his lap. His father entered the room and sat at the head of the table, as always.

"It smells delicious, Bernadette." He rubbed his stomach and grinned at Evan.

His mother beamed at his father and placed the plates in front of him and Evan. "I hope you enjoy it." She grabbed her plate and sat beside his father.

There weren't many words spoken as they ate, his father concentrating on shovelling forkfuls of food into his mouth. Evan could barely swallow anything but tried his best. He knew from experience that his father would comment if he didn't eat much, complaining that he didn't appreciate his mother's cooking.

When the main course was done, Evan gathered the plates while his mother plated the dessert. Sitting once more, he inhaled and said, "Could I please talk to you both?"

"Of course you can, dear," his mother said.

Evan glanced at his father, who narrowed his eyes at him, but despite the panic weaving through him, he said, "I'm...I'm...gay," he finished with a gasp.

His mother's spoon clattered to the table. His father glared at him, carefully putting his spoon back in his bowl and wiping his hands on the napkin. Evan waited for any words to come from either of them. His entire body trembled, his teeth rattling so hard it echoed around his head.

His father put the napkin back down and sat back. Meeting Evan's gaze, he said, "You have twenty minutes to pack whatever you can fit into the bags you own and get out of the house."

Evan's eyes filled, having never believed he would say it. Why was it okay that Dominic was gay but not Evan? "What?" he whispered.

"Twenty minutes and counting," his father repeated.

Evan glanced at his mother, seeing her gaze on her bowl, but she didn't refute his father's words. His breathing increased, and he gaped at them.

"Nineteen minutes," his father said.

Evan's chair scraped across the floor as he stood, his mother flinching at the sound, and after one more glance at them both, he raced for the stairs. Tears flowed freely down his cheeks as he riffled through the wardrobe for his backpack and suitcase. Flinging them on the bed, he stumbled as he rushed to gather what he could of his clothes and toiletries. He could barely think what he needed, just throwing in whatever his hands touched.

"One minute!" his father bellowed up the stairs, and Evan's heart pounded even as he cried harder.

Where was he going to live?

He zipped up his bags and carried them down the stairs. Slipping into his shoes and coat, he didn't even look back as he exited the house. There was nothing for him there now.

"Evan!" his mother called, but he didn't turn. Too little, too late.

He trudged down the streets, the frigid evening air freezing his tears on his cheeks. He strode up a path and knocked on the door.

Owen's mum smiled at him before taking in his appearance and then pulled him inside.

"Come on. The guest room is already set up for you," she said. "Owen is in his room. You go see him while I put your things away."

They climbed the stairs, and at the top, Sally dragged him in for a hug. "You're welcome to stay here as long as you need to, Evan. Okay?" She met his gaze, cupping his cheek. "This is your home as much as ours now."

Evan nodded but couldn't reply, his throat blocked by all the emotions bubbling up inside him. Owen came out of his room with a frown.

"What's happened?"

"Evan's staying with us now. Go on. Watch a movie or something." Sally pushed him towards Owen, and he went. He wasn't sure what else to do.

His breath puffed in front of his face as he wiped away the memory, weaving his way through the streets, no idea where he was going but needing to walk off the shock by carefully blanking his thoughts from anything other than pleasant thoughts.

It must've been those thoughts that brought him to Sally's door. Evan stared at it, not even knowing if she was at home because he didn't know her shift pattern. He licked his lips, contemplating walking back home when the door opened.

"Evan? Everything okay?" Sally said.

Evan blinked at her, his voice gone, his head back to all those years ago. Instead, he shook his head.

"Oh, sweetheart. Come inside. You look freezing. Where's the car?" She ushered him into the living room, taking his coat from him and pushing him onto the sofa. She dragged the blanket from the back of the sofa and wrapped it around him, and the scent of home sank into him, clearing some of the fog. He stared at the fireplace, though the fire wasn't burning like it would've been when they were younger, keeping the room nice and toasty. It was still warmer than outside, but not as hot as then.

Sally slid an arm around his back and rubbed up and down. "What happened, Evan?" she asked softly.

"I saw them."

"Who?"

He blinked and met her gaze. "My parents."

Sally's eyes widened, and then she sighed. "I hadn't heard they'd returned. Otherwise, I would've warned you." She rubbed his hand. "Where were they?"

"Book Drunk. I was having a coffee when I saw her. Made a mess and left Oscar to clean it up. I'll have to apologise to him."

"Don't you worry about that. I'm sure he understands."

"But—"

Sally shook her head. "No, he'll understand. As for you, I think you need hot chocolate and a nap. How about it?"

Evan found a smile for her, his shoulders lowering as the tension slowly left his body. "Sounds like a plan."

Sally disappeared, and Evan returned to staring at the fireplace. Memories of his teenage years flitted through his mind. Sleepovers in front of the fire, movie nights, climbing the trees in the back garden. Most of his good memories revolved around this house and Dominic's parents' house, not the house he grew up in. He'd believed himself to have quite a pleasant childhood until the moment he'd told his parents he was gay. An epic mistake if ever he'd made one.

Sally brought in a mug of hot chocolate and settled beside Evan, tucking her legs underneath her.

"I'm sorry for showing up unannounced," he said.

"Evan, you don't need to announce yourself. I told you then, I've told you over the years, and I'll tell you again. This will always be your home."

Evan stared into the swirling hot chocolate, his throat tight. "Thank you."

"Now, how about a Laurel and Hardy marathon before a nap?" she said, and Evan chuckled.

"Sure."

Sally was obsessed with the comedy duo, watching them repeatedly, and Evan had found an appreciation for them over the years. But now, more than ever, he needed that normalcy.

Five hours later, he woke, overly warm but content. He stretched, and his feet left the warmth of the covers. He pulled them back in and blinked. His old room came into focus, and memories resurfaced. His stomach churned, but he shoved everything aside, checking the time. Before he had dragged himself to bed, Sally had asked what time he needed waking so he wouldn't be late for his shift, so he knew he wouldn't be late, but he'd slept longer than he'd expected. He needed to get home so he could shower, eat and change for work.

He sat upright. "Shit." He reached for his phone and cursed again when he saw how many messages and missed calls he had from Owen. Evan should've been home three hours ago.

He swung his legs over the edge of the bed and held the phone between his shoulder and ear while he slid on his shoes. The phone rang and rang, but Owen didn't answer. It went to voicemail, and Evan said, "I'm sorry. I'm here. I'm alive. I'm coming home now. I'll explain, I promise."

He exited his old room and bounded down the stairs, looking for Sally. "Has Owen call—"

He stopped in the entrance to the living room, where Sally was curled up on the sofa—and Owen sat in one armchair, much the same way. Their gazes met, and Owen looked ravaged.

Evan dropped to his knees in front of him, resting his hands on him wherever he could reach. "I'm sorry. I should've called. I… My brain wasn't where it should've been."

Owen cleared his throat, glanced behind Evan at his mother and then back to him again. "It's okay. Mum explained. But…" He stared at his mother again, exhaling slowly. Evan looked at Sally, who nodded at Owen. "I thought you'd left," he whispered, and Evan's heart broke all over again.

"I'm so sorry. I didn't mean to. I truly didn't. I didn't even know where I was going when I turned up here. I just left the cafe and walked. I ended up here. I got your message and was going to reply, but I got distracted, and then everything disappeared into a jumble." Evan inhaled, trying to explain further, but Owen palmed his cheek.

"I know that now. I just wanted to explain where my head went. I'm not mad. I promise. I understand."

Evan lowered his forehead to Owen's knee, needing the connection between them. Owen's fingers raked through his hair, and Evan let himself go. His tears, however much unwanted, were cathartic after far too long of holding it in, which he hadn't realised he had been. Owen slid his arms around him, and they stayed that way until Evan's knees and back protested. Then he sat upright, sniffing, and stared at Owen.

"Thank you, and I'm sorry."

Owen smiled at him. "You don't need to be sorry. I understand."

"Doesn't make me feel better for worrying you."

Owen dropped his mouth to Evan's, the light caress bringing more tears to Evan's eyes but for a different reason. He wanted to tell Owen that he loved him. He wanted to tell him absolutely everything he was feeling, but it would be too soon for his best friend. Too much weight for him to deal with after Evan's shock disappearance. So, he kept it inside, keeping it for a time when he wouldn't have to worry about the time being right because he'd know. There would be no denying the words at that point. But for now, he could feel them. He could keep them inside and cherish them. Because he wasn't going anywhere now that he had Owen.

Nowhere at all.

11

Owen

The moment he'd kissed Evan, he'd known his mother would jump on it, and he held up a single finger behind Evan's head, asking her to hold her questions for later. She would. He knew she would, but there would be questions. He couldn't deal with the question right then, though. He needed to reassure himself that Evan was right in front of him and hadn't disappeared off the face of the earth again.

He needed to tell Evan how he felt. It was easier for him to acknowledge he loved Evan now that he'd heard Evan profess his love for him.

At least, he thought he had. The previous night's good time was a little blurry, but he was sure Evan had said he loved him. But even if he was making it up, Owen could feel the love between them. As if it was a tangible thing he could hold on to. And he wouldn't take the chance that Evan disappeared before he said it.

He did, however, want to make it a little special, so he held it in for the moment. He had plans.

He cupped Evan's cheek. "Are you ready to go home?" he asked.

Evan nodded. "I am." He turned to Owen's mother. "Thank you for everything."

Sally rose at the same time Evan did, her arms slipping around the waist of the taller man. "You are always welcome. You know that. Just take care of yourselves." She glanced at Owen and grinned.

Owen stood and enfolded her in his arms, and her mouth found his ear. "I'm so happy you finally got your head out of your behind. Love him fully, my boy," she whispered.

"I plan to."

They said their goodbyes, and Owen drove them home, fingers linked with Evan's. When they entered the house, Owen pulled Evan into the bathroom. "Time for a shower."

Owen undressed them both without fanfare and waved for Evan to get in first. It was a tight squeeze because their shower was not built for two large bodies—two smaller bodies, maybe, but not two large ones—but they managed. He draped his front against Evan's back and reached for the shower gel. Squirting some onto his fingers, he slid his hands across Evan's skin. As he was further under the water, the suds quickly washed away, but Owen repeated it several times until his front was clean. Then he stepped back a little, instantly missing the skin-to-skin contact, and washed his back, ass and legs. When he'd finished, Evan turned around and pulled Owen into his arms, resting his forehead against his shoulder. Owen just held him.

After a few minutes, he said, "Let's get out so I can feed you."

Evan said nothing, and that, more than anything else, worried him. There weren't many things that kept Evan from talking, but the topic of his parents was one of them. He dried off his best friend and himself and led him to the bedroom, helping him get dressed in his scrubs. He didn't think Evan was in the right frame of mind to be going to work, but he understood Evan's need for normality.

While Evan leaned against the counter, Owen reheated the enchiladas, dividing them onto two plates and taking them to the table. Evan followed and sat beside him. Owen fetched drinks and then took Evan's hand.

"You don't have to talk about it, but you do need to eat."

Evan met his gaze, the pain etched so deeply into them, and nodded. He picked up his knife and fork and ate. Owen watched, mirroring his movements to hopefully encourage him to eat more than he might've if he hadn't been there, and when they were done, he pushed the plates aside, reaching for Evan again.

Evan cleared his throat and sniffed. "I went to Book Drunk for a coffee, wanting to enjoy some time out of the house." Owen nodded. "I didn't see them at first." He frowned. "Or maybe they came in after. I don't know. I was looking around to see if I knew anyone and saw...her." He swallowed. "She looked right at me...and *smiled*." Heat rose in his voice, the anger finally beginning to show. "As if I would be happy to see her." He shook his head. "I could tell my father was there, too, though I didn't see his face. I saw the back of his head, which was enough. I stood to leave, but I knocked into the table and the plate shattered on the floor. Oscar cleaned it up and told me to leave." He blanched and looked at Owen. "Not like that, I mean. He could see I needed to go and told me I could."

"I know. He was worried about you."

Evan raised his eyebrows. "He was?"

Owen nodded. "He had no idea what had spooked you, but knew something had, so he called Christian, who called Freddie, looking for me. I wasn't there, though, so he called Brett, who tracked me down." He'd been in the middle of organising a surprise for Evan. "To begin with, I had no idea where you might go. I called and messaged, but you didn't answer. I came home, but you weren't here. I called Matteo to see if anyone at the hospital had seen you, but no one had." He sighed. "I will be honest with you. I was going out of my mind, but I knew I would find you, even if you didn't want to be found."

Evan tightened his hold on Owen's hand. "I did want to be found. I promise."

"I know."

"How did you know where I was?"

Owen chuckled. "Mum rang me. She said you were there, and she hadn't wanted to leave you alone until you fell asleep, which was why it took her so long to call."

Evan nodded, eyes locked on something to the side of Owen. "She called after me," he murmured. "Just like she had that night."

Owen's heart raced, like it always did when he thought about those two people and what they did. "What do you mean?"

"When I raced out of Book Drunk, she called my name. Her voice hasn't changed," he said distractedly. "She did the same when I left the house after they threw me out. I didn't stop to see what she wanted. Then or now."

"You didn't have to do anything you didn't want to."

Evan sighed. "I don't know if they moved away, and I've just been lucky enough not to cross paths with them before now, or if they've just returned from wherever they went."

"Does it matter?"

Evan frowned, seeming to think about his answer. "In some ways, yes. If it was just that we never crossed paths, it might be easier than thinking they moved away without saying anything." He exhaled. "I know it shouldn't matter."

"Don't do that. You can feel however you need to feel. There are no right or wrong answers to this situation."

Evan met his gaze, and Owen felt it to his soul. "Thank you."

Owen smiled. "You don't need to thank me, but you're welcome, anyway." He patted his hand. "Are you definitely going to work tonight?"

Evan nodded. "Yes. My mind is blown, but it's not splintered. I can still do the job, and I think it will help me recentre myself more than what you've already managed."

Owen's heart burst at the admission, making him feel ten feet tall. He had one more question for him before he left for the hospital. "Do you want me to find out what happened to them?"

Evan stared at him, worrying his bottom lip. "I'm not sure."

Owen nodded. "Okay. Just say the word if you do. You know what Felix is capable of."

"That reminds me," Evan said, reaching into his pocket. He checked his phone. "Felix sent me a message earlier..." He showed it to Owen, who smiled.

"I still think it's an admirer," he said, wanting to get Evan thinking of something else rather than what they had been talking about. "I'm not turning down thoughtful presents."

Evan rolled his eyes and stood, grabbing the dinner plates. "I bet you won't." He carried them to the kitchen while Owen took the cups.

"Come on. You have to admit that scarf is nice."

"I don't have to admit anything." He looked as if he'd swallowed a lemon.

Owen chuckled. "I can get rid of it if you'd prefer." He was deadly serious. Joking aside, he wouldn't want to hurt Evan in any way.

Evan sighed and faced him, sliding his arms around his waist. "No. It's fine. I suppose it is a nice fabric."

Owen hid his smile by joining their lips, the spiciness of the enchiladas still present on his lips. He wrapped his arms around Evan's neck, deepening the kiss into something they could easily turn into something more. After several air-denying minutes, they pulled apart, panting.

"That's a nice 'see you later,'" Evan said.

"And don't you forget it."

"Never," Evan promised. "But I really need to go."

Owen kissed him once more. "I guess I'll see you in the morning."

"Not if I see you first."

Owen chuckled at the reminder of the childhood retort and allowed Evan to pull from his embrace. He watched as he pottered around, collecting the things he needed for the night shift. His lover stopped at the front door and looked back.

"I'll miss you."

"I'll miss you more," Owen countered. "Be safe."

"Always am."

When the door closed behind him, Owen exhaled, finally allowing himself to feel everything he'd bottled up. That initial thought of Evan leaving him had coalesced into something bigger the more he hadn't been able to find him, but the moment his mother called, he'd let it all go. The trust issue was his problem, and no one else's. He needed to trust that Evan wouldn't leave, and as much as he thought he did, that had proven he still had a way to go. Even if Evan had left, Owen could've understood it. Seeing their estranged parents would've destroyed anyone.

With the rest of the lonely night ahead of him, he settled onto the sofa with a movie marathon in mind. If he stayed awake as long as he could, he could sleep with Evan when he came home instead of leaving the bed so the man could sleep alone. His mind went a mile a minute, and he finally caved and called Felix.

"Can you find out what you can about Evan's parents, please?"

"Consider it done."

Owen hung up. He was worried he'd made a mistake, but he didn't have to tell Evan what he'd found out. He wasn't a fan of keeping secrets, but he could if it was in his best interests.

He made it until four o'clock, when his body cried out for sleep, and he tumbled into bed. He'd obviously slept because a warm body wrapping around him woke him.

"Go to sleep," Evan said, kissing his cheek. "I'm tired."

Owen did as his sir ordered.

"When I agreed for Nick to plan the party, I didn't mean that he could keep it a secret," Owen grumbled as Evan tied the blindfold over his eyes. "What has he got planned?"

Evan chuckled. "I'm not telling. All I will say is that he should be a party planner with how he's pulled this off in eight days."

"That doesn't reassure me."

His stomach twisted, settling slightly when Evan's lips met his. "I'll look after you. I promise."

"You better."

Evan grasped his hands and squeezed before letting go. Owen grabbed the inside car door handle, hoping it would settle him a little.

"Ready?"

"What would you do if I said no?" Owen asked.

Evan chuckled. "Take you anyway."

"Exactly." He waved his hand. "Onwards, Jeeves," he said in his best posh accent.

Evan laughed again, which was worth the embarrassment. The car started, and Owen tried to figure out where they were from the turns and speed they were doing, but it wasn't easy. He was sure Evan was taking them back on themselves.

"Are you trying to confuse me?" he finally said.

"Of course. How else would this be a surprise? You're more than capable of figuring out our direction unless I take us on the long route and make a few random diversions," Evan said.

"Asshole."

He gave up trying and settled back, enjoying Evan's company. It had been a week since Evan had seen his parents, and there had been no sighting of them again. Despite Evan not knowing whether he wanted to know what his parents had been up to during their estrangement, Owen had received information from Felix, but he wouldn't share it with Evan unless he asked. His feelings about Mr and Mrs Montgomery were less than stellar than it had already been.

The car finally stopped, and Owen's ear strained for any hint of noise, but there was nothing other than the usual muted conversations from passing people.

"Can I take this off now?"

"Nope," Evan said. "And, on top of that, you now need to wear headphones."

He could hear the laughter in Evan's voice. "No way."

"Yep. Put them on." He placed them in Owen's hands, and Owen sighed.

"I'm going on record to say, this sucks."

"Duly noted."

He sighed again and put the damn things over his ears. They must've been noise cancelling ones because every bit of sound disappeared. It was unnerving. A displacement of air flowed around him, bringing with it a cooler temperature, and he startled when Evan grabbed his hand. Evan tapped his knees to get him to climb out, which Owen did, far more clumsily than he thought he would. Evan kept hold of his hand, leading him with an arm around his waist. A nudge to the back of his knee had him believing there was a step, so he carefully felt it out with his foot, finally getting up. He wanted to curse but was far too busy concentrating.

Evan pulled him to a stop, squeezing his hand.

"Can I take them off now?" he said, his voice loud in his own head.

Evan tapped twice on the back of his hand. Once for yes, twice for no. That's what he'd told him before. He exhaled, feeling completely out of his element. Evan squeezed his hand again and tapped once.

"I can take them off?" he checked. One tap. He reached for the headphones first, and the sudden onset of noise was overwhelming. He dragged off the blindfold, blinking repeatedly to get his eyes to work again. "What the fuck?" he said.

"Happy birthday!" everyone around him shouted.

He found Nick's gaze. The man beamed and came closer. "Are you ready for a night of debauchery?"

"Debauchery? It's a karaoke bar." His worst nightmare. "I thought we were going to a pub?"

"It's karaoke and cocktails night," Nick said. "What more could anyone want than booze and beats?" Nick shimmied his shoulders far more elegantly than Owen had expected.

"Definitely need the booze." Owen smiled tightly and then a little more widely when a sliver of uncertainty went through Nick's eyes. "It's great. Thanks, Nick."

His expression brightened. "Awesome. They made a special drink for you for your birthday." He reached for the bar and produced a very pink, very glittery glass, complete with purple umbrella and straw. "Try this. I've named it the Owenator."

Owen briefly closed his eyes, truly glad Nick had no control over naming things. "Thanks." He eyed the concoction. "What's in it?"

"You have to guess. There are four ingredients. If you guess right, we get a free round of drinks."

"No pressure," he murmured. He sipped the drink. Immediately, the grapefruit flavour hit him, followed by the heat of alcohol, maybe gin. He smacked his lips. It wasn't that bad if he was honest with himself. He sipped again. "Grapefruit." Nick smiled. "Gin." His grin widened. What were the others? He licked his lips for the aftertaste. "Prosecco?" Nick nodded. He had no idea about the last one. He drank again, eyeing the drink. Then he noticed the fruit floating in it and took a chance. "Raspberry?"

The guests cheered, and Nick high-fived them. Evan leaned closer. "I didn't realise you knew what prosecco tasted like."

"Blame Prince George. He made some cocktails for a party and insisted we try them. It's not too bad, although not my favourite."

Evan smiled at him. "You're a good friend to go along with this."

"It's my own fault. I shouldn't have given him free rein. I'm not singing."

Evan chuckled. "Good luck trying to stop yourself from getting up there after one too many *Owenators*."

Owen shook his head. "I'll stick to beer, thanks."

Nick returned. "I got you another Owenator. Can't wait to get this party really started."

Owen's stomach dropped. "Started? I thought it already had."

Nick waved him off. "I may have added a last-minute event to our night." He winked. "You'll love it, I promise."

Owen gulped the drink in his hand, wishing he had several more to follow it with. He wasn't sure he wanted to be sober for what was to come.

"I'll look after you. I promise," Evan whispered in his ear.

"Please don't let me do something stupid. I'll do whatever you want."

Evan smirked. "You already do everything I tell you to."

Heat kindled in his lower stomach, the kind that had nothing to do with alcohol, and if nothing else came of that night, he hoped he and Evan could visit a quiet corner somewhere and do something about the chub he now sported. Evan chuckled, probably knowing what was going through his mind, and kissed him. Owen followed when he pulled away, whimpering when Evan denied him. Evan pointed behind him, and Owen glanced over his shoulder, doing a double-take. He must be hallucinating.

"Is that Prince Freddie singing karaoke?"

12

Nick

Organising nights out was something Nick loved doing. Pleasing his friends and family with heartfelt, well thought out events made him happy. Why he hadn't gone into party planning instead of bodyguarding, he didn't know. Maybe he'd missed his calling.

What he hadn't expected was to have to do both things at the same time—nights out *and* bodyguarding—because Prince Freddie and Prince Damon were having far too much fun at Owen's party, and as Owen was usually Freddie's bodyguard, it fell to some of the others present to keep an eye on them. He had no idea how the prince had persuaded whoever it was to bring them there. If Malachi Sanders got wind of the event, he'd be here before anyone could stop him.

And Nick couldn't let that happen.

Video evidence of their friends in compromising *karaoke* positions was the most he wanted anyone to get hold of. Anything else was off limits. As much as Malachi loved the royal family, he wanted to grab a scoop before anyone else, and that way lay problems for some reporters to remember where the line actually was before they crossed it.

Brushing aside thoughts of the wayward reporter, Nick looked towards the birthday boy. Evan and he were best friends, but from the small touches and gentle smiles, Nick would be surprised if they weren't in a relationship before long, if they weren't already. He frowned. Had they told him they were together? God, he was so bad at remembering stuff like that. Give him stats and figures and he was in his element, but if he didn't write other things down to remind him, he would be afloat without a raft.

Surveying the room, his gaze focused on those who were not part of their birthday party. He couldn't have had the place closed down for them only because it had been too short notice, which meant they needed to be vigilant. Any one of these customers could be someone who would take a shot at the princes, or even the bodyguards who protected them if they wanted to make a name for themselves.

Especially someone like that guy. The way he kept shooting glares and clenching his jaw was a good indication that he could be a problem.

Nick headed to Locke, Freddie's bodyguard. He leaned into her ear so she could hear him. "There's a guy here not looking too happy. I think we need to get them out."

Locke nodded and spoke into her comms. "Edinburgh and Delta are going to be leaving. Places, please."

"See you tomorrow," Locke said before heading towards the princes. He watched as she spoke to Freddie, who nodded, linked hands with Damon and followed Locke to the entrance, but not before he hugged Owen goodbye.

When they were finally out of the building, Nick relaxed a little more. "A round of drinks on me!" he called, keeping an eye on the guy. But he never moved from his spot. Hopefully, that meant he was just having a bad day. Nick's phone vibrated against his leg, and he pulled it out and let out a breath.

LOCKE: *We're clear. Thanks for the heads up. Here's your own... Malachi is hanging around outside. Just so you know.*

Nick groaned. Just what they needed.

13

Evan

A lot of things happened that night, and Evan had plenty of them documented on his phone. Not only photos but videos, too. And he couldn't wait until he could share them with Owen when he was sober.

Evan covered his mouth, hiding his laughter as Owen took to the stage with Matteo, the pair having become firm friends since he'd introduced them several hours prior. The introductory notes of *I Will Survive* rang through the speakers, and Matteo slid his arm around Owen's back as they belted out the words—or at least, what he thought the words were in Owen's case.

Nick had gone above and beyond for the party, organising a karaoke competition, a best drag queen competition, and arranging for Owen to have a song sung directly to him by the local drag queen title holder themselves. The guests had overdone themselves with food and drink, most of them far beyond their alcohol limits, but Evan wasn't the only designated driver that night.

The song finished to raucous applause, and Owen bowed, Matteo catching him before he tumbled off the stage. His friend aided in manoeuvring Owen back to their table, and both finally dropped into their chairs with matching grins.

"Weren't we great?" Owen said, sipping his beer.

"Smashed it," Matteo added.

"Absolutely amazing," Evan agreed. "But it's time to go home now."

Owen gave him puppy dog eyes, which were extremely glassy, and shook his head. "No! We have more to sing."

Evan gave a sad smile. "The place is closing, unfortunately."

"Oh, no! Can we give them some money and help them stay open? I want to come back!"

Evan palmed his nape, getting his attention. "We can come back another day, yeah?"

"Yeah!" Owen said. He had always been a funny drunk, and that night was no different.

"Come on, then." He glanced at Matteo. "We can drop you off on the way if that's good for you?"

Matteo shook his head. "I have a taxi coming. I'm good." The man sounded decidedly more sober than he had been acting several minutes ago.

"Did you actually drink anything tonight?" Evan asked.

Matteo smirked. "Does it matter?"

Evan chuckled. "I suppose not. As long as you had a good time."

"Amazing. Can't wait to do it again with all these party animals." He looked around, raising his eyebrows.

Evan followed his gaze, laughing when he saw several bodyguards fast asleep against other members of their group, including Dominic asleep on Randall. Prince Freddie had indeed been singing karaoke when they first walked in, but he hadn't stayed for long. Whether any of Freddie's songs were leaked to the media in a day or two was anyone's guess. It would be hilarious to see the public's reaction to it.

He wrapped his arm around Owen's shoulders and led him from the building after a round of goodbyes from those sober and awake enough to notice them leaving. Getting Owen into the car was a task of epic proportions, distracted as he was by the lights and the stars and the passing cars and the people and...everything. Finally, though, they got into the car, and Evan leaned over to click Owen's seatbelt in place.

"I love you, you know?" Owen said as he pulled back, and Evan paused, meeting his gaze. His eyes were still glassy and drunk, but there was a solemness to him.

"I know," he said, but his words caught in his throat. He would've loved to hear those words when he was sober, and hopefully, one day he would. Closing Owen's door, he inhaled a cool breath and rounded the car before climbing in. Owen's forehead was already leaning against the window, and he would, undoubtedly, be asleep in five seconds.

The snoring that accompanied his driving was a testament to how much Owen had drunk—he only ever snored when he was drunk, but how that happened, Evan had no idea. Maybe it was because he was so relaxed. He didn't know, but it was cute in a nasally, old man way. Not that he'd tell Owen that. Not yet, anyway.

He parked the car outside the house and woke Owen. He grumbled but listened, walking himself to the door—after Evan corrected his direction once—and entering when Evan opened it.

"Time for bed, sleepyhead."

Owen snorted indelicately. "Sleepyhead." But he headed for the bedroom.

Evan followed, helping Owen strip and climb into bed. He wasn't going to get him to shower, not in his state, but once

Owen was in bed, he was out. Evan grabbed a glass of water, some paracetamol and a banana and put it on the bedside table, their past experiences helping him to know what Owen would need when he woke.

Evan left his man sleeping and headed for the bathroom, enjoying a luxuriously warm shower. As the water rained down on him, he considered everything that had happened over the past few weeks. He had wanted—though had never believed would happen—Owen to fall in love with him and they live happily ever after. And although they seemed to be heading in that direction, all the issues that had cropped up were far from happy.

Evan's incident with the drug user cutting his arm, seeing his parents and making Owen worry unnecessarily were all things he hadn't wanted to happen. But as life happened, so did little things they couldn't control. He hoped he could grab hold of those things they could control and guide their lives in the direction he wanted them to go.

Finished with his melancholic thoughts, he dried off and headed to bed. Despite Owen snoring like a tractor, he wouldn't sleep somewhere else unless it was impossible to fall asleep because, once he was asleep, nothing would disturb him. Usually. Owen's retching woke him, which was a surprise, but he darted from the bed to the bathroom and rested his hand on Owen's back.

"Sorry," he said between bouts.

"It's okay. Don't worry about it. I'll get you some water." He filled a small glass and set it on the back of the toilet, within reach. He then wet a cloth with cool water and placed it on Owen's nape. The groan that accompanied it sounded grateful, and he regularly turned it to keep the cool side close to his skin. When he stopped, Owen sank back against the bath, sweat dripping down his face. Evan rinsed another cloth and wiped him, handing him the glass when he was done. Owen's hands trembled, and Evan cupped them to help him get it to his mouth.

"Thank you." He blinked slowly. "Some birthday."

"You'll be fine about it once you're feeling better," Evan said. "Besides, birthdays shouldn't count until after we've woken on the day. Anything that happens before we sleep is not our birthday, even if it's after midnight."

"I like that theory." Owen sipped again and sighed. "I need more sleep."

"Do you think you'll keep down some paracetamol?"

"I can try."

"Come on, then." He took the glass, putting it aside, and pulled Owen to his feet carefully. Helping him to sit on the bed, he handed him the tablets, which Owen took with the water.

"Thanks."

"Get some rest." Evan tucked Owen back into bed, raking his fingers through his hair until the soft inhales of his sleep reached him. Then he went back to the bathroom and cleaned up before climbing back into bed.

The same thing happened twice more, but they eventually managed five hours' sleep in one go, waking far later on a Sunday than they usually did. Evan nuzzled his nose into Owen's neck, ignoring the boozy, sweaty scent coming from his skin. Underneath it, it was still him.

"Happy birthday, sweetheart," he whispered, not knowing how bad Owen's hangover would be.

"Thank you," he replied in the same voice.

They stayed snuggled together, dozing here and there, until Owen's phone began blowing up with chimes from messages. His friends and family were obviously up and about, and quite right, too. After all, it was eleven o'clock in the morning.

Evan kissed Owen's cheek. "Check your messages while I make breakfast. And no push ups today."

"Okay," Owen said, still sounding sleepy. It wouldn't surprise Evan if the man fell back to sleep, but it was his birthday, and he could spend it however he wanted to.

Evan slipped into some joggers and a T-shirt and started a fry up. One thing they always agreed on was that, despite not wanting to eat a full English breakfast, it was the fastest way to get over a hangover. While he worked, he heard Owen on the phone. He obviously hadn't gone back to sleep, which was good.

His voice drew nearer. "It was good... A little, yes... Maybe... Not on your life." Owen entered the kitchen, giving Evan a smile, even as he went pale, probably at the smell. "Mum's asking if you have proof of what happened last night."

Evan smirked. "That's for me to know and you to find out."

Owen glared. "No, he doesn't," he said to his mum. He rolled his eyes and left the room, which was probably a good thing. "You'll have to get it from him then."

Evan chuckled. He would expect a phone call or message from Sally in the near future. In fact, he was sure he would receive messages from several people about those photos or videos. Whether he shared them would depend on who it was.

He finished cooking and took two plates to the dining table, finding Owen staring at the news on the TV.

"Anything interesting?" he asked.

Owen shook his head. "Was Freddie really there last night?"

Evan snorted. "You know he was. You saw him before you started drinking."

Shaking his head, Owen stood and joined him at the table, his face paling again. "I'm trying to breathe through my mouth because this is terrible." His eyes widened. "Not your cooking! The smell."

"I know what you meant."

They ate in silence, Evan allowing Owen to come back to being a slightly less hungover man than he had been, and by the time they finished, Owen was smiling. "As much as I hate eating when I first start, I was ravenous by the end."

"You sound a little more human now. How's your stomach and head?"

"Stomach seems fine now. I suppose time will tell. My head is okay."

"Good. Oh, I was speaking to Damon last night. He was talking about that kid you mentioned from the charity?"

"Riley?"

Evan nodded. "Damon is sponsoring him to go to college to get his degree."

Owen grinned. "I knew he'd been considering it, but I hadn't heard that he'd decided."

"Yeah, he said he didn't see a problem with it, especially when Riley seemed so switched on and enthusiastic. Hopefully, this boy will do right by them."

"He will. I could see the intelligence behind those careful eyes. He didn't want to believe something good could happen to him but wanted so badly to."

"Did you look into it anymore?"

Owen shook his head. "I got distracted by some things." He smirked.

"Oh? What things might they be?"

"I wonder." He stared at Evan, eyes shining.

Evan grinned. "Now, birthday boy, what would you like to do today?"

"You mean you don't have any karaoke planned for today. Be still my heart." Owen placed a hand against his chest. Evan flipped him off, and they laughed. "To be honest, I don't really have any plans. Mum couldn't get the time off work, so she won't see us until Tuesday, and I didn't make plans to see anyone else."

"Do you want to visit Book Drunk for a coffee while we decide?" He couldn't decide if he was brave for suggesting it or an idiot.

Owen tilted his head. "Are you sure?"

Evan's stomach churned a little, but he didn't feel the need to shy away from the place. "Yeah. Even if they're there, we can get the drinks to go."

Owen nodded slowly. "If you're certain, yes. But there's one thing I want to do first."

"What's that?"

He scrunched up his face. "Shower."

Wrapping up warm, they left the house half an hour later and headed down the road to the cafe. Despite the sun shining down on them, the air was cold and brisk. The tourists were out in force, as they always were at all times of the year, but they ignored them and continued as if they weren't there.

When they entered Book Drunk, the warmth bled into him immediately, and Evan rubbed his hands together. The cafe bookshop hadn't been open on Sundays initially, but Oscar had made a sound business decision in doing so, and business had boomed. Christian hadn't been so happy about the extra hours, from what Evan had heard, and Oscar had to share the work with his best friend and assistant manager, Hilary.

"God, I need warming again after that," Evan said, shivering.

"I know just the thing," a voice said, and Evan glanced over his shoulder.

"I wasn't expecting to see you today," Owen said to Prince Christian.

Christian, the strong silent type, smiled. "I had nothing else to do, so I thought I'd keep my boy company."

It was no surprise to anyone that knew them that Christian was a Daddy and Oscar was a little, but they didn't advertise that outside of their friends and family for obvious reasons.

Christian frowned. "Wasn't it your birthday yesterday?"

Owen's cheeks flushed, and Evan winked at him. "It's actually today, but the party was yesterday."

"I heard on the grapevine that the karaoke bar is asking for a return performance," Christian joked, and Evan blinked, having not expected it from him.

Owen palmed his face. "Please don't agree on my behalf," he murmured.

Evan and Christian shared an amused glance. "Well, I need to get something warm to drink before my insides freeze," Evan said. "What do you want?" he asked Owen.

"Coffee?"

Evan shook his head. "I shouldn't have asked." He headed for the counter where Oscar stood, glancing around them, hoping not to see the people he saw those few days ago. When it was his turn, he ordered a hot chocolate and a latte, and added a slice of chocolate cake for Owen. He maybe should've checked how his stomach was before he did so, but he'd either eat it or not, depending on how he felt.

He carried them over to the table Owen had chosen and set them down. "One very strong coffee and a cake for the birthday boy," he said.

"Ooh, chocolate cake. Yum."

"I should've known your stomach would be better now." He sipped his hot chocolate, groaning as the warmth heated his stomach. "I think I just need to drink hot drinks all day, every day, from now on," he said. "I'm freezing. Anyway, what do you want to do for the rest of your birthday?"

Owen's forehead creased as he slowly demolished the cake, but when he took the last mouthful, it cleared. "I want to go to see Amy."

It wasn't what he expected Owen to say, but it was something he was totally on board with. "Okay. We can stop by and grab some flowers on the way."

"And a chocolate bar."

Evan chuckled. "And a chocolate bar, yes."

What that girl had gone through was unthinkable, and the tragedy had affected everyone close to them. It had changed everyone's lives, some for the better, some for the worse. Families had split, friends had lost contact, communication had dried up, but the girl at the centre of it had never been forgotten.

Owen, Evan and Dominic had been seventeen when Amy had been taken, and the worst of it was that they hadn't even realised it until three days after. Amy had argued with her parents and stormed off to her friend's house to sleepover. Something she had done many times in the past. No one had thought anything of it. Her parents and her friend's parents had an agreement that they would keep her there until she calmed down and let them know if there were any problems. More often than not, Amy returned a day or so later. Three days wasn't unheard of, but it didn't happen often. Amy was usually quick to anger, quick to calm.

Unfortunately, what no one had realised was that Amy had never arrived at her friend's house in the first place. Her friend hadn't been expecting her, and Amy's parents hadn't expected to hear from her friend's parents. So both thought Amy was with the other. It was only when Sally decided to check in with Amy's friend's parents that they realised something was wrong.

Three days was a long time to be with a bad guy like that. It had taken a further two days before the police had found her, and by that point, she was dead. The man responsible chosen the coward's way out and was killed by police. It was a bad time for them all, but Owen had taken it particularly harshly. From that moment, he'd begun training, wanting to protect other people from whatever came their way. Evan went the other direction and trained in first aid so he could help those who got hurt.

It destroyed so many lives, but on the other hand, they wouldn't be where they were today if it hadn't happened. So, as much as it pained him to say it, maybe it was all meant to be. He just wished Amy hadn't had to suffer for it.

14

Owen

T he need to visit Amy came out of nowhere, but it felt right. Owen hadn't visited her for a few months, but he wanted to share his birthday with her. As they set out, Evan linked their fingers, their other hands holding flowers and chocolate. They should've probably taken the car with how cold it was and how unsteady he still felt from the previous night, but he wanted to walk. It only took half an hour, and the sun was still shining. Besides, they worked up a sweat by the time they reached the cemetery.

As they drew closer to where Amy rested, he remembered the time she borrowed his sleeping bag to take on a school trip, and he filled the bottom with plastic snakes before giving it to her. Apparently, her scream had sent many people running to their room. She had cursed up a storm when she returned.

He stopped beside her gravestone, the marble still looking clean and fresh. His mother visited at least once a month and cleaned it up whenever she did. Owen did it sometimes, too. Only the best for his pain in the ass sister.

"Hey, bumblebee," he said, crouching and setting the flowers down. He undid the wrapper, and Evan handed him the multipurpose tool he kept in his pocket to help cut the stems down. "Can you believe the news about me and Evan?" he said, glancing over his shoulder. "I remember you shouting at us many times and saying we should be together. It wasn't the curse you thought it was because I'd always wanted him. I played it close to my chest, though. Not many people knew. But by god, Amy, you were one smart cookie." He shook his head, placing the cut flowers into the vase built into the stone.

"You were a pain in the butt, little sis, but we love you," Evan said. "Dominic does, too. No matter what we do, you'll always be a part of our family. It's a shame you didn't get to see May grow up. Dominic's little sister is a spitfire, and I'm sure you would've been thick as thieves." He crouched on the opposite side, laying the chocolate bar in front of the flowers.

Owen chuckled. "They would've been a menace together. Absolute dynamite." He finished the flowers, including the ones Evan brought, and it brightened up the black marble. He sighed. "Fuck, Amy. Life can be so unfair."

Evan stood, and they met at the base of the grave. Evan slipped his arms around him, and Owen relaxed against him. He stared at the grave for a long while, but finally, he noticed Evan's chattering teeth, and he pulled away, his own body feeling the chill. The sun was deceptive.

"Sorry. Come on. Let's go back home and get warm." He winked, and Evan chuckled, his breath puffing a cloud around them. He turned back to his sister. "See you soon, bumblebee."

They wandered back to the street and towards the house, a little quicker than their usual walking pace, and when they made it inside the house, they both stamped their feet, trying to get the circulation back into them.

"Go jump in the shower to warm up, and I'll get the coffee started."

Owen shook his head. "No, you go." Evan narrowed his eyes, and Owen's breath hitched. "Okay, I'll go," he mumbled, heading for the bathroom.

He would've loved to have Evan in the shower with him, but they probably wouldn't warm up as quickly because the water wouldn't reach part of them. So it made sense to do it separately. As he stood under the spray, he closed his eyes. Birthdays were for celebration, but he often found himself thinking about his life and what parts of it he was happy or unhappy with. This year, there were a lot more things he was happy about. Last year, he had wished for Evan to return home, and he had. What could he wish for that year? Long-lasting love? The chance to show Evan how sorry he was? He wasn't sure, but he wanted everything. And the only way he was going to get that was by taking a chance.

He switched off the shower and dried off, dressing in clean clothes and went to find Evan. May as well start now. Evan was in the kitchen, leaning against the counter with his hands wrapped around a coffee mug. Owen stopped right in front of him and took the cup from his hands before cupping his jaw.

Meeting Evan's gaze, he said, "I love you."

Evan closed his eyes, a shiver working its way through his body that Owen believed had nothing to do with being cold. Owen brushed his thumbs across his cheeks, and Evan's fingers gripped Owen's waist. He waited. He didn't need Evan to reply because he'd heard what he'd whispered the other night, even if he had been half asleep at the time. He wasn't the only one taking a chance, and that made it easier to acknowledge.

Evan opened his eyes again, heat building inside them. "I love you, too." He inhaled. "If you ever push me away again, I won't survive it, Owen. You're it for me. It's always been you. And it will destroy me if you back out. I need you to be sure. I know we've been together already, but I'll be honest, I've held myself back. If you are at all unsure about this, you need to tell me now."

Owen gulped. If Evan had been holding himself back, what the hell was Owen in for? But there was no sliver of doubt inside him. "I'm yours. There's only one way we're stopping this now…" He didn't finish the sentence, but Evan understood. He could see it in his eyes.

"That was your final chance to let go. Are you ready for what being mine entails?"

Owen swallowed again and nodded. "Yes. No matter what it is, I know I can take it, and I know you'll never hurt me." Evan opened his mouth, but Owen put his finger over the top. "But remember, if I can't back out, you can't leave."

A wave of sadness passed through Evan's eyes for a moment before it was gone, and then he nodded, and Owen removed his finger so he could speak. "There is nothing on this earth that can make me leave. Not now."

Owen crashed his mouth to Evan's, the latter letting him for a few seconds before grabbing his jaw and pushing him back. Evan's eyes had hardened. "Who's in charge?"

"You are," Owen gasped as Evan's fingers tightened, his thumb sliding into Owen's mouth.

"This is the last chance for you to give your opinion before I take over and give you what you need. What do you want?"

Owen sucked on Evan's thumb before closing his eyes. Evan pulled his thumb free, and Owen said, "I want whatever you want to give me."

"Good boy." Evan smashed their lips together, biting at his lower lip and sliding his tongue around his mouth as if reacquainting himself with his taste. Owen relaxed his neck, his head falling back, trusting Evan to hold him up. He whimpered when Evan pulled back. "On your knees."

Owen dropped to the floor like a marionette, uncaring of the hard surface. Opening his eyes, he met Evan's blazing gaze, waiting for instructions. Evan's hand brushed across his cheek.

"You look beautiful on your knees for me, bruised lips, wild hair, glassy eyes. Only I can see you like this." Owen didn't reply. It hadn't been a question. "Take me out."

Owen's fingers fumbled with the button and zip of his jeans, but eventually got them open and his boxers down enough for his cock to stretch for the ceiling. His mouth watered, but he didn't make a move to suck him, as much as he wanted to. He licked his lips, though, and then transferred his gaze back to Evan's face.

A slight curve to Evan's lips was all the amusement he saw before Evan's hands gripped Owen's hair and pulled him closer. "Hands behind your back and lick."

Owen's tongue was out before he'd even registered the order, and he licked every inch he could reach without using his hands. His saliva ran down his chin in rivulets, but he didn't care. His eyes darted from the red, straining erection in front of him to Evan's eyes, watching as his expression tightened with every millimetre that his arousal grew.

"My balls," Evan growled.

Owen used his chin to push the jeans and boxers down further, exposing him further, and then focused his attention on the sacs. It would've been easier with his hands, but his tongue seemed to do a fine job of it, especially when he focused on the area between them.

"Suck them," Evan said, his voice hoarse.

Gladly. He opened his mouth as wide as he could and sucked, using his tongue as well. Then he transferred to the other one. His cock was pressing against the zip of his jeans, and he felt so close to coming handsfree.

Evan pulled on his hair, and his ball popped free. "Go to the bedroom, undress and wait for me on your back on the bed."

"Yes, Sir," he said, scrambling to his feet and racing to the bedroom—Owen's bedroom, as that seemed to be where they tended to go whenever they were together. He undressed in record time, putting his clothes on the chair to sort out later, and climbed onto the bed, flopping to his back. His chest heaved, his eyes darted to the door and ceiling alternately, and he needed—god, how he needed—everything that Evan was hopefully going to give him.

"So well behaved," Evan said as he entered.

Owen wasn't sure where he was supposed to look, so he locked gazes with Evan again. His lover grabbed the lube from the bedside table and tossed it to the bed.

"Get yourself stretched while I get undressed. Be quick about it. I don't have time to waste."

Owen's heart pounded so hard he thought it would jump right out of his chest, but he grabbed the lube and squirted some onto his fingers. Spreading his legs, he reached between his legs to his hole, his body already shivering in anticipation. Evan's eyes were on him even as he pulled the T-shirt over his head. Owen massaged, pressed and stretched his channel as much as he could in the time it took Evan to undress, and when the man crawled between his legs and batted his hands away, Owen's stomach fluttered.

"Keep your legs high."

Evan didn't bother checking his hole to see if he was ready, and Owen loved it. His master held his cock at his pucker and pushed. One long, steady thrust, where he slid through any resistance Owen might have had, until his balls hit Owen's ass. Owen bit his lip, trying to keep his groan contained.

"Fuck, you feel so tight."

Evan's fingers gripped Owen's nipple as he withdrew and slammed back in again. The pleasure/pain balance was exquisite, and Owen's eyes watered at how good it felt. His hands kept slipping against the back of his thighs, but he repositioned them again, keeping his legs high. Evan changed his position, and Owen saw stars, the man nailing his prostate with each thrust.

"Ah, there we go," Evan grunted. "Just the right spot."

Owen's orgasm tingled down his spine. "Please, Sir?"

Evan kept up the speed. "Please, what?"

"Please, can I come? Please? I'm not sure I can hold on." Owen licked his lips, his breathing choppy.

"You can hold on a bit longer."

Owen wasn't sure about that, but he tried. He closed his eyes, blocking out the sight of Evan destroying his hole.

"Look at me! Look at us," Evan ordered, and Owen's eyes snapped open, meeting his gaze. Then Evan lowered his eyes to where their bodies joined, and Owen followed.

"Fuck, fuck, fuck," he said, his control right on the edge of slipping.

"That's it. See how well we fit? No one can give you this," Evan said, slamming his hips forward. The slap of skin heightened Owen's arousal further.

"Please! Oh, fuck, please!"

Evan let go of Owen's nipple, and a tingling sensation flooded the area. "Come for me," Evan ordered, and Owen let out an undignified screech as his climax barrelled through him. His eyelids fluttered closed, his hearing disappeared, everything went offline while waves of pleasure washed over him.

When he came back, his brain filtered things in slowly. The complete relaxation of his body. The scent of sex. The sound of panting. The taste of sweat on his lips. And finally, when his eyes opened, the sight of Evan on top of him, waiting to meet his gaze.

A smile crept across his face, and Evan returned the gesture. "Are you okay?" he asked.

"More than," he croaked.

Evan's smile grew. "I'll get you a drink. Stay there."

He climbed off him, and though Owen wanted him to stay, he also needed to get clean. He couldn't make his body move. He'd planned to be at least upright by the time Evan returned, but he'd barely moved his pinkie finger. Evan placed a straw at his lips, and sweet, tart orange juice flooded his mouth. He drank as if he'd been in a desert for the past two weeks. The effort that took wiped him out again, and his head thumped back to the pillow. Evan wiped a cloth over his body, and it felt divine. He rolled his head to the side when the bed dipped and Evan stretched out beside him. Evan threaded their fingers together, and Owen smiled again.

"How are you feeling?" Evan asked.

"Like I won't be able to move for a few days."

"Well," Evan said, "sorry to burst your bubble, but you have to work tomorrow."

Owen gasped, over-exaggerating. "It's my birthday! Stop being so unkind!"

Evan chuckled. "I apologise. You don't have to go to work tomorrow. I was lying."

Owen laughed and finally gathered the energy to roll to his side, snuggling up against Evan. "Thank you," he murmured.

"For what?"

Owen shifted his head so he could look at him. "For knowing what I need and want without having to ask and for giving it to me."

Evan brushed their lips together. "I'll always give you what you need."

"I know. And that's just one reason I love you."

Evan grinned. "And what are the others?"

"Ah, you'll have to wait and find out."

"Find out when?"

Owen smirked. "As we work our way through our years together." He studied every inch of Evan's face, finally acknowledging that there were more lines on his face. A reminder they were getting older. But never too old for love.

"I'll gladly wait for that."

Owen snuggled into Evan's embrace, closing his eyes. He was wrung out, but he didn't want to fall asleep yet. He'd already wasted too many hours by sleeping late that morning.

"What do you want to do for dinner?" Evan said, proving he was a mind reader.

"Hmm. I don't know what I fancy."

Evan swung his legs over the bed, leaving Owen colder than he was. "We'll order in. Curry? Pizza? Chinese?"

"Ooh, Chinese sounds good."

"Done. I'll order it now. Come on out whenever you're ready."

Evan disappeared, clad in only his boxers, and Owen rolled to his back, staring at the ceiling, unable to stop his stupid grin.

While he lay there, he heard music and singing, enough that he wanted to know what Evan was listening to, so he reluctantly dressed in joggers and a T-shirt and headed to the living room. Evan sat on the sofa, looking at his phone.

"What's that?" Owen asked.

Evan turned a bright smile to him and patted the seat next to him. Instead, Owen climbed into his lap. Evan chuckled and pressed play. It took Owen a minute to realise it was him on stage at the karaoke bar the previous night.

"Oh, my god. I can't believe you recorded that, you ass!" He backhanded his chest. "Delete it. Right now!"

Evan shook his head. "No chance. That stays with me forever. A reminder that although the most amazing, gorgeous, clever, wonderful man is all those things, he also can't sing for shit. You have to have some flaws, Owen. It's only fair."

"Well, I don't see you having any," he replied.

"Oh, I have flaws. Without a doubt." Evan gestured to the phone. "It's also got Matteo on it, too. He can't carry a tune, either.

You're a perfect match in the karaoke world." He switched to a different video. "You might like to see this, though."

Owen, again, was on the screen, but there was a drag queen beside him, crooning to him in their gravelly voice. He smiled. He'd always loved the idea of drag shows, but he'd never actually met one. Frowning, he muttered, "Typical. The one time I get to meet someone and I'm too drunk to remember it."

Evan's arms came around him. "Well, it just goes to show how nice these people are. You have a free ticket to attend a drag show of your choosing. They," he gestured to the screen, "said you probably wouldn't remember it, and they wanted to give you a second opportunity."

Owen glanced at him, eyes wide. "Really?" Evan nodded. "I can't wait."

Evan chuckled and palmed his cheek, bringing their mouths together. "You are so easy to please and such an enigma at the same time."

"I'm one of a kind."

"You truly are. And you're mine."

Owen wrapped his arms around Evan's neck, straddling his lap, and kissed him again. By the time the doorbell rang, his lips felt bruised, and he fell back onto the sofa while Evan grabbed the food. He touched his lips, smiling.

Best birthday present ever.

15

Evan

E van hit the ground running when he entered the hospital almost two weeks later. A car accident victim had just been brought in, and they needed help. He shoved his things behind the nurses' station and washed up quickly before helping the doctor. There were so many cuts and bruises already forming, and they had to work fast. Evan set up an IV for fluids and medicine to help with any pain the person might feel—though, hopefully, because they were unconscious, they felt little.

They worked tirelessly until the person was as patched up as they could be, and then the doctor exhaled. "Now we've stopped them from bleeding out, let's look at what needs doing first."

By the time they sent them for the tests the doctor needed, it had been over an hour. Evan cleaned up and grabbed his things, telling Marie he would be back in five minutes. He strode for the staff area and locked his belongings away. He grabbed coffees on the way back, handing one to Marie.

He had little time to drink it. A&E was rammed—it always was, but there must've been something in the air that day because it seemed overly busy compared to usual.

Evan groaned, dropping into a chair behind the nurses' station. "I need lunch. I'm already starving!"

"It's not even eleven o'clock yet," Marie said, shaking her head.

"That means it's lunchtime *somewhere*, doesn't it?"

She threw something at him, which he caught instinctively. "Eat that. It'll tide you over if nothing else."

He stared at the muesli bar, wrinkling his face. He hated muesli, but needs must and all that. Ripping open the wrapper, he swung his chair around to watch the news on the screen as he chewed.

"*—been confirmed that there has been a shooting in Windsor. There are no confirmed fatalities, but several people are injured.*"

Evan gestured to the screen. "Have you seen this?"

Marie glanced at it and then at him and nodded slowly. "Yeah, it started ten minutes ago."

"Wonder who it is?" He stared at the screen, trying to read the scrolling words along the bottom.

Marie put a hand on his shoulder. "Evan—"

The words on-screen registered, and he dropped the bar as he stood, moving closer to the TV.

"Evan..." Marie said again.

"*—shots were fired towards Prince Freddie and his husband, Prince Damon. Their bodyguards got them secured quickly, but not without injuries. We don't have confirmation of who is injured, yet.*"

Evan raced around the desk, grabbing his phone and dialling. "Come on, come on, pick up, pick up," he muttered.

"Evan, he'll be okay."

He glared at her. "You knew, didn't you?"

Marie nodded. "I can't distract you when you're working, Evan. You know that."

The call turned to voicemail, but he ended it and dialled again. "Pick up, you asshole." No answer again. "Where the fuck is he?"

"He's probably taking care of securing the prince," Marie said. "He'll be fine."

"Incoming GSW in five minutes. Patient is unconscious. We believe it may be a concussion but will need confirmation. Vitals are stable. Please note, we need additional security at A&E when we arrive."

Evan didn't need any other confirmation. Whoever was coming in with a gunshot wound was either royalty or royalty was coming in with them. They would usually use a different entrance, but sometimes, it wasn't possible. He dropped his phone to the desk, bracing his hands and lowering his head. His heart pounded, and he couldn't breathe, but he needed to. He visualised helping Owen to breathe and followed his own phantom instructions.

The five minutes dragged by, but eventually, the ambulance pulled up. The paramedics raced out just as more security guards entered A&E, and within seconds, they wheeled the gurney in. Damon walked in behind it, along with Locke, and Evan's heart dropped. It was either Freddie...or Owen.

Damon met his gaze, his eyes pained. He nodded at him, and Evan swore his heart stopped. He stepped towards the gurney, Owen's face coming into focus.

"Fuck, no," he said, grabbing Owen's hand. "Owen?"

"He's unconscious," the paramedic said, as if talking to an idiot.

"I can see that," Evan snapped. "Owen, sweetheart. Come back to me."

"Oh, shit," that same paramedic murmured, seeming to realise Evan knew the patient.

"Bay three," Marie said. "Evan, go with him, but don't get in the way. If you do, I'll have you removed. Understand?"

Evan nodded and walked beside the gurney as they wheeled it into the bay. He couldn't take his eyes off him. There was so much blood on his clothes. He glanced at Damon, who had also come with them.

"What happened?"

Damon sighed. "We were shot at as we left Windsor Castle. Not sure if they were aiming for Freddie or me, but they missed. Unfortunately, the bullet sliced along the side of Owen's head."

Evan couldn't see the wound because of the bandages he had on, but there was a lot of blood. He knew head wounds bled a lot but seeing it on his boyfriend was a whole other matter. He stepped aside when the nurses took over from the paramedics, and he wrung his hands. He had to survive. He just had to.

Watching as Dr Wallis removed the bandages, Evan gasped when the wound came into view. There was a line going from his temple to halfway towards the back of his head. He could just imagine Owen flinching away from the pain, which might just have saved his life.

If he woke up.

Concussion could be a bitch.

"It looks fairly superficial, though the blood shows differently. I want him to have an MRI to check for internal bleeding or bruising," Dr Wallis said. "Keep the fluids going and add more pain relief to it. When he wakes up, he's going to have a stinking headache."

The nurses bustled around, and Evan knew he needed to walk away and let them do the job, so with a kiss to the back of Owen's hand, he whispered, "I'll be right here when you get back."

A porter wheeled Owen out of A&E and towards the MRI testing room, and Evan rested his hands on his hips, reminding himself to breathe. Damon squeezed his shoulder.

"I'm sorry," he said.

Evan couldn't reply. He knew it wasn't Damon's fault, but he couldn't help but briefly wish Owen had a different job. One where he didn't put himself in danger every single day. One where Evan wouldn't have to worry if that day would be the day he didn't return home to him. He dropped his head. Owen wouldn't be Owen if he didn't do what he could to protect those around him. Even if he wasn't a bodyguard for royalty, he would've found something to do that would put him at risk. It was who he was.

Finally, he glanced at Damon. "Is everyone else okay?"

Damon nodded. "Yes. Freddie is back home now, and they've increased security for the moment. We're waiting on information about where the shot came from, but I've not been told anything yet. I wasn't really thinking of looking around when everything happened."

"It's not your fault," Evan said, meaning it that time. "It's the shooter's fault. I think you should get back home. Take an update to Freddie because I bet he's worried."

Damon nodded. "If you're sure?"

"Yeah, it's okay. I'll let you know when I get some more news."

"All right. Let us know if you need anything at all."

Locke stepped closer. "He'll be fine, Evan. He's a stubborn son of a gun."

Evan huffed a laugh. "That he is." He wandered back to the nurses' station after they left, sitting and dropping his head into his hands.

"He'll be fine," Marie said.

"I know, but this is always what I worry about."

"And I'm sure Owen worries similarly about you."

"But my job doesn't involve guns," he said, glaring at her.

"No, but it does involve scalpels." She looked pointedly at his arm, where the scar was still visible from his altercation.

Evan sighed. She wasn't wrong, but it wasn't what he wanted to hear right then. Even if he *needed* to hear it. He waited impatiently for Owen to finish, and when he tried to work, Marie told him to sit his butt down. Apparently, he was off rota for the moment. It wasn't a terrible decision because he wasn't sure he would've been any good to anyone, and no one deserved a distracted nurse tending to them.

He monitored the news, but apart from repeating the same information they already had, they had nothing new. He checked news reports on his phone, too, but had the same results.

Finally, while Marie was talking on the phone, she glanced at him, and he straightened.

"Yes, I'll tell him. Thanks." She put the phone down. "They've taken him to room twelve."

"Thank you!" He kissed her cheek and raced down the corridors to the room. He knocked before entering and found Owen awake and talking to Dr Wallis. "Oh, fuck," he whispered, sagging against the wall.

Owen smiled at him, though he winced with it. "Hey, you."

Evan shuffled closer and dropped into the chair beside the bed, reaching for Owen's hand. "How do you feel?"

"I was just asking him the same question," Dr Wallis said, making Evan jump because he'd forgotten he was still there.

Owen winced as he moved his head. "I have a headache and some dizziness when I move too fast. Almost like I'm drunk and everything is moving slower than my head is."

"Do you feel sick?" Dr Wallis asked.

Owen paused, then nodded and winced again. "Yes, but only when I move my head. When I'm still, it's okay."

"Any ringing in your ears?"

"I don't think...maybe a little." He yawned. "Sorry."

Dr Wallis smiled. "Being tired is to be expected. I need to ask you a few questions to see where your level of confusion lies, okay?"

"Sure."

The doctor went through several seemingly random questions, like asking who the king was and what year it was, plus asking for family members' names and what he did the day before and earlier that day. Both long-term and short-term memory questions to figure out if he had any amnesia symptoms.

"Good news. You don't seem to have any memory loss, apart from that initial confusion when you first woke, which is expected. You have a concussion, without a doubt, and I'm going to look through the MRI results once more to double check there are no issues in that head of yours. But if everything checks out there, you'll have the go ahead to return home." He held up his hand. "On the understanding that you will not work for at least three days. I want to see you again in three days' time so I can check you over before I say you're ready to go back. Understand."

"Thanks, doc," Owen said.

"Do you have any questions for me at the moment?"

Owen shook his head and winced. "I really need to stop doing that."

Dr Wallis chuckled. "That'll fade soon enough, but you need to rest." He glanced at Evan. "I assume you'll keep an eye on him."

"I sure will. Thanks, Dr Wallis."

"I think you can call me Edward by now."

Evan chuckled and refocused on Owen as Dr Wallis—Edward—left. He blew out a breath, his heart finally returning to the level it should be. "How are you really?"

Owen smiled. "I promise, I'm okay." He reached his other hand to cover Evan's, squeezing. "I'm here, baby."

Evan dropped his head to their joined hands, his eyes letting go of the tears he'd wanted to shed for far too long. Owen removed his hand and raked his fingers through Evan's hair until he pulled himself together. He lifted his head and grabbed a tissue from the bedside table.

"Sorry about that," he said wetly.

"Never be sorry for showing emotion."

Evan choked on a laugh and mopped up. "Can I get you anything?"

"Some water?"

He stood and filled a glass with water, handing it to him. He could see the tightening of Owen's eyes whenever he moved, so he helped him as much as Owen would allow, knowing it would take a little time for the symptoms to ease. Most concussion symptoms disappeared after a couple of days, but others lasted weeks. It all depended on the situation and the patient. He hoped Owen was in the former group because he knew how much he hated being relegated to the sidelines.

"Shall I switch off the lights for a little while so you can rest until Dr Wallis comes back?" he asked.

The sigh that followed his words gave the answer before Owen said the word, and Evan flicked the switch by the headboard, plunging the room into darkness, save for a small light by the door. He reclaimed Owen's hand but kept quiet so Owen could rest, and by his light breathing, it didn't take him long to fall asleep. Thankfully, there was no longer a requirement to wake people who had a concussion, so Owen could sleep as long as he needed.

Evan pulled his phone from his pocket and dimmed the brightness as much as he could so it wouldn't hurt Owen's eyes if he woke. He sent a message to Brett, asking him to pass on Owen's condition to Damon and Freddie because he realised he didn't have either of their numbers or Locke's. Brett replied, saying he would and asking Owen to listen to the doctor's instructions and not to contact him for at least the length of the time the doctor said. Evan chuckled quietly. Brett knew Owen very well indeed.

He messaged Matteo, explaining what had happened and apologising for cancelling their dinner plans that day, and Matteo initially replied with the middle finger.

MATTEO: *Of course I don't mind, dick dweeb. Look after your boy. I might pop round tomorrow with something to keep him occupied while he's off. He seems like the kind of person to hate being inactive. Take care of yourself, too. X*

Evan smiled and shook his head. As much as Matteo pretended to be hard-headed and standoffish, he cared deeply for those he considered friends. He also contacted Dominic, who had sent several messages to him.

EVAN: *He has a concussion, but he's awake and alert, so it's a win. We're waiting on the results of the MRI, but the doctor is hopeful that it's fine. He'll be going home today, I'm sure.*
DOMINIC: *I'm glad to hear it. Can't wait to find this fucker and give him a piece of my mind. There's been enough shooting in this world lately. Let me know when you get home and if you need anything.*

Trust Dominic to be by his phone and reply straight away. Evan agreed and scrolled to the news again. There still didn't seem to be any more information except that the shooter seems to have been in one of the buildings opposite Windsor Castle.

Dr Wallis returned a couple of hours later. Evan gently woke Owen, but they kept the lights low.

"Everything looks fine on the MRI. I don't have any concerns. Keep doing what you know he should and shouldn't be doing, Evan, but he can head home now. I have a prescription for pain relief for him, too." Owen signed the discharge papers.

"Thanks, Dr...Edward. I appreciate your help."

Dr Wallis smiled and left, and Evan glanced at Owen. "Will you be okay with the lights, or would you like me to grab some sunglasses when I collect my stuff?"

Owen opened his mouth to undoubtedly say he was fine, but he paused. "Sunglasses, please."

"Got it." Evan stood and leaned over, pressing his lips to Owen's. "I'll be back in a few minutes. Don't go anywhere."

"I'm more than happy sleeping here for the moment," Owen joked.

"The beds aren't bad, are they?" Evan replied with a smile. "I won't be long."

He headed for the staff room, collecting his bags and coat and dropped by the nurses' stations to update Marie and grab some sunglasses from lost and found—he'd return them later—before heading back to collect his man. He helped Owen into Evan's coat, knowing the cold would be worse for him, and aided him as they walked towards the exit. He settled Owen by the door and fetched his car, helping him inside. The journey was short but quiet, Owen leaning his head against the window, reminiscent of his drunken birthday party.

When Owen sat on the sofa, Evan fussed over him, but Owen grabbed his hand. "I'm fine, Evan. Just sit with me until it's time for bed."

So Evan did. And despite the silence, despite the darkness of the room, despite his mind replaying events of the day, he held his best friend, his boyfriend, and watched over him.

The day could've ended so differently, and he had to be glad of the result. Everyone had survived. He couldn't ask for more than that. Even if he wanted to. He closed his eyes and rested his cheek against Owen's head, listening to his breathing and reassuring himself several times that he was with him, alive and almost well.

And if he shed a few tears, who would know?

Owen was still with him.

And Owen loved him.

And Evan loved Owen.

They had their lives ahead of them, and Evan intended to spend it loving the man who had made him whole.

151

16

Brett

Why was Brett still doing this job when it was just pain after problem after darkness after...everything that was not light and fluffy happiness?

He was sick and tired of having his men caught in the crossfire, and although it was their job to protect the royal family, lately it seemed to be focused more on his bodyguards. It was just a hunch, though. He had nothing concrete to substantiate his ever-flowing thoughts, but something wasn't right.

He couldn't even ask Felix to check anything because Brett had no idea what to search for. His gut was doing the talking, but it wasn't telling him what the threat was, and that pissed him off.

"Boss," the man himself said. "The police have been up and around the potential location of the shooter, but so far, they've found nothing. When things have died down a bit, I'll hover around where Owen was hit and see if I can figure out the trajectory. They might be looking in the wrong place."

"Or whoever it is has expert training in cleaning up their own messes and you won't find a thing," Brett said.

Felix glanced at him, a slight furrow in his brow. He opened his mouth, but Brett's phone beeped. Brett glanced at it and sighed.

"We have half an hour before Christian and Oscar need to leave. Let's make it count."

Felix nodded and went back to his computers, and Brett watched him for a moment before reaching for the next set of paperwork he had to complete. Soon, he was going to have to choose whether he was a bodyguard or whether he was the boss. He wasn't sure how much longer he could take, not only the workload, but the painful reminders of those he lost. Every time someone went out into the field, there was the chance they wouldn't return. Like Owen today. He was bloody lucky. An inch or two to the left, and he'd be dead. Like far too many others since Brett had taken over.

Would it be easier as just a bodyguard or would he beat himself up because he wasn't the boss and taking control of the situation?

He sighed and focused on the paperwork. The answer would appear at some point. Either that or he would burn out and someone else would be making the choice for him.

17

Owen

Concussion sucked.

To begin with, whenever he moved, his head pounded and swirled as if he was on a rollercoaster, his stomach joining in on the game. But with every hour that passed, it lessened. What remained was the sensitivity to light. Even sitting in the near dark and watching TV made his head ache and had him squinting. Evan reassured him, time and again, that he was just healing and it was the process, but Owen was fed up with it. He wanted to be back at work. He was bored. Never again would he complain about downtime, sitting outside the suite. Maybe.

By the time he reached the three-day mark, everything seemed better, although he was pissed that he'd had to miss Prince Douglas's party the night before. Evan had said they could attend if he wanted, but Owen could see in his eyes that he wasn't as sure as he sounded, so Owen had relented and stayed home. It was the right decision, but it didn't stop it from sucking.

And the other thing that sucked? No sex. As much as he was horny, whenever he had coerced Evan to try something, his head had told him, *fuck no*, and he'd had to stop.

So, in all honesty, concussion fucking sucked.

Evan had even commented on how many times he'd used the word sucked in the last few days, but Owen couldn't help it. There wasn't a word strong enough to explain how shit it was, and he hadn't swallowed a bloody thesaurus.

So, while he internally ranted about how he couldn't work yet, he plotted. It was coming up on Valentine's Day and though he didn't agree with the hype there was every year, he would never let the day go without celebrating it. And therefore, he plotted and planned.

When he woke the following day with no tremor of pain or nausea, he almost wept with relief. He knew Brett wouldn't allow him back to work that day, but the moment he entered the bathroom and switched on the light with no negative response, he called Evan.

"What's wrong?" Evan said, racing into the room in just his boxers.

Owen grinned at him. "I'm okay."

"Good, but why did you shout me?" He frowned.

"Because I'm okay," he said more slowly, raising his eyebrows so Evan would get his meaning. He'd give him a break; he *had* woken him.

Evan cupped his face, looking into his eyes, checking his responses. "Any nausea?" Owen shook his head, relieved when the motion didn't hurt. "Any pain?" He shook his head again. "What about the wound site itself?"

"It just aches, as any wound would."

Evan grinned. "I'm glad. We'll get that appointment with the doctor today and then you should be cleared for basic duty."

Owen huffed. Basic duty meant anything that was inside Windsor Castle. He wouldn't be going out on active duty until his wound had healed completely. Which he could understand.

He showered—with Evan helping—and grabbed some breakfast. Evan had called Dr Wallis, and they drove to the hospital that afternoon. Dr Wallis wouldn't usually see patients who weren't part of A&E, but he'd made an exception for them. While they waited for him, Owen caught up on his messages and emails, now that the screen didn't burn his retinas, even on the highest brightness. Evan had dropped back the sunglasses he'd borrowed for Owen. Hopefully, no one had come looking for them before he'd taken them back.

A knock sounded, and the door opened. "Good afternoon," Dr Wallis said. "How are you feeling today?"

"Good. First day I've woken with no pain."

"Glad to hear it. Let's get you checked over so you can get out of here."

He went through the normal examination, checking his eyes, his ears, his wound, asking questions and more. Eventually, he settled back into his chair.

"I don't see any lingering effects of the concussion, so I believe you are well enough to resume your duties. Just remember, take it easy for the first few days, and the moment you have any pain, let me know so we can check you out. There are instances of delayed issues, so be cautious."

Owen nodded. "Thank you. I will."

Dr Wallis redressed his wound—he would need to keep the bandage on until it healed properly to stop the chance of infection. They said goodbye and drove home, but Owen stopped short of entering the place. "I've been cooped away for too long. Can we go to Book Drunk for a coffee?"

Evan smiled. "Sure."

Owen threaded his fingers through Evan's and led the way, enjoying the sun straining to reach them through the clouds. He glanced across at Windsor Castle as it came into view, being opposite Book Drunk as it was, and he paused, studying the surrounding buildings.

"Everything okay?" Evan asked.

Owen nodded. "I was expecting a little trepidation about being here, but I feel nothing except anger." He turned and pointed at the building the police believed the shooter had been squatting in. "That's where he was." He sighed. "It could've ended so differently."

"Don't remind me," Evan murmured, and Owen glanced at him.

"I'm sorry." He repeated the words he'd said many times during the last few days.

Evan smiled. "You don't need to be sorry for who you are. I wouldn't have fallen in love with you if you weren't."

Owen chuckled. "Come on. I think it's time I treated you to a large coffee for putting up with my grumpy ass."

They'd had a regular roundabout of visitors recently: Dominic and Randall, Matteo, Sally, Nick, Felix, Brett. Freddie and Damon, even. But it was nice to get out of the house.

Entering Book Drunk, Owen's stomach immediately growled as the scent of food hit him. It must've been fairly loud because Evan grinned at him. They headed for the counter, but when Oscar looked up and saw them, he dropped what he held and came running around the counter and threw his arms around Owen's neck.

"I've been so worried! Are you okay?" He pulled back, staring at him. "You were so brave."

Owen flushed, not used to being the centre of attention like that. He swallowed hard. "I'm okay now. Back to normal."

Oscar pointed to his bandage. "That says otherwise."

Evan slipped his arm around Owen's shoulder. "It's just to keep it clean. He's doing a lot better. Cleared for basic duty."

Oscar put his hand on his chest and exhaled. "I'm so glad. Anyway, come on in. Whatever you want is on the house today."

"No, it's—"

"It's not up for debate. I know." Oscar grinned. "What can I get you?"

Knowing there was no dissuading him, Owen ordered a coffee and a panini, and Evan ordered a coffee. They settled at a table near a window, and Owen leant back, sighing. It was good to be out and about again, even if he had noticed Malachi hanging around outside the cafe.

"You need to call Brett and tell him," Evan reminded him.

"I'll do that after this." Then he had a thought. "Actually, let's grab some coffees to go after this and take them over. I can speak to him in person instead. He's more likely to believe I'm okay if he sees me."

Evan chuckled. "True."

All Owen needed to say to Oscar was that they wanted drinks for Brett, and he filled several to-go cups with drinks and put them in a large takeaway tray. He waved away payment again, and Owen vowed to return the favour one day. They wandered across the road to the castle, ignoring Malachi's questions. The guards waving them in, and headed to Sec HQ. As they passed Randall's office, they popped their heads in.

"Hey, stranger," Randall said, rounding the desk and hugging him. "How are you doing?"

"A lot better, thanks. We brought drinks."

Randall groaned and held out his hand. "Gimme!"

Owen laughed and handed the one with Randall's name on it. "I'm assuming it's correct because Oscar made them."

Randall sipped it and closed his eyes. "Oh, god, yes."

Evan chuckled. "He makes the best coffee."

"Nope. That boy is a tea god." Randall sipped again, humming. "What brings you here, anyway?"

"Just thought we'd pop in as we got drinks. I'm heading to speak to Brett about starting back."

"That's good. Don't push it, though, yeah?"

Owen smiled. "I promise."

"Good. Dominic would have everyone's hides if you got hurt again."

They spoke for a few more minutes, and then they continued down the corridor. At Sec HQ, he knocked and entered. The room had several guards working, heads down or staring at screens, but they all looked up when the door opened. Second nature and all that.

"I'm back!" Owen shouted, and everyone cheered.

Brett glanced at him and held out his hand—not to shake his hand, but as if he held a cup, and Owen took that to mean he wanted his drink.

"Here you go, boss." Evan handed out the rest of the drinks.

"Thanks." He sipped. "To what do we owe the pleasure?"

"The doctor has given me the all clear to return to work." Brett raised his eyebrows, and Owen sighed. "Fine, limited duty work."

"Glad to hear it. You can start back tomorrow. Duties around Windsor only. Understood?"

"Yes, boss."

"While I have you both, though..." Brett nodded at Felix, who came over. "We've had an interesting development from the gifts you've received."

Owen settled into a seat. "What's that?"

Brett waved at Felix, who leaned against the desk. "I was looking a bit deeper into the calendar. You know, where it was bought from, that kind of thing. And I found something weird. It's not readily available anywhere."

Owen frowned. "What does that mean?"

"It means the calendar was specially made. There are no indications of where, no copyright or business details anywhere, which should've clued me in, really." Felix's forehead creased and then cleared again. "Anyway, I delved deeper, looking at the photographs and realised something."

Brett sighed. "You really need to get to the point."

Felix glanced at him, pursed his lips and continued, "The photos are all of coffees made by Book Drunk."

Owen's heart dropped. "What? How is that possible?"

Felix shrugged. "Maybe they know you like going there."

"Am I the only one who thinks this is weird? Like *weird* weird," Evan said.

"Not the only one," Brett mumbled. "Felix is going to see what else he can find out, but because the photos are copies of the original, he doesn't think he can get much else from them."

Originally, Owen hadn't been too fussed about receiving gifts from a stranger, but with each piece of information they found, he was beginning to think this person was a stalker rather than a nice admirer. He wasn't sure how to react to that, so he pushed it aside. He had received nothing else, so maybe he should be grateful.

"Okay, thanks. Anything I need to know before tomorrow?"

Brett shook his head. "Go home and rest for the last day. I'll catch you up with everything in the morning."

Owen shook hands with them both before leaving, Evan following.

"I'm not convinced the admirer is a good person," Evan said.

Owen reached for Evan's biceps, stopping him. He cupped his face. "I'm not sure, either, but let's hope for the best and plan for the worst."

"Which would be?"

Owen pointed to Sec HQ. "They're already doing it. Tracking evidence, following leads, seeing where it takes them. If there's something hinky about whoever this is, Felix will find it."

Evan nodded, and his mouth quirked. "Hinky?"

Owen snorted and kissed him. "Shut up."

They headed home, and even though Owen was feeling better, that brief excursion had worn him out. As they settled down to watch a movie, he fell asleep. Evan woke him a little later for dinner, and then they headed to bed for an early night. And although Owen wanted to tease Evan and bring him off, he didn't have the energy. He promised to make it up to him.

"You don't need to make anything up to me. You're healing. I'll be more than happy when you're back to being one hundred per cent, and then we can catch up on us. Sleep."

Being back at work was both a curse and a blessing. He was glad to be out of the house and seeing his friends again, but he was just as bored as at home, but only while sitting there. Brett had, indeed, caught him up on everything that had happened, including the shooting. They still didn't have any suspects, and there didn't seem to be any CCTV around that caught anything that could help them. The police were still investigating, but they'd put it down to it being a fanatic. That didn't help them figure out who was the target.

As he sat outside Freddie and Damon's suite for his short stint covering Locke's lunch break, the door opened, and Freddie beckoned him closer.

"Yes, Your Highness?"

Freddie pursed his lips at him, but Owen just shrugged. There was no way he would ever lose the honorific when addressing him. "Come on in. I want to catch up with you."

"I'm fine, Your—"

"Inside. Now."

"Yes, Your Highness," he mumbled, entering the prince's domain. He stood awkwardly. "How can I help?"

"You can sit down, let me get you a drink and tell me how you are feeling," Freddie said.

Owen sighed, knowing he wouldn't get out of it and, if he was honest with himself, didn't want to. He sat down, and Freddie handed him an apple juice.

"How are you?" Freddie asked as Damon settled beside him, rubbing a hand over Freddie's back.

"I'm okay. Doctors have given me the all clear. Just need to wait for this to heal." He gestured to his head. "The bandage is purely for infection reasons."

"Glad to hear it. As much as I know this is part of your job, it still makes me sick when something like this happens and the bodyguards take the brunt of it." He shook his head. "It's one part of the job I hate."

That was one thing about Prince Freddie. He took his role as a job rather than a birthright, and Owen loved him for it. The man was so down-to-earth because he didn't believe the hype that he was destined to be great, and although Owen believed he was, Freddie didn't. He didn't even want the job. Not really. That made him perfect for it. His mother had always said, it was those who didn't want to be leaders and politicians who should be.

"We do this job knowing what we signed up for. We don't have any problems with it," he reminded him.

"I know. I don't have to like it, though."

Owen chuckled. "That's true. Were you both okay? You didn't get any ricochet or anything?"

Damon shook his head. "We were fine. You pushed us aside, almost instinctively. I think you felt the burn and moved without realising it."

Owen thought back to the day. "I remember heat blazing across my head and shoving at you, but I remember not having a clue why I did it. Even now, I can't explain the need to get you out of the way."

"Well, whatever instincts you had saved our lives," Freddie said.

"I'm glad. People would use my face as a dartboard if anything happened to you."

Freddie sighed but sat back. "We're keeping a low profile for a little longer. Damon has to travel the day after tomorrow, but he's going with several guards, whereas I will stay put and help Father to recover from his Valentine's Day plans."

Owen chuckled. "Big plans?"

Freddie blew out a breath. "Extensive. But I suppose he has two people to think about, not just one." He patted Damon's knee and smiled at him. "Are you doing anything?"

Owen cleared his throat. "I have an idea, but whether I can pull it off is another thing."

"Anything we can help with?" Damon asked.

Owen opened his mouth to decline but thought better of it. "Possibly." He detailed his plan, and Freddie and Damon grinned at him.

"We can help with both those things. I know just the thing," Damon said.

And so he spent the next couple of hours planning with the two princes, even after Locke had come back and knocked on the door because she was concerned that Owen hadn't been at the door only to roll her eyes when she saw them. When everything was settled, he thanked them profusely and headed back to Sec HQ.

"I hear you've been distracting a couple of princes?" Brett said.

Owen frowned and waved his hand. "Is that a problem?"

Brett chuckled. "No, because they were driving us mad, wanting to help with the investigation. Whatever you did to distract them helped." He tilted his head. "What did you do?"

"They were helping me plan a surprise for Valentine's Day. I haven't had much chance to do it. Sorry for doing that on work time."

Brett waved him away. "As I said, time well spent." He pointed to Owen's desk. "There is your next report."

Owen groaned and sighed. "Okay."

"I think you'll like this one."

He opened it, read it and grinned. "Yep."

The reports Brett had him reading and taking notes on were events from the past few years. They were trying to create a database of the different attacks on the royal family to see if there was any rhyme or reason to them. Initially, Owen didn't think there would be, but with each new report he went through, he found similarities. It was almost as if people were researching past attacks and using them as a springboard for their own version. The one he'd just been given was the third of the same type of attack—a shooting at a charity event. As much as he first thought it to be a waste of time, he was beginning to see why Brett wanted this done. Owen had already found two attacks that, when looked at individually appeared to stand alone, yet when they were compared to another, Owen had found the attacker's family member was to blame. It was fascinating in ways Owen hadn't expected.

But his mind kept wandering to the following day, hoping Evan liked what he had planned. He'd never had to think about Valentine's before, so he was flying blind.

18

Evan

E van startled awake as pleasure streaked down his spine towards his groin. His eyes crossed as the suction on his cock increased, sending licks of fire to his balls. Palming the head going to town on his dick, he rolled completely to his back, giving Owen more access.

Owen pulled off. "I was wondering when you were going to join in the party," he rasped, his voice changed either from the swallowing of his shaft or the early morning hours or both. He dropped down again, sliding Evan's dick deep in his throat.

"Fuck," Evan breathed, rubbing his face to clear the sleepiness away. He didn't want to miss a minute of this unexpected gift. Staring down at his man, he watched him work, his arousal increasing tenfold with the visual. Owen paused with just the head in his mouth, peered up at him and flicked his tongue at the nerves underneath. "Oh, shit!"

The unexpected orgasm shook him to his core, his lungs stopped working, and his mind blanked. When he finally came back to his body, his chest ached as it worked for oxygen and his head pounded from the lack of it.

"Holy..."

Owen grinned and climbed up his body, kissing him briefly. "Happy Valentine's Day."

Evan huffed a laugh. "Definitely happy."

Owen bit his lip. "I have a bath ready for you. You relax in there while I get some breakfast ready." He climbed off the bed.

"I'd prefer to take a bath with you," Evan murmured.

"Later maybe. I want to spoil you today."

"Aren't you supposed to be at work?"

Owen shook his head. "Brett gave me the day off."

Evan raised his eyebrows. "Aren't you the lucky one?"

"Truly." He braced his hands back on the bed, leaning down. "I get to spend the whole day with you and spoil you rotten."

"What about you? Don't you get spoilt?"

Owen kissed him again. "I get joy from watching you get spoilt." He strode for the door and pointed to the bathroom on his way. "Bath."

Evan wasn't usually one for taking baths, mainly because his six-foot frame didn't fold into standard baths easily, but he could make it work. Owen was obviously trying hard to make the day a good one, so who was Evan to argue? He slid into the warm water, humming when the heat seeped into him. He rested his head back against the bath pillow he hadn't known they'd had and closed his eyes.

He had his own plans for Valentine's Day, but nothing like what Owen seemed to have. All Evan had planned was for them to have a walk along the River Thames before getting onto the boat for a quick ride. He would happily cancel that, though, if Owen had different ideas. He'd imagined this day many times over the years, but nothing had seemed right for their relationship when the day actually arrived. They were completely different people than who they were when they were younger.

Owen tapped on the door and poked his head in. "Breakfast is almost ready."

Evan smiled. "I'll just dry off and I'll be with you."

"I can bring it in here if you'd like?"

Evan shook his head. "I'm good. Won't be long."

Owen stepped closer, leaning down to kiss him, and then backed away again. "See you in a minute." He closed the door, and Evan sighed in contentment.

"If only life was always as easy as this," he muttered.

He climbed out of the bath and drained the water, drying and dressing before going to find Owen. He aimed for the terrible singing, a smile creeping across his face. Getting them back to that karaoke bar would be essential at some point.

"Hey!" Owen said, wiping his hands. "Right this way, kind sir."

He led the way into the living area where the coffee table had been covered with a tablecloth and two lit candles stood on each side.

"A candlelit breakfast. That's new," Evan said, dropping to the floor cushion where Owen indicated.

"Only the best for you. I'll be right back." He jogged back to the kitchen, and Evan took out his phone, taking a photo of the setup. He had no intention of showing anyone what Owen had done, but he wanted a reminder of the effort he'd put into it.

"Here we go. The breakfast of champions. Well, brunch. Or even lunch, as it's nearly midday."

"Wow," Evan said.

He took a slice of breakfast quiche, a spoonful of fried vegetables and some toast. There was more than enough to have several portions of each. Taking a bite of the quiche, he moaned as the flavour burst over his tongue.

"How did I not know you could make a quiche like this?" he mumbled.

Owen's cheeks flushed. "Well, I can't. Mum made it for me. Us."

Evan smiled, though his cheeks were full of food. He swallowed. "It's the thought that counts. Maybe we can practise making it together one day."

"I'd love that. For some reason, I've never been very good at quiches."

"You make up for it with the other stuff you cook."

Owen grinned, chewing his food. "So," he said once he swallowed, "I do have a couple of other plans for today, but as I was making breakfast, I had a thought that maybe you had plans. I hadn't taken that into account. So, do you?"

Evan sipped his orange juice and tilted his head back and forth. "Well, yes, and no. I had an idea for something we could do, but we don't have to if you want to do something else."

"What is it?"

"A walk and a boat ride on the Thames."

Owen's eyes lit up. "I haven't been on a boat ride since I was a kid. Yeah, we can do that. Do you have tickets already?"

Evan nodded. "Three o'clock."

"Awesome. Well, do you want to know what I have planned, or would you prefer to be surprised?"

"Surprise me."

Owen grinned. "Okay."

They chatted as they finished breakfast, and once Owen had cleared the plates away, he straddled Evan's lap as he sat on the sofa.

"I want to get you off again," Owen murmured into their kiss.

Evan grabbed Owen's lower lip between his teeth and pulled it away from his teeth before letting go. Owen's breathing increased, and Evan slid his hand up Owen's chest to wrap loosely around his neck.

"No. My turn." He tightened his hold, and Owen's eyes widened. "You're going to come while I'm deciding if you can or can't breathe." Owen's pulse beat a rapid tattoo against his palm. "You like that idea?" Owen nodded, but Evan raised an eyebrow.

"Yes...Sir," he gasped, inhaling deeply when Evan released his hold a little.

"Good. Get your cock out for me."

Owen scrambled to do as he'd asked. When Owen's already-leaking dick hung between them, Evan wrapped his hand around it, wanting to bring him to the edge as quickly as possible. Not send him over, just bring him to the edge. He repositioned his hands where he wanted them—one curved around the side of Owen's neck with his thumb across his Adam's apple, the other encircling his dick.

He stroked the length, twisting when he got to the head, and rubbed his thumb up and down his neck. "Shall I make you come?" he asked.

"Please, Sir."

The next time he twisted his hand, he tightened his hold, restricting Owen's air supply and focused solely on the bundles of nerves beneath the head of his shaft. Those same nerves that sent Evan over the edge in bed that morning. Two can play at that game. Owen wrapped his hand around the forearm close to his neck, his nails digging into Evan's skin, his mouth opening as his face deepened in colour. Evan stroked his palm down, tightening his grip on his cock but loosening it on his neck. Owen gasped, his hips jerking.

"Yeah, you like this."

He repeated the same actions over and over, tightening around his neck and focusing on the nerves before tightening around his cock and loosening his neck. Owen's gaze was glassy, but he never lost his focus on Evan, despite being denied his orgasm so many times.

When Owen was a dripping mess—both from sweat and precome—Evan said, "You get to come this time." Anticipation shone in his eyes, and Evan smirked. "If you can do it before I let go."

He tightened his hold and stroked a fierce rhythm, and Owen fucked his hand even as his air ran out. Evan watched him, taking note of every pulse of his heart, every dilation of his pupils, and just as it reached the fine line he would never cross, he loosened his hold. The moment he did and Owen sucked in the first molecule of oxygen, Owen came. A river of come flowed over Evan's hand and pulsed onto his shirt.

He held Owen in the same position until his entire body relaxed, and then Evan pulled him close, ignoring the mess between them. He kissed Owen's temple, rubbing his back and allowing him to come down in his own time. He wasn't too worried about his sugar levels as they'd just eaten, but he would need to be reassured and held as he came back to himself.

Evan had experience with air restriction, not from a relationship standpoint, but from when he'd visited a club in Italy. He'd been intrigued, and a Dominant there had seen it and had trained him in the art of it. It didn't interest him in that *he* wanted it, but to be given that amount of trust from a partner was overwhelming.

When Owen shivered, Evan grabbed the blanket from beside him and draped it over them, making sure Owen was tucked in tight against him. "I'm right here, sweetheart. I'm not going anywhere." He pressed his lips to Owen's head, brushing his mouth over his skin and bringing him back slowly.

Owen moved his head to Evan's shoulder rather than chest and whispered, "Thank you."

His voice had a little rasp to it, but it shouldn't last too long. The only thing he wasn't clear on was whether Owen's neck would bruise. It was something he should've thought to ask before they started.

"How do you feel?"

"Blissed out," Owen said.

Evan smiled. "I'm glad."

They stayed in their cocoon for a while, chatting quietly about everything and nothing, and then Owen pushed upright, wincing.

"We really need to clean up."

Evan laughed. "Come on. I'll help."

Owen chuckled. "Or you'll hinder."

"One or the other." He shrugged, unrepentant.

An hour and two orgasms later, they headed out the front door, wrapped up for the cold weather. Mid-February was warmer than January but still not warm. The boat ride might be a little chilly. He slid his gloved hand into Owen's, smiled at him, and they headed down the road. It wouldn't take them long to get to the river, but they weren't in a hurry. They slipped into shops they wanted to explore as they went, commenting on the things they saw. To be honest, Evan couldn't remember the last time he'd taken more than a few minutes to look at the local shops. It was a wonderful feeling to be able to support the smaller businesses instead of throwing money at the bigger corporations, who only added to the billions they already made.

In one shop, he found a scarf, similar to the one Owen's admirer sent him, but in a slightly different colour, and couldn't resist buying it. After all, he didn't have one, and the one he'd been sent was still with Brett and Felix. Once he'd paid for it, he pulled the tag off and wrapped it around Owen's neck, pulling him closer for a brief kiss.

"Happy Valentine's."

Owen grinned, and they continued down to the river. He'd been right. It was a little chilly. Okay, more like bloody freezing, but they chose a bench, tucked their arms around each other and watched the scenery.

"After this, I have plans," Owen said, and Evan chuckled.

"I don't doubt it. We'll head home to warm up as soon as we dock."

Owen bit his lip and raised his eyebrows. "There's an idea."

Evan frowned, not following his thought process. "What is?"

"Docking." He waggled his eyebrows, and Evan huffed another laugh.

"You're such an adolescent."

"Takes one to know one."

As beautiful as the trip was, Evan was ready for home when it ended. He grabbed Owen's hand and sped home, shoving him against the door once it shut behind them, and kissing the ever loving hell out of him. Then Owen pushed against him, and Evan stopped and asked the question with his eyes.

"I have a surprise, remember?" Owen panted.

Evan licked his lips, eyeing Owen's bruised mouth, but stepped back, palms held up. "Okay."

"Will you wait in the bedroom while I get it ready?"

Evan nodded, smiled and retreated to the bedroom. Settling with his back to the headboard, he scrolled on his phone, checking in with people and returning emails he'd received. When Owen finally called him, he'd been in there for over half an hour. But when he left the room, his eyes widened.

The living room had been transformed. The sofas had been pushed back to the walls and the coffee table had been set aside, and in their place was a large blanket with pillows and cushions spread around it and a mountain of food on one side.

"You did all this?"

Owen nodded. "I had a little help to obtain some things, but yeah."

Evan pulled him in for a kiss, wishing there was more he could put into words, but he could only repeat what he'd said before. "I love you."

Owen beamed. "And I love you." He tugged on Evan's hand. "Come on." He led him over to the blanket. "There are actually a few blankets under this big one, but if it's not comfortable, let me know."

"It's perfect."

They settled opposite each other. "I chose a lot of finger foods so we could pick and choose during the afternoon and evening. None of it will spoil if it's left out. Hopefully."

He picked up a strawberry and held it to Evan's mouth. Evan bit into it, the sweetness bursting over his tongue. "Delicious." Owen dipped the strawberry into a bowl of chocolate and held it out again. Evan took the last bite, making sure to lick Owen's fingers as he did.

Evan studied the food, choosing a grape and placing it between his teeth. He crooked his finger, and Owen leaned closer, lips closing over the grape, and Evan pushed it into his mouth with his tongue. He kissed him, leaning closer to deepen it when the doorbell rang.

Glaring at where the offending sound came from, Owen patted his cheek and rose. "I'll get it."

Evan rested back, adjusting his dick. He was going to be sore if they kept going at it as much as they had that day. Owen closed the door, and Evan said, "Who was it?" Owen didn't reply but came into the room with a box. Evan stood. "Is that what I think it is?"

"I think so. It's addressed to me."

He wandered over to the table and put the box down. When he got it open, inside was a box, similar to the original one he received. Taking an audible breath, he lifted the lid. It was another scarf.

"They've already sent one. Why do I need another?"

"What does the note say?"

This may be an OLD memory, but any memory is good, right?

Owen put the note down and studied the scarf. "Old memory?" He checked the label. "This is an old scarf. It's not new." Evan watched as he checked the label and froze. "This is *my* old scarf. From school. I haven't seen this in years. Look, you can see my faded name."

"Who the hell is sending you something of your own?"

"The last time I remember seeing it was at Mum's house. She must've donated it or something."

Evan wasn't so sure, but before he could answer, the doorbell rang again. "What the hell is going on?"

This time, he went to the door, and when he opened it, he wished he hadn't. He stared at the two people on the other side, his mind blanking on what to do or say.

"Evan? Is it another parcel?" Owen stopped behind him and cursed. "What the fuck are you doing here?"

"You'll remember your manners, boy—" Evan's father started.

"I'll do no such thing," Owen retorted, pushing Evan behind him. "What do you want?"

"To talk," Evan's mother said. "Please."

Owen glanced at Evan, who finally shifted his gaze from his parents to Owen. He didn't have an answer to his unasked question. Owen nodded, though, and threaded his fingers through Evan's before turning back.

"You can come in, but the moment you say anything nasty, you're out. Understand?" Owen said.

Evan's mother nodded. "Yes, of course. Thank you."

"And you will stay in the living room until my mother arrives, because there is no way you are talking to Evan without her being here."

"We have every right—" his father said.

"That's fine," his mother interrupted, and his father glared but said nothing more.

Owen tugged Evan to one side while his parents entered, then he closed the door and faced Evan. "We're going right past them into the kitchen, okay? No talking to them."

Evan thought he nodded, but he couldn't be sure. His brain had gone on holiday, apparently.

19

Owen

The nerve of those people. Not only knocking on the damn door in the first place, but believing they had the right to. Fuckers would get what was coming to them if Owen had anything to say about it.

He led Evan into the kitchen, pushing him against the counter and pressing his body against him, hoping to give him something tangible to hold on to. While he held him, he pulled his phone from his pocket and dialled his mother.

"Hey, everything okay? I'm at work," Sally said.

"I know, and I'm sorry. I need you to come to mine. Evan's parents just turned up, and I don't trust myself with them."

Sally mumbled something just out of earshot, which he assumed wasn't for his ears, and then she spoke more clearly, "I'm on my way."

"Thank you."

"You don't have to thank me for this. It might be you pulling *me* off them instead of the other way around. I'll be as quick as I can."

He ended the call and put his phone on the counter. Cupping Evan's face, he brought his glazed gaze to his and brushed his thumbs over his cheeks.

"I'm here, sweetheart. I'm here."

Evan dropped his head forward, dislodging Owen's hands but snuggling into his neck and wrapping his arms around him. He still said nothing, which was understandable. Shock was too minor a word for what he probably felt right then.

Owen kept his arms around him, running a hand up and down his spine and mumbling nonsense. He really wanted to give them a piece of his mind, but he held back. When he heard the doorbell, he pressed his lips to Evan's head. "I'll be right back. Stay here, okay?"

Evan nodded and gripped the counter behind him as if he needed it to keep him upright. Owen headed for the door, stopping halfway through the living room when his mother walked in with Evan's father behind her.

"Next time, wait for the person who lives here to open the door. You have no right—"

"I knew who it would be."

"I don't give a damn. You wouldn't have let us do that in your home, so don't do it here," he bit out.

Evan's father clenched his jaw but said nothing as he returned to the sofa beside his wife. Sally ushered Owen back into the kitchen and went straight to Evan, who collapsed into her arms when she reached him. Owen could hear them murmuring, but it wasn't his business. Their relationship had grown in the time Evan had lived with them, and the intervening years had not stopped that. Evan might not consider Sally to be his mother—mainly because he was scared of being too much for her—but Sally was happy to claim Evan as her son.

"Are you ready?" she asked them both.

"Not really," he said, "but I suppose."

They entered the living room, one of them on either side of Evan, and settled onto the opposite sofa. It was a squeeze, but Owen was not letting him face it without support.

"What do you want, Bernie?" Sally asked.

Evan's mother raised her head. "I want to know my son."

"Isn't that a bit of too little too late?" Owen asked.

"He's sitting right there. It's not like he's dead," Paul said, glaring at them.

Owen's blood boiled, but Bernadette placed a hand on Paul's arm. "Please."

"Why now?" Sally said. "He wasn't good enough for you when he came out as gay. What's changed?"

Bernadette wrung her hands but stared at them. "We were wrong." Paul scoffed, obviously belying her words. "We were."

"It's been twenty-three years. Why now?" Owen snapped.

"I want to know who my son has become."

"You have no right to know that. You threw that away when you threw *me* away," Evan suddenly yelled. He scooted forward on the sofa, his hands clenched into fists. "Why the hell should I give you *anything* you ask for?"

Bernadette looked down at her hands. "Because..."

"Oh, for god's sake. Our daughter needs medical help, and we need to see if you are a match," Paul said.

Silence descended as they all processed the new information. Their *daughter*? When did they have a daughter?

"What?" Evan murmured.

Bernadette lifted tear-filled eyes to them. "Jessica was born a year after you...were gone. She was a happy accident. She's twenty-one now, but she's been in and out of hospital for years, and no one could figure out what was wrong with her. She's recently been diagnosed with a rare form of leukaemia. We wanted to ask if you would be tested."

So, it had nothing to do with getting to know their son. It was all about their daughter. The daughter none of them knew about.

"That's why you moved," Owen said. "To hide the pregnancy." Paul's gaze flashed to him, surprise in his eyes, and Owen grinned. "I work for the royal family. No information is beyond my reach. Remember that," he warned. Paul's lips thinned, but he said nothing.

Owen glanced at Evan, who was staring at his mother. Silence descended for a long while, and Owen wasn't sure he was going to say anything. After all, he owed them nothing.

But Owen knew what his answer would be, so he wasn't at all surprised when Evan nodded. "Of course I'll get tested." He cleared his throat. "Does she know? About me?"

Bernadette nodded. "Yes, but we told her we were estranged."

"Yeah, can't have a gay son out there in the world. Much better to have one who's a shit and doesn't call," Evan spat and stood. "I'll get tested when I go back to work." He headed for the bedroom, and Owen stood, ready to send them out the door.

"Will you tell her?" Bernadette asked, and Evan paused.

Evan faced her. "I will not do it anonymously, but...I won't go out of my way to see or talk to her. However, if she finds me, I won't turn her away." He glared at her. "I'm nothing like you." He disappeared and closed the door behind him.

Owen faced them. "I think it's time you left. No matter what happens, you are no longer welcome here. If you have anything to ask or say to him, you can leave a message with the hospital. Understood?"

Paul stood. "I thought you would've brought your son up with better manners than this, Sally."

Sally rose, stepping closer. "My son has more manners than you have in your entire family line. I don't think I need to worry about him." She turned to Bernadette. "I've always liked you, Bernie, but you need to grow a backbone. He's not worth it, but your children are. Both of them." She pointed to the door. "Now, get out."

Evan's parents left, and Owen locked the door behind them for good measure. When he entered the living room again, Sally was setting up the cosy nest he'd made for them before all hell broke loose.

"I wouldn't worry about that now. I don't think either of us are in the Valentine's mood."

"I'll put the food in the fridge, but the rest can stay. Maybe you'll feel better tomorrow and can pick up from the beginning again," she said with a smile.

"Thank you, Mum." He kissed her cheek.

"You are always welcome. Now go check on him. I want to see my boy before I leave."

Owen entered the bedroom, finding Evan curled up on the bed. He slid in behind him and wrapped his arms over him, slipping his leg between Evan's, and pressed his lips to Evan's nape.

"I won't ask how you are. Is there anything I can do?"

Evan sniffed. "Not really." He exhaled. "I have a sister," he whispered.

Owen tightened his hold. "You do." And it made Owen wonder if Felix knew about her. He hadn't mentioned her when Owen had asked for basic information about what Paul and Bernadette had been up to during the years, but that didn't mean he hadn't purposefully withheld that to protect them. It was the kind of thing Felix would do. "Do you want to know more about her?"

Evan didn't answer for a moment, but then he said, "Yes. I will do as I said, but I want to know about her. Jessica."

"Okay. We'll find out what we can about her. I'm sorry I didn't tell you what I'd found out."

"It doesn't matter." Evan turned over to face him, his face streaked with tears. "She's ill, Owen." His voice was broken.

"We'll do what we can to help. Okay?" Owen's own eyes filled as he made the promise. They would do whatever it took to help Jessica with the leukaemia. And if it was the last thing he did, Evan would get to know her. Owen had made no such promise to his parents to not involve himself with his sister, and he would do everything to make her understand it was not Evan's fault that he wasn't in her life. It doesn't matter that there were sixteen years between them—it wouldn't matter if there was one hundred and sixteen years between them—they would look after her because there was no telling what her life was like with them as her parents.

He kissed Evan, brushing the leaking tears from his cheeks, and cupped his cheek again. "Mum wants to say goodbye. In her own words, 'I want to see my boy before I leave.'" He grinned, trying to lighten the mood a little.

Evan gave a watery chuckle and rubbed his face. They headed for the living room, and Sally enfolded him in her arms as soon as they were within reach. He heard them murmuring, but yet again, it wasn't for him.

"Right. I'm going to head back to work. If you need anything at all, call me, okay? I love you both." She patted both their cheeks and left.

"I think we need movies and ice cream," Owen said.

Evan snorted. "Ice cream makes everything better."

"And don't forget it."

When Evan finally fell asleep the previous night, Owen went into planning mode. He got in contact with Felix and asked him to find out whatever he could about Jessica Montgomery, and though he didn't outright say it, he implied he knew about her. He didn't have time to be mad, but he might be later. He had to plan a belated Valentine's Day.

He woke Evan with gentle kisses and touches, bringing him from his slumber. "We have places to be, Mr Montgomery. Time to rise and shine." Evan opened one eye, glaring as much as he could with it, and Owen laughed. "Come on. I'll even share a shower with you before we leave."

By the time they'd had a shower, climaxed and eaten breakfast, they were already behind schedule. Owen ushered him into the car.

"Where are we going?" Evan asked for the tenth time since they'd got up.

"You'll have to wait and see. I'll give you one clue. It'll take around an hour and a half to get there."

Evan huffed as Owen pulled out onto the road. "That could be anywhere." He fiddled with the radio, finally settling back on the original station they always listened to.

"You'll figure it out the closer we get."

He hoped that by taking Evan to a place of good memories, a place Owen's mother used to take them, would help take his mind off everything that was happening. It wouldn't work for long, but they had the day ahead of them, and they could let the rest of the world tick along without them for a little while. Today was for them. Tomorrow, reality could intrude if it had to.

It took Evan around an hour to finally guess correctly. "Brighton?"

Owen grinned. "Well done."

"Can we visit the Upside Down House? I read about it when I came back and knew I wanted to see it at some point." Evan bounced on his chair as if he was a little kid, rubbing his hands together.

Owen laughed. "Yes, we can. Other than dinner at the marina when it starts to get dark, I don't have any set plans for us. We can wander around, find new places, revisit old ones and basically do whatever we want to."

"Sounds great. I'd love to see how much the open market has changed over the years. When was the last time we went?"

Owen frowned. "I think it might've been for my twenty-fifth birthday. The three of us went to the theatre, though I can't remember what we went to see."

"I can't either. Maybe Dominic will remember. We'll have to ask him later."

Owen parked the car in a long-term parking spot and locked it up before donning his coat. It was significantly cooler on the coast than further inland, but it wasn't as cold as he'd been expecting. Still, he wrapped the scarf Evan had brought him around his neck and took Evan's gloved hand.

"So, where to first? The market? The aquarium, though, we'll have to get some photos for Randall. He'll be so jealous."

"I'm sure Dominic will bring him one day," Evan said. "He's already taken him to the London one, remember?"

They wandered towards the market, spending time looking around the wares and buying little gifts for their friends. When Evan paused at a small snow globe with Brighton Pier inside, Owen knew who he was thinking of. Despite not knowing his sister had existed, she would never be far from his thoughts now.

"She'd love it," Owen whispered in his ear, and Evan sent him a small smile and paid for it, tucking it into his pocket for safekeeping.

Owen bought a Laurel and Hardy mug for his mother, a mini plastic aquarium game for Randall, a boxing glove keyring for Dominic—now he was back to training with them—and couldn't resist a cuddly teddy bear in a tuxedo complete with a crown for Princes Freddie and Damon.

"That'll give them a laugh, if nothing else," Evan said.

"You're one to talk. Why would Matteo need a Daddy's boy T-shirt?" He raised his eyebrows.

Evan grinned. "That's for him to tell you if he wants to."

"I don't think I need to ask. The question I do need answered is who?"

"Again, a question for him. But I'm not truly unconvinced that it's a terrible choice." Evan shrugged. "I always thought the guy was straight, but after seeing him lately, I'm not so sure."

They spent a couple of hours at the aquarium, grabbing some lunch when they were finished, and then aimed for Brighton Palace Pier. Owen loved rollercoasters, and thankfully, so did Evan. They would never be too old to ride them, and he had visions of them riding them when they were old and grey—if the attendants let them.

After far too many turns on the turbo coaster, twister and waltzers, they grabbed some candy floss, once more acting more like kids than adults, and Owen loved it. He also loved the easiness and relaxation on Evan's face. It was what he'd hoped for, and although he knew it would return when they arrived home, he was happy for the reprieve.

They took a walk down the beach, removing their shoes and socks, and Owen wiggled his toes in the cold sand and breathed deeply.

"I don't know what it is about the seaside, but it makes everything better," he said.

"I thought that was ice cream?" Evan grinned at him.

"That, too."

"I guess we're going to have to go for the trifecta of candy floss, hot dogs and ice cream, then."

Owen bit his lip. "I want space for dinner."

Evan tilted his head. "Maybe we should go for ice cream after dinner?"

"A treat for the car journey home," Owen agreed.

They walked to the marina and brushed as much sand off their feet as they could before putting the socks and shoes back on.

"I think I might regret that. Walking on sandy feet is never pleasant," Evan said.

Owen gave their name to the host and settled at the table, draping their coats on the back of their chairs. The view from the window was as amazing as he remembered, the lights from the pier and the boats glowing brightly in the distance, giving them a sense of romance, especially with the dim lighting in the restaurant itself.

"Thank you for this," Evan said.

Owen smiled. "You're welcome. I think we both needed this. A reminder of who we were with a bridge to who we are now. Despite everything in between, we're still those people. I don't want to forget anything about our journey, but if I could go back to that morning and change the outcome, I would."

Evan covered his hand. "I've been thinking about that, and I think we had to go through that to become the people we are today. If we hadn't done that, I'm not sure we would've stayed together."

"What makes you say that?" Owen frowned.

Evan leaned on his forearms, lowering his voice. "What we've been through changes us inside. I think we were far too in the clouds to see each other properly. I honestly think we would've caused each other more harm and possibly lost our friendship completely when we broke up."

Owen thought about it. "Possibly. We still had a lot to learn about each other, that's for definite."

"And now we're older, a little more dented, yes, but we can appreciate things a lot more."

Owen exhaled. "I love you for saying that. I'd never thought about it that way. I still regret doing it."

Evan smirked. "I'm sure I can make you feel better about it. Some kind of punishment might help you to forget."

Owen's body heated, and his cock thickened beneath the table. He swallowed hard and sipped his glass of water. "Okay."

And if his voice cracked at the potential for that night, no one else would know.

20

Evan

A phone ringing woke Evan from his sleep. He fumbled for his phone on the bedside table and dragged it towards him. Without checking who it was, he rested it against his ear.

"Hello?" he croaked.

"Evan? I'm so sorry to call. It's Edward. Dr Wallis. I... I need some help."

Evan's mind cleared the more the man said, and by the time he asked for help, he was wide awake with Owen stirring beside him.

"Edward? What's wrong?"

Dr Wallis's voice hitched. "It's my daughter." He sniffed. "Someone's taken her. I know it's not really what you do, but you know people. I need someone to help me because the police aren't doing much."

Evan swung his legs over the edge of the bed and raked a hand through his hair, still trying to get his brain to fire properly. "How do you know someone's taken her?" The bed beside him depressed, and Owen settled against him, so Evan put the phone on speaker.

"She won't have left without me. Her mother and I separated amicably, and Anika chose to stay with her mother, but she stays with me whenever I'm off shift. She wouldn't have left without telling me. That's not her."

"How old is she, Edward?"

"She's fifteen."

"And she's not just gone out to see her friends or gone to a party without telling you?" Evan glanced at Owen, who shrugged and nodded as if he agreed with his train of thought.

"No, she wouldn't. I don't mind her going to parties and seeing her friends. She knows all she has to do is tell me where she's going." His voice was straining, as if he was losing the will to explain again.

Owen cleared his throat. "Dr Wallis, it's Owen Morris. I understand you trust your daughter, but we need to be sure. Have you tried contacting her?"

"Of course I have! I called her a thousand times already and there's no answer. I've called her mother and her friends, and no one has seen her. The police say we need to leave it before we can say she's missing, but I *know* her. She won't have gone willingly without telling us where she was."

Evan and Owen shared a look, and Owen nodded again, climbing off the bed and grabbing his phone before disappearing into the living room.

"Okay, Edward. We're going to look into it. I can't guarantee anything, but make sure you keep trying Anika's phone. In the meantime, send me all the information you have about her last movements that you know about, and we'll see what we can find, okay?"

"Thank you. Thank you. I just need to find her."

"We will do our best. I'll call you if we need or have any more information."

"Thank you, Evan."

He ended the call, and Evan sighed, dragging on some joggers. He had no idea where to start looking, but hopefully, Owen would have some thoughts on that. Entering the living room, he saw Owen pacing across the space with his phone to his ear. He was only in his boxers, so Evan returned to the bedroom and grabbed a pair of joggers and took them to him. Dropping to his knees with a smirk, he held them open for Owen to step into and pulled them up his legs, snapping the band around his waist.

"Thank you," Owen mouthed and then returned to his call. "Yes, Anika Wallis, fifteen years old. Father is Edward Wallis, a doctor at the hospital. Mother's name is unknown." He listened for a minute. "Yeah, maybe. The police have given their standard answer that they have to wait a certain time before they can file a missing person's report, but we're not doing that, Brett. We can't." His voice broke, and Evan wrapped his arms around him.

There was no way they wouldn't help Edward try to find Anika. It was too close to home for them to ignore it and let the police do their job. It might be too late by then.

"Okay, thanks." He hung up and inhaled. "He's going to get Felix on it and see if he can find anything on any CCTV cameras. It's a long shot, especially as we know little about where she was and what time she disappeared. Brett is going to call in a favour with a police officer he knows to get the ball rolling." He glanced at Evan. "We have to find her."

"We will. We have resources we didn't have before," Evan said, tightening his hold. "Let's get dressed, and we can head over to Brett. We might be able to help more there."

By the time they walked into Sec HQ, the place was a hive of people. Evan hadn't expected so many people to be around at four in the morning, but it was busier than Windsor's streets during a royal event.

"Brett, do we know anything yet?"

Brett glanced over and shook his head. "We can't find any sight of her on CCTV so far. There is more to look through, but the last we see of her is when she finished school and her father picked her up and took her home. We don't have evidence of them entering their home, but the cameras can see them turning onto their road. This was at three-thirty this afternoon."

Owen looked at Evan. "Did Edward mention if they went out last night at all?"

"No. Let me call him back."

Brett held up his hand. "I think it might be better if you visit him. You can see the house and see if there are any signs of entry anywhere."

"We're not forensic experts, Brett," Owen said.

"I know. That's why you'll be taking Roger with you. He is." Brett gestured to a tall, lanky guy who had blue overalls on and looked more like a medical examiner than a forensic expert.

Evan and Owen shook his hand. "Nice to meet you," Evan said.

"I wish it was under better circumstances," Roger said.

"Head over to Dr Wallis's house and see what you can find. Keep me updated." Brett moved away, effectively dismissing them.

"All right, then." Owen headed for the door, and Evan and Roger followed, the latter grabbing a large bag, which Evan assumed contained the equipment he needed to do his job.

They said little on the quick journey, and when they finally pulled up to the house, Evan was surprised that no one else was present. He would've thought the police would already be there. When he voiced his thought, Roger said, "Brett requested the police stay back until I've done my investigation. Too many cooks, and all that."

"Understandable, I suppose," Evan murmured.

They headed to the door, and Evan knocked. Edward flung it open, and seeing the hope fall from his expression tore Evan apart.

"Evan," he said.

"Edward. Can we come in?"

Edward seemed to come back to himself and gestured for them to enter. "Yes, sorry. Would anyone like anything to drink?"

"No, we're good, thanks."

They followed him into a living room, where a woman said on a sofa with a blanket around her shoulders. She went to stand, but Evan stayed her.

"Please, sit. We have a few questions to ask if that's okay?"

Edward settled beside what Evan assumed was Anika's mother. "Of course. This is Rebecca, Anika's mother."

"First, I'm sorry to be here under these circumstances," Roger said, "but I'm a forensic scientist. Would you allow me to look at your daughter's room, please?"

Rebecca nodded and wiped her face. "Of course. I'll take you." She stood, pulling the blanket tighter around her body, and they disappeared.

Evan refocused on Edward, who wrung his hands in his lap, staring at the coffee table. "Edward, can you walk us through when you last saw Anika?"

He blinked at them, sniffed and nodded. "Yes. Um... We had dinner at six-thirty. Just me and Anika. We watched a movie after doing the dishes, and then she headed to bed. That was about ten o'clock. Usual time for a school night."

"Did she seem her usual self?" Owen said. "No arguments or upsets she mentioned?"

Edward shook his head. "When I picked her up from school, she was happy and laughing with her friends. She usually walks home when she's not at my house, but I like picking her up because it gives me more time with her. She says she doesn't mind." He glanced at them. "Do you think she does and is putting on a brave face for me?"

Evan could understand the man focusing on random information instead of the details they needed, but he couldn't stop himself from reassuring him. "If she's anything like you've mentioned, I'm sure she would tell you if there was a problem."

"So no arguments?" Owen asked.

"No, none. Like I said, she was happy and laughing."

"Did she mention anything about upsets at school or with her mother?"

Edward shook his head. "Nothing."

"Has she ever disappeared before?"

"No."

"Been somewhere she wasn't supposed to be? Or lied to you about her whereabouts?" Owen asked.

Edward started shaking his head and paused. "Only once that I'm aware of. She said she was going to Gemma's house—Gemma's her best friend—but the pair of them actually went to another friend's house. That was when we told her we wanted her to be truthful about where she was."

"When did you find out about that lie?"

"That same night. She was supposed to stay at Gemma's house, but she came home instead and told us where she'd been. That friend had alcohol, and Anika hadn't liked the idea of it but felt pressured to try some. But then she came right home and told us what happened."

"Is she still friends with that person?"

"Not that I'm aware of."

Owen pulled out his phone. "We're going to need their details as well please."

Edward nodded. "Of course." He gave Owen the details, including a phone number he had for the girl's parents.

Evan took over the questioning because he needed to ask something Edward might not have thought about. He shuffled to the edge of his seat. "Edward, have you had any problems or arguments recently? Maybe a patient or a patient's family? Other hospital staff? Anything you can think of?"

"Not that I can think of. We get the usual upset when things don't go the way patients want them to, but mostly, no."

"There's no one you can think of who might hold a grudge against you?"

Edward stared at him, and Evan could see him thinking through his interactions. "I honestly can't think of anyone."

"And no one has approached you outside of work for any reason?"

Edward looked dazed but shook his head. "No," he murmured.

Roger and Rebecca returned, and Roger said, "I'm going to check around outside."

Owen and Evan quickly went through similar questions with Rebecca, to no avail. From what they said, there was no reason for Anika to have disappeared on her own, and no one could remember anything that might point to someone kidnapping her.

"Okay. The police will visit shortly. They'll probably ask the same questions we did, and I'm sorry about that, but the more times you talk it over, the more chances there are that you might remember something important," Owen said.

"It's fine. As long as it helps find her," Edward said.

"We'll be in touch if we learn anything new," Evan said, standing.

Edward rose and held out his hand. "Thank you, Evan. I appreciate this, especially as you didn't have to help."

Evan gave a small smile. "No problem."

They headed outside and leaned against the car as they waited for Roger to finish his job.

"What do you think?" Evan asked.

Owen blew out a breath. "To be honest, there's nothing here. We've not got anything to go on unless Roger finds something."

Evan could hear the pain in his voice, but he was, unfortunately, right. They had nothing. The only way for the girl to disappear was through her father's front or back door while he was watching TV or through her bedroom window. It didn't leave a lot of options for someone to forcibly take her if she put up a fight. Which potentially meant she had been unconscious. He shared his thoughts with Owen.

"I agree. If she didn't leave of her own volition, she must've been unconscious at the time. It's the only way she could've disappeared without Edward knowing."

And that didn't bode well for her.

"Unless he knows more than he's saying," Owen added.

Evan stared at him, rearranging things in his head to leave space for that option. It was something he hadn't thought about. "Do you think he does?"

Owen blew out a breath. "I'm not sure. There's nothing to show that he does, but it's not impossible."

As Roger returned, a car stopped beside them, and two men climbed out.

"Are you Owen and Evan?" one said, holding up his badge. "Detectives Acton and Burrows."

Owen stepped forward, holding out his hand. "Owen Morris. This is Evan Montgomery and Roger..."

"Coulson," Roger finished. "Forensic scientist."

"Sorry to meet under these circumstances. Brett mentioned you know the father," Detective Acton said.

Evan nodded. "Yes. He's a doctor and I'm a nurse at the hospital. We have spoken with them, but we have nothing to go on."

Acton nodded. "Okay, leave it with us and we'll keep you updated. Coulson, did you find anything?"

"I've taken some fingerprints, but they might come back as family. I don't have a reference for them right now, but I'm going to head back in to get the parents' prints for our records. Other than that, there wasn't anything amiss that I could see, either in the bedroom or outside the window or in the back garden."

Burrows sighed. "So we have nothing."

"Pretty much," Roger agreed.

"Let's speak with them. Like I said, we'll keep Brett updated as we go."

Roger said, "Can I get a lift back with you, Detective?"

"Sure."

"Thanks, Roger," Evan said. "Let's get back. I'll drive."

He took the keys from Owen and climbed in, Owen a little slower than him. This had to be bringing back awful memories for him. It was bad enough for Evan because he thought of Amy as a little sister, the same as he thought of May, Dominic's sister, but it must be ten times worse for Owen. He was purposefully ignoring that his sister was ill for the moment. He didn't have enough brain power for that right then. They were silent as he worked through the streets, heading back to Windsor. The guards waved them through, and they trudged through the corridors to Sec HQ.

Filling in Brett took little time because they had nothing, but they still gave him everything they had. Felix had found nothing else on the cameras in the time they'd been gone.

"It's as if she's disappeared off the face of the earth," he muttered, frowning.

"It's too clean," Owen added. "Have you looked into the father?" he asked Brett.

"Felix?" Brett called. "Edward Wallis?"

Felix joined them, holding a tablet. "Edward Wallis, doctor at Windsor Hospital for eight years. Before that, he worked in London. He amicably divorced Rebecca Wallis two years ago and has joint custody of Anika Wallis, who is now fifteen. Edward has lived in the same house since they moved back to Windsor, and Rebecca lives in a smaller house a short distance away. No criminal record for any of them, not even parking tickets."

"This doesn't feel right," Owen said, and Evan couldn't agree more.

As much as he didn't want Edward to be part of it, for someone to disappear so easily without leaving a trace at all was almost impossible. It was feasible, just unlikely.

"Did you check any property cameras?" Felix asked.

Evan shook his head. "I didn't think about that."

"I'll call Acton to ask him for the footage," Brett said, dialling already.

"I'd hate to think he was involved," Evan said. "He seemed too distraught to be part of it."

"Maybe he's a good actor," Felix said. "Or maybe he's not involved at all. Whatever it is, we'll figure it out."

"And get his daughter back. Regardless of the outcome," Owen said.

Evan's heart broke all over again, and he rested his hand on Owen's nape, squeezing gently.

"Acton said Wallis has given them access to the door cam footage. Cameras are on the front and back door, and on the back gate to the garden and garage door. No footage is showing on any of them. There's either nothing to see or it's been deleted."

"If she was taken from the house, the footage would've been there undoubtedly. I'm going with it being deleted. Which means it was either deleted by the parents or hacked and deleted by whoever took the girl," Felix said.

"And can we get them back?"

Felix was already shaking his head before Evan finished asking the question. "Unless the footage was automatically downloaded to local storage, the files are impossible to recover once they're deleted."

"That's a dead end, then," Brett said.

Felix held up a finger. "What about other door cam footage? Surely they're not the only ones with door cams on that street?"

Brett dialled his phone again. "Acton, you might want to ask the neighbours if any have door cams. Maybe they caught what happened." He paused, listening. "Okay, thanks."

"He's going to get some officers to visit the neighbours and see what they can find. I'll keep you updated."

"I need to do something," Owen said.

"You need some sleep," Brett said. "Go home and come back in at least four hours. I doubt we'll have any information before then."

"I can't," Owen said, his voice breaking completely.

Brett sighed. "Okay. Help Felix with tracing the last steps of them both. I want it on a map so I can see everything."

It wasn't much, but at least it would keep Owen busy, which was what he needed.

21

Owen

Owen knew it was busy work he'd been given, but as long as he *was* busy, he could deal with it. It couldn't be happening again. He couldn't let another child disappear and be murdered while he might be able to do something to stop it.

He could still remember the worry and uncertainty he'd felt when Amy went missing. It was an almost tangible memory that would be with him for the rest of his life. And the gaping hole in his chest when he'd been told Amy wasn't coming home would never be filled. It grew smaller with each passing day, but it would never close completely. He was glad the guy who'd taken her was dead—suicide by a police officer was the coward's way out, but the result didn't bother Owen one bit. He deserved it after what he did.

Spending an hour mapping out the Wallises movements the previous day helped to visualise where they'd been. But once they'd arrived home, they hadn't exited again. So it only helped up to a point. He took it a little further and got the blueprints to the house itself and the maps of the property line and then mapped their movements within the house, too.

Once he was done, he stepped back, crossed his arms over his chest and studied the scattering of pins and lines. He focused on the stairs, which showed several lines, meaning they'd used the stairs several times during the evening.

"Can someone find out if the stairs in the house creak in certain spots?" he called to no one in particular.

"On it," someone called back.

Evan came up beside him. "What are you thinking?"

"Well, most stairs have certain spots that creak, don't they?" Evan nodded. "So, if Anika left by herself, she would've probably avoided the creaks because she knew where they were, right?" Evan nodded again. "And if someone took her, they probably wouldn't know where the creaks were."

"And therefore, maybe Edward heard something but didn't know he did?"

"Maybe. It would be a moot point if the people who might've taken her had cased the property before. It wouldn't be impossible for them to take the time to locate the creaks and avoid them, but it seems overkill if they were just wanting to take her."

Evan pointed to a neighbouring property. "Would they have seen something?"

"I supposed it depends on who was awake at whatever time it happened."

Owen's heart skipped, and he stared at Evan. "We didn't ask him how he knew she was missing."

Evan's eyes widened, and he headed for Brett, who immediately got on his phone. Owen turned back to the board. "What happened to you, Anika?" he murmured, studying the plans and trying to see something he hadn't figured out yet.

"Acton said Edward had gone to check on her when he'd heard a noise but couldn't figure out where it came from. This was just before he called me," Evan said, appearing back at his side.

"What noise?"

"He wasn't sure. Something just that was different from the quiet noise of the TV. He couldn't explain what it was."

"So would that have been when she went missing, or was it just a random noise?"

Evan shrugged. "I doubt we'll ever know."

Owen focused on the map again. "Is there going to be a ransom request, or is this an opportunistic event?"

"Edward's not received anything about a ransom, but that doesn't mean he won't. Some requests don't come through straight away, do they?"

Owen raked his fingers through his hair. There was so much they didn't know, and most of it, they couldn't find out until possibly too late. "I need coffee."

"Come on. Let's go grab some and have a breather for a few minutes," Evan said, sliding an arm around his shoulders and tugging him towards the door. "We'll be back soon," Evan called out.

Owen let his better half lead him from the room, even though he wanted to stay and do more, but what else could he do? Until they had more information from the police or anyone Brett had brought in to help, there wasn't much anyone could do. In the break room, Evan headed for the coffee pot and poured two mugs, handing one to Owen when he returned. They settled at a table.

"Talk to me, Owen," Evan said.

Owen exhaled and shook his head. "I don't know, Evan. My head's both all over the place and viciously clear at the same time."

"It's understandable."

Owen stood abruptly, knocking the table and spilling their drinks. He cursed and grabbed some napkins, cleaning up the mess before throwing the wad of wet towels in the bin. Pacing across the floor, he raked his fingers through his hair again and again.

"One minute, I'm pissed off. The next, I'm sad. The following, I'm angry. I'm all over the place," he said again. "I *need* to find her."

"We will. We will find her, Owen. We will."

"But we have nothing!" Owen flung his arms wide. "We have fuck all to show for the hours of work we've put into this. Nobody has any fucking clue who took her or even if she was taken. How is that helping us?"

He put his hands on his hips, head lowered, and breathed hard. It wasn't Evan's fault, but he couldn't stop himself from exploding at the impotency he felt. Evan slid his arms around Owen, and he sagged into the embrace, clutching at the back of his T-shirt.

"We have to find her," he said into Evan's neck. "We have to."

"We will," Evan promised, and though Owen knew he couldn't make a promise like that, he clung to it.

The door slammed open. "Wallis just received a phone call for a ransom!" someone shouted at them and disappeared again.

Owen and Evan raced back to Sec HQ, stopping when Brett held up a hand. A choked voice came through the phone.

"I want to know my daughter is okay," Dr Wallis said.

"That's not how this works, Dr Wallis," a robotic voice answered. "You will do what I tell you, and then—and only then—will you see your daughter again. One million pounds in twenty-four hours."

"I don't have—"

"One million, twenty-four hours."

The call ended, and Brett spoke into the phone. "Dr Wallis, are you still there?"

"Yes," came the broken reply.

"Quick thinking on including us in the call. Thank you for that. We'll get looking into it, and we'll be in touch."

"What about the ransom?"

Brett clenched his jaw. "Don't worry about that. We'll sort it."

Brett spoke to the doctor for a few more minutes, but Owen had spaced out, recalling the words on the phone, and he froze.

Evan leaned closer. "What is it?"

Owen met his gaze and murmured, "He said, 'see your daughter again,' not 'see your daughter alive.'"

Evan raised his eyebrows. "You think he said it like that on purpose? That he's planning to kill her, anyway?"

Owen shrugged, though his gut was telling him that, yes, that's exactly what he thought. The robotic style voice wasn't giving away the person's identity. Although it sounded fairly masculine, that meant nothing at all.

He crossed his arms over his chest and tried to bury all the emotions bubbling at the surface. While Evan had been in Italy, Owen had buried everything he'd been feeling, sometimes coming across as emotionless—which for his job had been a good thing—but it also meant he'd not been able to feel the hurt, the loss, the grief for anything that had hurt him. Since Evan's return, his emotions had risen to the forefront, and it was that much harder to shove everything back down. It clouded his thoughts, and he really needed that clarity right then.

Nick came up to them. "Felix is just working on seeing if he can get a location from the phone call. Hopefully, he will and we can break down the door and grab them." He clenched his fists. "Anyone who hurts kids deserves a funeral."

Owen had an idea. "Would it be better or worse for the criminal to get publicity for this?"

Evan and Nick stared at him. "What are you thinking?" Evan asked.

Owen gathered his thoughts. "First, answer the question."

Nick shrugged and turned to Brett, asking the question Owen had voiced. Brett joined their small group. "I suppose it depends on how much of a trigger point they have. Publicity makes things that much more black and white. If they get frazzled, they're likely to do one of two things: either blow up and kill her or give her back and slink off into the shadows. Why?"

"I was trying to figure out whether leaking something to the media would be beneficial for us."

"Leaking what?" Brett glanced over at Felix, who was busily working away at his computer, a frown on his face.

"Just the disappearance and that there has been a ransom. Would it put the right kind of pressure on them or not?" Owen asked. He honestly thought it would be a good option, but he wasn't the expert. There had been no ransom for Amy. Just the grief of finding her body.

Brett rubbed his chin, his mind going a mile a minute—Owen could almost see the steam rising from him. "In this instance, I don't think it would work in anyone's favour. Whoever was on the other end of the phone did not sound the least bit concerned. About anything."

Owen nodded. Brett would know better than he did.

"Brett!" Felix called, and they all looked over. "Couldn't trace it." He sagged, visibly upset about it.

"I didn't think they would be that stupid," Brett said. "You did good."

Owen could see Felix didn't believe him because when something like this happened and you didn't get results, it felt like a physical blow.

"I want you both to get some rest," Brett said, glaring at him and Evan. "You've been up for long enough."

Owen crossed his arms over his chest again and shook his head. "It won't happen."

Brett peered at him. "Just because you think you're the *best in the business* doesn't mean you don't have a breaking point."

The reference to the words he'd said to Dominic wasn't missed, and he found a smirk to send Brett's way. "You wouldn't like me if I wasn't just a little bit like you."

Brett's mouth twitched, but then wiped clean like it was never there. "In which case, start checking through those hospital records to see if anyone Dr Wallis treated sends up a red flag."

"Yes, sir," Owen said.

Brett glared at him but turned away, and Nick blew out a breath. "You seriously said that? Man, you have balls of steel."

"I was actually talking about me and Locke." Owen laughed, the first moment of levity he'd found all morning.

Nick tilted his head to the side as if thinking about something and then nodded. "I can see it. Although I don't think Dominic or Viola would like to be relegated to second best."

"The truth hurts," Owen quipped, feeling his humour already disappearing as he headed for the computer and the extensive list of patients Dr Wallis had seen over the last six months.

He struggled to focus, to begin with. Visions of the time between realising Amy was missing and finding her flashing into his mind. The race to search everywhere they could think of that she might've gone. The panic when she was never at them. The slight hope when they remembered somewhere else she liked going, and the distraught sense of failure when she was, again, not found. Then the call that sent their family into a tailspin of grief. Then the call that ended everything. The call that carved a hole in Owen's heart to never be filled again.

He inhaled and refocused, needing to concentrate and get through the details. It was tedious, but important, and so he did his duty, spending his time triple-checking the patients were as benign as their injuries.

"Felix!" Brett hissed, gesturing for him as he held the phone to his ear. "Send it to this phone number, and we'll see if we can trace it. Okay. She's alive, Dr Wallis. Let's be thankful for that at the moment. We'll do what we can from this end." He hung up. "Dr Wallis received proof of life. A photo of Anika in front of the news on TV, which shows the date and time. It was taken an hour ago, according to that. Can we trace it?"

Felix hesitated but then nodded. "We might be able to if I—"

"Then do it," Brett said. Felix raced back to his computer. "Nick, you're needed with His Majesty. Take Landon with you as well. As much as this takes precedence—on the king's orders—he still has duties to uphold and needs his guards."

"I'm on it," Nick said and disappeared out of the room.

Owen glanced between Felix and Brett, his heart pounding. Would they find the location? Would they be able to find her? Evan's hand rested on his nape, making him jump, and he stared at his boyfriend, taking the strength he needed from that steady and reassuring gaze. He inhaled and nodded, returning to the hospital records.

He wasn't sure how long he'd been working when Felix whooped, scaring the shit out of nearly every person in the room.

"I've found the fucker!" he yelled.

Owen scrambled over to him. "Where are they?"

"A house on the outskirts of Windsor."

Owen noted the address and raced for the door, Evan close behind him.

"Owen, stop!" Brett ordered, and Owen paused by the open door.

"I'm not letting them get away with this," Owen said.

"We need to wait for the police to join us at the address. There's no point in going vigilante on this. It might make things worse, not better."

Owen shook his head, his stomach cramping. "I'm not waiting, Brett."

Brett narrowed his eyes. "You leave, Owen, and you won't have a job to come back to."

Owen swallowed, his chest aching at the thought of losing the job he loved, but the girl was more important than he was. He nodded and left. Evan followed.

"Owen, let's think about this, yeah? We would do better with support. We can't face them on our own. We'd have a much better success rate if we had help."

"I can't wait, Evan. I just can't."

Evan was silent for a moment. "Can we at least get some more guns or something?"

Owen sighed. "Brett would've already made Felix change the codes to the armoury, so we'll have to go with what I've got." He glanced at Evan. "You can stay here. You don't have to be part of this."

Evan hit him, a sharp punch to the biceps. "Shut the fuck up, asshole. Do you remember the conversation we had not long ago? About having each other's backs?"

Owen's throat tightened as they exited Windsor Castle and climbed into the car. The guards stopped them at the gate.

"Brett says we're not to let you through," he said apologetically.

"Hayden, as much as you need to take orders, if you do not open this gate, I will crash through it, leaving the royal family at risk. You don't want that, and neither do I. Just let us go."

Hayden bit his lip, hesitating, but finally nodded and lifted the gate. The poor guy would be in so much trouble for that, but he'd made the right choice. As much as Owen wouldn't want to risk the royal family, he needed to get to the location as fast as he could.

The drive took about fifteen minutes, and he parked down the road, just able to see the house from where they were. In his boot, he had two bulletproof vests and two hand guns with several clips of bullets.

"Stay alive," Evan said. "You die, I'll bring you back and kill you myself. Understood?"

"Yes, Sir," Owen said. "Be safe."

"Always am."

They shared a tension-filled kiss and then headed for the property, using the trees and hedges as cover. There were no cars in the driveway, but that meant nothing. The closest house to it was around two hundred yards away, giving the property a sizable acreage for its location. They chose to approach the property from the corner of the house, hopefully as out of sight of the windows as they could be. Sliding along the wall of the house, Owen peered into the window but couldn't see anything. He continued, Evan at his back. The second window held nothing, either.

He glanced back at Evan and pointed to the front door. Tension bracketed Evan's expression, but he nodded. He motioned for Evan to go around the back, and he disappeared. Owen tried the door handle, and it opened with ease. His stomach roiled, but he continued forward, sweat dripping down his spine and face. Holding his gun out in front of him, he headed towards where he could hear a TV, his steps slow and soft, testing each move before putting his full weight on it. His eyes scanned around him, but he couldn't see anything amiss.

Stopping in front of the door where the sound of the TV was coming from, he held his gun forward and twisted the handle. He got a glimpse of the room before there was a click, and he cursed.

22

Dominic

Dominic's phone chimed, and he reached for it before he had any idea he'd done it, putting his book aside. It was an unknown number, but that wasn't unheard of in his line of work. He clicked it and it opened a photo. It was a dimly lit room with just a lit TV screen. But what caught his attention—what he zoomed in on—was the white square on the wall of the room with the black #2 written on it.

Flashes of the day he'd been shot and left for dead flew through his mind, and he glanced up at Randall, needing to double check he was with him and alive. Which he was and playing with that damn mini aquarium Owen had bought him.

He studied the picture again, seeing nothing else of importance. But he hadn't been sent the picture on a whim. There was a message behind this one, and Dominic knew that whoever was behind his attack was behind this, too. Was it another attack or was it a threat?

He stood and headed to the door, poking his head out. "Colt, could you sit inside? I need to visit Brett. I'll get him to send someone else if I'm not coming back."

"Sure." Colt stood and entered.

Dominic peeked his head in to Randall. "I'm just heading to see Brett. I'll be back soon."

Randall frowned at him. "Everything okay?"

"I'm not sure."

He raced down the hallways to Sec HQ, almost forgetting to knock before entering. "Brett! I've just received—"

"Holy shit!" Felix yelled, raking his fingers through his hair. "It blew."

Brett stood up, his chair cracking backwards. "Tell me it didn't."

Felix stared at him. "The house blew. I don't know if Owen and Evan were there or not. I couldn't get an answer from them."

"Where are Owen and Evan? And has this got something to do with this photo?" Dominic held up his phone.

Brett gritted his teeth. "They went to the location we found from the proof of life. No backup." He took the phone from Dominic, looking at the photo. "It's the same as what was left with you."

Dominic swallowed, not ready to believe something had happened to his best friends. "I think Owen and Evan have walked into a trap."

"We need to get there! Now!" Brett ordered, and every available guard raced from the room.

23

Evan

E van reached for the handle to the back door, just as he heard a crash of glass, when he was thrown five feet in the air away from the house with a blast of heat so powerful, he doubted he'd ever feel cold again. When he hit the ground, he blacked out.

He groaned, coughed and groaned again when his body told him not to move or even breathe. What the fuck had happened? Where the hell was he?

"Evan? Evan!" someone shouted, and he strained to hear whoever it was.

He rolled to his back, blinking up at the sky as pain caused his lungs to stop working while he got the pain under control again.

"What the fuck happened?" he croaked. At least, he thought he did.

"Thank fuck." Evan blinked again, and Nick's face appeared in front of him. "You with me now, Evan?"

"Yeah. I think. What happened?"

Nick's mouth twisted, and he glanced over his shoulder towards something. Evan followed his gaze, but all he saw was black smoke circling to the sky.

"An explosion."

In a rush of memories, everything came back to him, and he scrambled upright, staring at the rubble of the house he and Owen had been casing. His breath stuttered as he took in the pile of bricks that sat in front of him. His chest ached, and he couldn't breathe.

"Evan, fuck! Brett, I need help here!" Nick turned back to him. "Evan, breathe for me, man. Fuck."

A slap on his cheek made him blink, giving him an excuse to turn away from the disaster that waited for him to acknowledge.

"Breathe, Evan," Nick repeated.

Evan stared at him as he followed his breaths, the lightheadedness finally receding a little. Brett crouched beside him.

"Where's Owen?"

Acknowledging what had happened was obviously something he had no choice about, but he couldn't say anything. He just pointed. At the house. Or what was left of it.

Brett followed his finger and cursed, racing back to the fire engines that stood nearby. Evan couldn't hear what they said, but more people came running, some with protective equipment, some without, and they started digging through the rubble.

Nick slid his arm around him and helped him to stand. "We need to get you checked out."

Evan already knew he had a concussion, what with the dizziness and ringing ears, and plenty of scrapes and bruises littering his body, but he didn't care. He needed to find Owen.

There was no way he could've survived that explosion, but if nothing else, he needed closure. He needed to be able to bury him alongside his sister. His steps faltered as he thought of Sally. This would destroy her. Burying one child was bad enough, but now she had to bury a second one.

Evan didn't get as far as the ambulance when shouts sounded from behind them. He paused, making Nick stop, too. They faced the team, watching as they all congregated on one area of the rubble. When two men reached down and pulled, a body came free.

Evan's knees went out from beneath him, and Nick helped him to the ground again. He stared at the body being carried closer. It was Owen. He was covered in dust and grime, but Evan realised his eyes were open—and not in the bad way.

"Fuck," Evan gasped, his eyes filling as his brain caught up with what he was seeing. "How the fuck is he alive?" he wheezed, close to breaking down and losing it.

Nick grabbed him and pulled him upright again. "I have no fucking idea. Come on. Let's get to the ambulance so you can see for yourself."

Each painful step reminded Evan of what had happened.

"Nick! Nick! What happened? Is this a royal attack again?" Malachi yelled from behind the tape that had been put up at some point. Nick ignored him, so Evan followed suit.

When they finally reached the ambulance where Owen was being tended to, he'd decided that running a marathon had nothing on this. The paramedics wouldn't let them into the ambulance because they were still working on fixing Owen up, but his boyfriend's gaze never left his.

"Are you okay?" Evan mouthed.

Owen nodded and winced, saying something to the paramedic, which made them look at Evan and nod back. The paramedic helped Evan onto the seat at Owen's head, leaving Nick outside, and continued tending to Owen while they talked. Unfortunately, due to the ringing in his ears and the dizziness, Evan couldn't decipher most of it. He felt himself listing to one side, and the next thing he remembered, he was horizontal next to Owen, staring across the small space between them.

"Don't fucking scare me like that, asshole," Owen said, and Evan was finally able to hear him over the ringing.

"Huh?" Evan said, having no clue what he was talking about. After all, who had been the one to walk into a building that exploded?

"You blacked out and scared the shit out of me," Owen said, his expression tightening before relaxing again.

"You're both as bad as each other. Now shut the hell up and get to the hospital so you can be patched up," Brett ordered from outside the ambulance.

"Wait!" Owen said, trying to rise but hissing and flopping back again. "There was no one there."

"We know, Owen. It's okay," Brett said.

"No, wait." Owen closed his eyes and inhaled before continuing. "There was a TV paused on the news. When I opened the door to the room it was in, it was empty. Except for a white piece of paper with #2 on it."

"That's great, Owen."

"How did you get out?" Nick said.

Owen sighed. "I heard the click and knew what it was. I jumped through the window just as the place blew. Unfortunately, it still all came down on me." He met Evan's gaze. "I hoped you hadn't entered the house because I didn't have time to call a warning."

"It blasted me away from the house," Evan mumbled, but unconsciousness was pulling him under. He didn't hear another thing.

The next time he woke, he was in a dimly lit room, and his body hurt like nothing he'd ever felt before. He hissed when he breathed in too deeply, and a voice from beside him made him jump.

"You finally decided to join me again," Owen said.

Evan rolled his head to the side, closing his eyes and letting his head settle before opening them again and seeing a sight he'd hadn't believed he'd ever see again.

"I thought I'd lost you," he whispered.

"And I you," Owen replied.

Evan took in what he could see of his boyfriend. A cast on his arm and a bandage at his temple was all he could see. "What's the damage?" he asked.

"Surprisingly, not much. Broken arm, cuts and bruises. I was able to protect my head from the falling debris, and the bulletproof vest helped protect my torso. How I don't have a broken leg or something is beyond me."

"Concussion?" Evan asked, the nurse in him taking over.

Owen shook his head. "No. Unlike someone I know. How are you feeling?"

"Like I've been run over by a fire engine and then they backed over me again."

"Ah, not too bad, then," Owen joked. Then he sobered. "Are you okay?"

Evan met his gaze. "Not even a little."

"Me either. No boxing for us for a while."

"Or push ups." He paused. "It was a setup, wasn't it?"

Owen nodded. "Brett came after us when they realised. From what I heard before we got whisked here, Dominic received a text with a picture of an empty room with the TV and the white number on the wall, exactly what I saw when I walked into that room. They put two and two together and realised it was a setup."

"Dr Wallis set us up?"

Owen shrugged. "We're not sure yet. That number two was exactly the same that had been thrown on Dominic when he was shot and left for dead last year, remember? But he had a number one."

Evan did remember. Owen had called Evan back from Italy to help him cheer Dominic up after everything that had been happening to him, and it was pure luck he'd still been there when Randall had been kidnapped and Dominic had gone off half-cocked to rescue him. Evan winced when he realised they'd done exactly what Dominic had done, and the result had almost been worse.

"So this event is related to Dominic's last year? How?"

Owen shrugged again. "We don't know yet. Brett is currently talking to Dr Wallis about everything."

"I would hate to be on the end of that wrath."

"Oh, we've got it coming," Owen warned.

And boy, did they.

"The next time you disobey me, Owen Morris, will be the last time. Understood?" Brett said a few hours later.

"Yes, sir."

"And taking Evan with you... What the hell were you thinking?" Brett held up a hand and sighed. "Don't answer that. I know what you were thinking, and while I understand, it could've all been prevented. If. You. Had. Just. Waited."

"What happened?" Evan asked, hoping Brett's wrath wouldn't come down on *his* head.

Brett's glare didn't feel good, but then his expression hardened for a different reason. "When Dominic received the photo of the room and we figured out the connection between them, we got in contact with Dr Wallis. After several long minutes of saying he knew nothing, he finally broke down and told us everything." He leaned his hip against the bottom of Owen's bed and crossed his arms over his chest. "Dr Wallis is being blackmailed into all of this. His daughter being kidnapped is true, but he received a phone call just before the one he connected with us. The initial phone call detailed a plan to get you," he pointed to Owen, "to that house so he could 'talk' to you. All Wallis had to do was to connect the next phone call to us as a so-called ransom, and then the kidnapper would send a proof of life which we could trace." Brett stared at them both. "The kidnapper knows you well enough to know you'd go racing in if you heard the girl was in danger. You played right into their hands and nearly lost your lives."

"Did Dr Wallis know he was trying to kill Owen?" Evan asked, an ember of anger burning in him.

Brett shook his head. "From what the kidnapper said, he just wanted to talk to Owen, and as soon as Wallis kept up his end of the bargain, they would return his daughter."

"She's back home?" Owen asked.

Brett frowned. "No. We're assuming the kidnapper had eyes on the explosion, and when they saw you were still alive, they changed their minds about giving Anika back. Maybe she's still useful to them."

"They've lost the element of surprise, though. We know they're after me now. What would be the point of keeping her?"

"Leverage. We won't want her hurt, so they have sway with us," Brett said.

Owen dropped his head back to the bed and sighed. "This is fucked up."

Evan frowned and then wished he hadn't. "So, Dr Wallis knew Anika had been taken?" Brett nodded. "Did he let her go?"

Brett shook his head. "He honestly didn't know they had taken her. That part is true. He was only told afterwards why she had been, which is what he kept from us."

"Were there any results from the neighbours' door cams?" Owen asked suddenly.

"No. Again, either nothing was recorded or they were deleted. I'm leaning more towards each of the cameras being hacked and evidence deleted because it seems far too coincidental for them all to not have something."

"So the kidnapper is either a tech whiz or has someone on their payroll who is. Would that limit the number of people it could be?" Owen asked.

"Felix is already looking into it."

"Was there any evidence from the house left?" Evan asked.

Brett sighed. "Well, we have people going through it with a fine-toothed comb, but we're not holding out much hope. The place was set up to be detonated by someone who knew what they were doing."

"If I never speak to Dr Wallis again, it will be too soon," Evan muttered, closing his eyes.

"He did what he had to for his daughter," Owen said.

Evan didn't answer because he could see the reasoning behind it, but he was still sore about the injuries Owen had from it. It would take him a while to forget about what that man let happen.

"Anyway, rest up. We're still helping the police to search for her. Wallis hasn't heard from the kidnapper again." Brett's expression was grim, which told of the potential of a negative outcome of the search.

Someone slammed through the door, and they all braced for something, but no one was ready for the storm that was Sally Morris. Brett nodded and introduced himself before escaping, but they had no such recourse.

"So, why is the first I'm hearing about this coming from a nurse when I've just come onto shift? Why did neither of you call me?"

Evan lifted his hand. "I was unconscious." Sally's face tightened, but she nodded at him before glaring at her son.

"I was in and out in the ambulance, Mum. And they've been testing me while Evan's been sleeping it off."

Sally's face crumpled, and she hid it behind her hands. Her shoulders shook before she inhaled deeply and wiped her tears. "Did you find her?" Evan raised his eyebrows, and Sally snorted. "One of your colleagues recognised me and filled me in on what happened. Felix, I think his name was."

Felix was a god, Evan decided.

Owen sighed. "We didn't. It was empty." Evan waited to see if Owen would expand on what Brett had told them, and when he didn't, Evan took his cue from him. No point upsetting Sally more than she already was.

She grabbed Owen's chart, checking things. "You seem surprisingly okay, considering you had a building dumped on you."

Owen chuckled and groaned. "God, don't make me laugh. My ribs ache."

Evan snorted, and then he wished he hadn't. Sally moved onto his chart. "Cuts, bruises and a concussion." She sighed and shook her head. "What am I going to do with you both? You're too old to be grounded, but by god, do I want to."

She crossed her arms, and Evan couldn't help but laugh again, even though it hurt like hell. The moment of levity was much needed, and his tear-filled gaze met Owen's, and he blinked, letting his tears soak into his pillow. He could've lost him. Sally could've lost him. As much as he loved providing backup for Owen, he wasn't sure his heart could take it. They'd never been in a life and death situation before, not really. Even with the situation with Dominic, where he'd been shot and left for dead, they themselves hadn't been in danger.

Sally moved between them and fiddled with the dials, and within seconds, a hazy lethargy came over him at the same time the pain eased. She brushed his hair back from his forehead and kissed him there. "Sleep. You need your energy," she whispered.

Before he succumbed to the inevitable medicated sleep, he watched as Sally climbed onto the bed beside her son and took his hand. They spoke softly—or Evan's ears had stopped working—but then he saw Owen's blinks lasting longer.

They were both so tired.

But when he woke, he would help them find the girl, and if he got the chance to give Dr Wallis a piece of his mind, he would.

24

Owen

When Owen had woken after the sleep his mother had made him have, he lay thinking everything through as he listened to Evan's breathing. As he thought about what he and his mother spoke about before he fell asleep, he remembered the scarf from his so-called admirer. Had whoever that was entered his mother's house and grabbed the scarf? Or had his mother sent it to the charity shop? Owen hadn't asked her yet, but he needed to. The idea that someone had entered her house, regardless of whether or not she was in the house, was troubling. But it was something he could deal with once they found the girl.

Later that evening, after arguing for several hours, they were discharged from the hospital on the understanding that someone needed to be with them for at least the first twenty-four hours. His mother took it upon herself to remake the bed in the room Evan had been using and left them to their devices, on the understanding that she would be interrupting them at random times to make sure they were okay.

It was the following day, when his body ached more than ever before, that Brett called him with an update.

"Wallis received another message, this time with co-ordinates. After checking things over, a team investigated. Nothing bad happened, but they found Anika. She was a little bruised from rough handling, but apart from that, she's doing well."

Owen exhaled, closing his eyes, and arms came around him from both sides. His mother and Evan. "That's good news."

"It is, but we have another issue."

Owen straightened. "What?"

"I'm sending you some photos."

He waited for the few seconds it took for the pictures to download, and when he saw the first one, his heart dropped. Anika sat on a chair, bound, gagged and blindfolded, and in front of her was what looked like a kitchen knife embedded into the table with a blue bow on it. There was definitely a threat in that display. He swiped to the second one and froze.

Have you enjoyed the game? You should be able to put all four clues together now. But I doubt you'll find the ENEMY in time. Enjoy your gifts.

The note was in the same handwriting as the notes sent by Owen's admirer.

"I guess I don't need to be worried about it being an admirer anymore," Evan muttered.

"What do you mean?" Sally said.

While Evan filled his mother in on the gifts Owen had received, he stared at the photos, at least until Evan mentioned the second scarf.

"Mum, did you send that scarf to the charity shop?"

Sally shook her head. "I've kept things like that in the cupboard under the stairs. You know that. Whenever people came to visit, if they didn't have something, I'd go digging in there to find a spare."

"That's what I was worried about," he said.

Sally's eyes widened. "They were in the house."

Owen nodded. "You'll be staying with us for the moment. At least until we get your house more secure." He finally remembered Brett was still on the line. "Brett, did you catch all that?"

"I did. We'll get someone over to your mother's house to check it out and see if we can get forensics."

"Do you still have all the notes?"

"Yes, why?"

"The words in all capitals, what are they?"

Brett rustled around before coming back on clearer. "Year, Old, New, Enemy."

"That's not the order they were sent in, though, was it?" He tried to remember. "New was first. I got the calendar second, which meant year is next. Old related to the second scarf, and now enemy. Shit, Brett. *New year, old enemy.* Who the fuck is this?"

Brett cursed a storm down the line, and he heard him shout, "Get me everything about Dominic's situation last year. EVERYTHING! Owen, we'll figure this out, okay? We were already going back over what happened when we saw the number two, but this just points more towards that."

"Send us everything, too. We can't do much else except research for the moment," Evan said.

"Will do."

Brett hung up, and Owen stared down at the note still visible on the screen. "So if these two events are connected, that means they went after Dominic, and now they're after me. Does that mean the situations connect us as bodyguards or friends?" He met Evan's gaze, a wave of panic flowing through him. He couldn't let anything happen to Evan. He couldn't lose him again.

Evan cupped his face. "No matter what the answer is, we're together. We'll figure this out." He dropped a kiss on his lips. "But first, I want to speak with Dr Wallis."

"Are you sure that's a good idea, Evan?" Sally asked.

"I need to hear the story from his side, Sally. I'll be able to tell if he's being honest or was only in it for something else."

She nodded slowly. "Don't go on your own, though."

Owen felt torn. He wanted to go with Evan, but he wanted to be with his mother in case something happened to her. In the end, he called Brett back and asked for someone to stay with her while they went to Dr Wallis's house. Nick turned up a little while later, holding a Chinese takeaway and a case of beer.

Owen raised his eyebrows, and Nick sighed. "She doesn't drink beer?"

He snorted. "Oh, she does, but you only brought one case?" He clapped him on the shoulder and left. "Good luck, man."

Nick would soon find out that his mother could hold her beer with the best of them, and no one had yet to drink her under the table, including him, Evan or Dominic.

They got a taxi to Dr Wallis's house, neither of them fit enough to drive, and when it deposited them on the man's driveway, Owen double-checked that Evan wanted to approach him now.

"Why not? It's not going to make it any easier, is it?" Evan sighed. "Sorry. I didn't mean to snap."

Owen slid his arm around Evan's waist. "You don't need to apologise. We're all up and down at the moment. It'll level out soon." He kissed his cheek. "Ready?"

"No." But he headed for the door.

When Dr Wallis opened it, his eyes immediately filled, and he swallowed hard, stepping back to allow them in. They entered the living room to find Anika sitting on the sofa with a blanket covering her. Her eyes widened initially, and then she jumped up and flung her arms around Owen. Owen froze for a second before returning the hold, unsure why he was the recipient, but more than happy to reassure her as much as she needed.

She stepped back, gripping his shirt. "I'm so glad you're okay."

He frowned and glanced at Dr Wallis for an answer. He shrugged. "Why would I not be?"

"The guy kept talking about you. About how you would be the second cog in his revenge. I can still hear his laughter when the house exploded."

"You saw that?"

She nodded. "He had a camera on it all the time. He made me watch as you went in." Her breathing laboured. "Made me watch as it exploded." Tears streamed down her face. "I hadn't wanted to be the reason you died."

Owen pulled her in for another hug, tightening his hold on her this time even as his heart bled for her. She had been through so much for being fifteen years old.

"I'm okay, Anika."

"No thanks to me," Dr Wallis said.

Despite the slight distance between them, Owen felt Evan tense, and he let go of Anika to grab Evan's arm. "Evan," he whispered. His boyfriend stared at him, sighed and nodded. Owen focused on Dr Wallis. "We'd like to hear what happened."

Dr Wallis nodded slowly. "Anika? Would you go and help your mother in the kitchen, please? You don't need to hear this again."

Anika nodded but glanced back at Owen. "Please don't leave without saying goodbye."

"I won't." He would discuss the other aspects of her words later.

She disappeared down the hallway and Dr Wallis gestured to the sofas. "Please." They settled on the sofa, and the doctor sat in an armchair, his hands wringing together. "I'll answer whatever questions you have, but please can I just say I am so sorry."

Owen had already forgiven him, but he knew it would take Evan a while longer, so he just nodded. "What happened, Dr Wallis?"

"Edward, please. I don't feel much like I deserve the title."

"You don't," Evan snapped, and Owen gripped his knee. Evan sat back, crossing his arms over his chest, his expression mutinous.

Edward nodded. "I completely agree with your sentiment, Evan." He sighed, long and hard. "When I found Anika gone, there was a note left on her bed. It just said, 'wait for a call.' I wasn't sure what else to think. So I waited, thinking it was a joke Anika was playing on me. When the guy called, he explained what he wanted me to do. I was to call you, Evan, and request help with finding Anika. The guy joked that you had the means to get her back for me. He said if I did everything he asked, Anika would be returned unharmed. And then he told me to wait for another call, reminding me that I couldn't tell anyone about the note or him. I had to make it look real." He licked his lips, shaking his head. "I honestly didn't think about what could happen. I was solely focused on getting Anika back, and I'm so sorry."

"You didn't hear her being taken?"

Edward shook his head. "I've recently had the stairs redone because the boards were bad. So we had new boards and new carpets. There were next to no creaks on the stairs, and Anika said she remembered someone grabbing her neck and nothing else. I'm assuming they used her pressure points to make her unconscious. I didn't hear a thing. Well, only one sound, but I couldn't figure out what it was. Some sort of click."

Owen could see the guy was beating himself up for everything that had happened, and he was likely to do that for a long time. After all, Owen was still beating himself up for what happened to Amy, and that was over twenty years ago.

"And you received a second phone call?"

Edward nodded. "Same guy told me I would receive a third call from him, which I would connect to your boss for him to listen to. I had to pretend to be scared—which wasn't hard."

"How did you have Brett's number? We didn't give it to you."

"Detective Acton gave it to me. Told me to call him if he couldn't get hold of him." Owen nodded and gestured for him to continue. "So when he called back, I added your boss, and did what the guy told me to."

"How do you know it was the same guy? The voice we heard was robotic," Evan said.

"He'd said he'd sound different to hide his identity."

Owen glanced at Evan, wondering if that was a lead they'd need to look into. If the guy needed to hide his voice from them, was it someone they knew?

"What other instructions had he given you?"

"He was going to ask for a ransom, but that was fake. I didn't need to 'worry' about that. Um... that he'd send a proof of life that I had to tell you about. He said it didn't matter if you located him." Edward frowned. "I didn't really understand that bit."

"It was because it was a setup," Owen said. "He wouldn't have been there no matter when we arrived. Whoever entered that house would've been in for a nasty surprise."

"What does he want with you?" Edward asked rubbing his forehead.

"If only we knew," Evan said. "I understand why you did it, Edward. I truly do. But you have to understand it's going to take me time to brush it aside. We nearly died."

Edward rolled his lips inwards and nodded, barely holding onto his tears. "I know. But no one can make me feel as bad as I make myself feel. I will never forgive myself."

Surprisingly, Evan crouched in front of Edward, resting his hands on his knees. "You don't need to forgive yourself yet. But I'm telling you now, if you even consider doing anything to stop your pain in the permanent way, you need to call me. I will *not* let you leave that girl without a father. Understood, doctor?"

Edward nodded. "I wouldn't. I couldn't. I'm too much of a coward."

Evan caught his chin, meeting his gaze. "You're not a coward, but that result doesn't help anyone."

Tears overflowed, and Evan stood, settling back beside Owen. Owen clasped their hands and squeezed. "Good job," he whispered. "Do you need to ask anything else?"

"Did he say anything about *why*?" Evan asked.

Edward shook his head, wiping his cheeks. "Nothing. He kept giving me orders, but he never completely said why he wanted me to do it other than to get you to the house. I didn't know he had it rigged."

"Okay. Thank you for talking to us," Owen said and stood. "I need to say goodbye to Anika."

Edward stood. "I'll fetch her." He turned and paused before facing them again. "I don't know what he told her about you or his plan, and I don't think she's ready to discuss it. She's going to be visiting a psychologist, and I'm going to suggest that she allow pertinent information to be shared with you if that's okay?"

Owen nodded. "Only if it won't affect her. I won't hurt her any further than she already has been."

Edward left, and Anika came running in. "Dad said you're going."

"Yes, we need some sleep." Owen smiled. "It was nice to meet you, Anika. I'm glad you're back home." He wouldn't add safe because home was supposed to be a safe place, and neither her house nor his mother's house was now considered safe.

"The guy mentioned...your sister. Amy." Owen's throat closed up, but he nodded. "She died, right?" He nodded again. "I'm sorry. He wasn't. Not even remotely. But I am. I'm sorry you had to deal with this situation just because he was being an asshole."

"Anika!" a woman's voice scolded.

Anike smiled but shouted, "Sorry, Mum!" She lowered her voice. "But he was. And I'm sorry for it."

"You don't need to be sorry, Anika. I really am happy you're home."

Owen opened his arms, cast and all, and they hugged again. "I don't have a brother, but if I did, I'd want you," Anika whispered in his ear, and it took every ounce of restraint to not burst into tears.

"Thank you."

They left after a brief goodbye from Edward and his ex-wife. The taxi picked them up, and Evan waited until they were on their way before asking what Anika had said. When Owen repeated it, he cried. That girl was going to be a force of nature, and one of the wisest people on the planet, if he had to guess.

Edward hadn't given them a huge amount of new information, but when they arrived home, Owen spent a few minutes on the phone with Brett, relaying what he'd said. He also brought up the connection between the two cases again, explaining his thoughts about if the connection was between the three friends, and therefore, was Evan next, or if it was about the bodyguard side of their relationship. Brett hummed a bit but didn't offer his own thoughts on that. He probably had so much information rolling around in that head of his that he could see hundreds of smaller connections that none of them had.

He joined his mother and Evan in the living room with Nick, and they put a reality TV show on, which Owen hated, but after several episodes, he found himself throwing comments into the mix, too. It was nice to relax with people and not worry about someone coming after him. At least for a little while.

His brain occasionally brought up that Evan might be next, but something about that scenario didn't seem to fit, his gut told him. He considered the bodyguard side of things, but apart from their job, nothing connected the guards, except for him and Dominic. Did that mean that they were the only ones focused on? Or was there another connection that he hadn't figured out yet?

Going around in circles was nothing new, but it tired him out, especially as he was still recovering from the explosion. Evan fell asleep during an episode, and when it finished, Owen nudged him and guided him to bed. Nick said he'd stay for one more episode and then let Sally get some sleep.

After curling himself around Evan under the covers, he tried to turn his brain off, but it was easier said than done. There were so many what-ifs in the situation. But there was one thing for sure—Evan and he were together for the long haul. He knew it deep in his soul, and there was nothing he wouldn't do for him. Maybe he needed to lock him down so he couldn't leave him again. Not that he would. It had been Owen pushing him away that sent him running, and he couldn't blame the guy.

Would Evan agree to marry him if he asked? Wasn't that the million pound question? He didn't want to think about the result being negative, so he concentrated on the good points of their relationship. The way they knew each other completely. The way they could finish each other's sentences. The way they understood what the other was thinking, just with a look. Owen couldn't imagine growing old without Evan being there with him—and he didn't want to. He wanted Evan all to himself. Forever.

It was definitely something to consider. Well, he didn't need to consider it because he was going to do it, but he needed to consider what he wanted to do to propose. Would it be better if it was when they were with family, or would it work better alone where they wouldn't be disturbed? Would Evan want to go away for a weekend or something, and Owen could propose at a special dinner? Or should he prepare a dinner himself and offer his skills as a way to persuade Evan to say yes?

So many questions, so little time.

Because he wanted all the time he could have, and he wouldn't be satisfied if any of it would be cut short for whatever reason.

"Stop thinking so loudly," Evan grumbled, and Owen chuckled, pressing his lips to Evan's nape.

"Sorry."

He blanked his mind, concentrating on Evan's breathing and following it with his own. The heat of his skin bled into Owen's, warming more than his body, and Owen smiled against his back. If he had this forever, it would still not be enough time.

There was no going back from this.

He loved Evan with every fibre of his being, and god help anyone who tried to take that away from him.

25

Evan

Concussion sucked.

Evan had borrowed Owen's phrase, and it truly was perfect. He had it a little easier than Owen had, but the lights and the headache were the worst. He couldn't remember the last time he'd spent so much time off work but these past couple of months had been a test of their limits, for sure.

He settled on the sofa, closing his eyes against the bright TV screen but still listening to it. He'd been catching up on the news stories, but they were so depressing, so he'd turned it to a daytime morning show instead. Owen would get a kick about that if he saw him. However, his boyfriend was back at work—even with a cast. He couldn't begrudge him the time, though. Owen was pissed as hell about the incidents, and he was determined to find out what was going on. If he'd been more certain of who was potentially the next target, he might've been a little more relaxed, but Owen was determined to protect Evan in case it was him. And to do that, he needed to be at work, working.

Evan groaned when the doorbell rang. He'd put everything he might need within arm's reach so he wouldn't have to move for a few hours, but he hadn't thought about answering the door. He sighed, contemplating ignoring whoever it was, but then the doorbell rang again, the sound slicing through his head. They'd only keep pressing it if he didn't answer.

He shuffled across the floor, careful not to move too fast, and looked through the peephole. A woman stood there, but he couldn't see any parcels or anything. He opened the door, careful to keep the chain on—he would prefer not to be murdered and then have Owen complain to him about it.

"Hello?" he said, squinting into the sunlight.

"Um, hi. Um, I'm sorry to bother you, but I'm..." She trailed off, and Evan studied her again, his stomach fluttering when he understood who she was.

"Hold on," he said, closing the door enough to remove the chain and opening it again. When he faced her full on, there was no denying who she was. "Jessica?"

Her shoulders lowered, and she exhaled heavily. "You know who I am?"

Evan licked his lips. "Kind of. I was recently told your name, that's about it." He could fudge the truth a little, but it was for her sake, not his parents'. "There's no denying it now I've seen you." He gestured to her. "Come on in. Despite the sunlight, I can feel it's not warm out there."

Jessica stepped across the threshold and rubbed her hands together. "You're right about that."

"The heating is on, so you should warm up quickly. Can I get you a hot drink?"

"Tea would be great if you have it. Otherwise, water is great." She glanced around.

"I have tea. Please, make yourself comfortable. It won't be long." He headed for the kitchen but paused. "Oh, I can put the light on." He reached for it, but her words stopped him.

"No, it's okay. I heard what happened to you. You have a concussion, right? Lights bother you?"

Evan nodded and then wished he hadn't. He cleared his throat, calming the nausea. "Yeah, a bit, but I don't want you to trip over anything."

She waved him away and sat on the edge of the sofa. "I'll be fine. In fact, do you want me to do the drinks?" She rose again.

This time, Evan waved her away. "No, it's okay. It won't take long."

Look at them being all polite. He entered the kitchen and braced himself on the counter, taking a few deep breaths before setting the kettle boiling and fetching two cups. While he waited for the water, he messaged Owen.

EVAN: *Jessica just turned up on our doorstep. Not sure what it's about, but I'll keep you posted.*

He put the phone down and made the drinks, making sure to leave the milk and sugar on the side in case she didn't use them. He put it all on a tray, and then his phone chimed.

OWEN: *Do you want me to come back?*
EVAN: *No, it's okay. Let me see what's going on first.*
OWEN: *Okay. Call me if you need me. Love you.*
EVAN: *Love you, too.*

He grinned as he picked up the tray and carried it into the living room, setting it down on the coffee table. "I didn't put any milk or sugar in, but help yourself to whatever you need."

"Thanks."

He sat on the other end of the sofa and cradled his tea. He wasn't usually a tea drinker, but he knew that for some cancer patients, the scent of coffee was nauseating for them. Plus, his stomach would probably thank him later.

After a tense silence, during which Evan couldn't think of a thing to say—well, he could but nothing polite about his parents—she faced him more fully. Even in the dim lighting, he could see the strain in her body. The darker circles beneath her eyes, the paler skin. He hated that for her.

"You're probably wondering why I'm here."

"A little, though I'm not unhappy about it."

Her mouth curved at the corners, a gesture she must've got from their mother. "I heard about what happened to you, and I wanted to check you were okay. I know... you don't get along with our parents, and they have no idea I'm here."

"Don't get into trouble for me, Jessica."

She straightened, and some of the Morris backbone entered her spirit. "I am my own person. I might need extra support than some at my age, but I make my own choices."

Evan smiled. "Good. But I'm not worth causing a rift."

Jessica put her cup down and slid a little closer, resting her hand on his forearm. Her eyes bored into his. "Yes, you are."

He swallowed hard, never once expecting anything nice to some from a family member, not after having his parents throw him out. "Thanks," he croaked.

She settled back again, picking up her cup. "I don't know anyone who would go after the people who took that girl, and when I found out it was you, I was so proud of you. I couldn't not visit to meet the person who I've always wanted to get to know. I'm sorry if you don't want me here."

Evan sighed. "I want to get to know you, too. Our parents... they're a difficult subject for me. I'm not sure what they told you, but we didn't part on good terms."

She studied him, biting her lips. "They threw you out, didn't they?" she whispered. Evan snapped wide eyes to hers, and she nodded with a sad smile. "It doesn't surprise me, but I hate that they did it. I had my suspicions because Dad has never been quiet about his hatred for anything but the 'norm,' as he calls it."

"How did you know I was gay?"

"I came to the hospital after you were brought in, and I saw you with the other guy—I can't remember his name." She beamed. "I could see how you looked at each other. There's no denying that connection."

"Owen," he murmured. "His name's Owen."

She smiled again. "I'm happy for you." Her smile faltered. "There is another reason I'm here, and I feel so selfish about it."

He waited for her to ask about the blood test, like their parents did, but she surprised him.

"I have little time left in this world, Evan. But I wanted to meet you before it was too late. It means that we'll just get to know each other, and then I'll leave you again. And I'm sorry, but I really wanted to know my brother." Her voice cracked.

Evan put his drink down and moved closer, gently enfolding her in his arms and resting his cheek against her head. "You are so far from selfish. I've only known about you for a few days, but I wanted to get to know you. I wasn't sure if it would be harder for you, though."

She lifted her head, tear tracks on her cheeks. "You didn't know about me?"

Evan shook his head. "No one told me you even existed. Otherwise, I would've probably introduced myself."

"How did you find out?" Evan looked away. "They asked you to go for tests, didn't they?" She cursed and pulled away, wiping her face. "I told them not to! It's not fair to you to be used as a pincushion."

He cradled her jaw, making sure she saw his sincerity when he spoke. "If it would help, I would be a pincushion every hour of the day. I'd already agreed to be tested. I just haven't managed it yet because of what happened. I'm sorry. I'll get there as soon as I can."

She shook her head. "It's okay. You don't need to worry. Even if they find a match now, it's too late."

He frowned, letting her go when she pulled away. "Why is it too late?"

She sighed and rested back against the sofa, staring at the ceiling, the defeat in her posture bringing tears to his eyes. "I went to my appointment this morning. I've passed the stage where anything can help now." She rolled her head to stare at him. "That's why I'm selfish. Because we haven't got long together, and it's not fair to you."

Evan couldn't speak. His heart pounded so hard, he thought he was having a heart attack. Those assholes had purposefully made him lose time with his sister, and he would never forgive them for it. Never. What they'd done to him and Jessica, keeping them apart, was worse than throwing him out. They were done.

"It's okay, Evan. I've made peace with it. I just want to spend the rest of my time however I want to spend it. No appointments, no treatments, no pincushions." She grinned, though it was tired. "I want to get to know my brother so I can take that information with me when it's my time to go."

"How long?" he croaked.

"A month or two."

He tried to swallow the lump in his throat, but it wasn't moving. She reached a hand across the space, and they clung to each other.

When he finally got his voice working again, he said, "Whatever you want, wherever you want to go, whatever you want to see, just ask, and I'll make it happen."

"Thank you, but I don't need anything apart from to get to know you. And Owen if I can?"

Evan reached for his phone and called his boyfriend.

"Hey, everything okay?" Owen asked.

Evan cleared his throat, though his voice was still raw. "Yeah. If you have time, can you come back? There's someone I want you to meet." He met Jessica's gaze, and her smile lit up the room.

"Sure. I'm on my way."

Evan hung up and smiled across at her. "He'll be back soon."

"I didn't mean to pull him away from work."

Evan chuckled. "He shouldn't be at work anyway, but he's trying to figure some stuff out. He's tenacious."

Jessica laughed. "I think we'll get on just fine, then."

"Would you like another drink?"

"Yeah, go on then." She tucked her legs under her, and Evan grabbed the blanket from the back of the sofa, draping it over her. She smiled. "Thanks. I hate being cold."

"Me, too."

Just before he entered the kitchen, he turned back and asked, "Does the smell of coffee bother you?" She shook her head. "I'm glad about that because Owen without coffee is like a bear after honey."

Her laughter followed him, and he grinned, though it fell when he was out of sight. He leaned back against the counter and dropped his head into his hands. There was so little time for them, and it was unfair. He didn't blame her at all. She wasn't selfish; she was human. He wasn't sure how he would manage without her, even though he'd only known her an hour, but he promised himself right then, he would cherish every moment, and remember her forever.

He heard the front door, and he popped his head out of the kitchen, watching Owen bypass the sofa with a glance, and Evan realised Jessica had fallen asleep. She was likely to be exhausted all the time.

When Owen entered the kitchen, Evan's composure fell. He wrapped his arms around Owen and tucked his face into his neck as the tears flowed. Owen just held him, rubbing his back and rocking them gently from side to side. It took him a long few minutes to calm, and then he lifted his head.

"Sorry."

"Don't be. Just confirm that you are physically okay, right at this minute?"

Evan chuckled and reached for some tissue to wipe his face. "I'm fine." He blew out a breath and checked on Jessica again before explaining the situation with her. "So, she only has a month or so left."

Owen cupped his face. "I'm so sorry, Evan."

"It's okay. I love that I'll get to know her. I hate that I'll lose her, but at least I know who she is."

They made the drinks and took them into the room, talking quietly between them so they didn't disturb her. When she woke, after only half an hour, she apologised.

"Power naps are what get me through the day," she explained. "But they can happen when I least expect it."

"Don't ever worry about falling asleep on us. We'll look after you," Owen said, leaning forward to hold out his hand. "I'm Owen."

"Jessica." Her jaw dropped. "You're..." Her hands covered her mouth, and she glanced at Evan.

"I'm...?" Owen frowned.

"You're Prince Frederick's bodyguard."

Owen and Evan chuckled. "Yes, I am."

"Wow. I love the royal family, but I've never been so close to royalty."

Owen boomed a laugh. "I'm about as far from royalty as you get."

"No, I mean proximity. It's difficult for me to attend events and things, so I've never had the chance to see them up close or in passing. It's nice to meet you."

"I'm nothing special," Owen said, but Evan glared at him.

"You are to me," he said, and Owen swallowed hard.

"Aww, you two are so cute." Jessica reached for her drink, and Evan passed it to her. "So, tell me about you two."

They spent the next hour talking about anything and everything, catching up on all the things they'd missed by not being brought up together. They seemed to have the same taste in music, but whereas Evan couldn't carry a tune, Jessica had a lovely voice. She also used to play the piano but couldn't keep up with it.

When she stood to leave, Evan gave her carte blanche to come over whenever she wanted, and after Owen disappeared for a few minutes, he came back and offered her a dream.

"I've cleared it with my boss that we can give you a tour of Windsor Castle whenever you have the time. You might get to meet some royals if they're there on whichever day you choose."

Jessica's eyes widened, and she covered her mouth again. "Seriously?" Owen nodded, and Evan could barely withhold his grin. "*Any* day. I do nothing, so I can come any day."

Evan glanced at Owen, who nodded, and he turned back. "Tomorrow?"

"Yes!" she squealed, and Evan pulled her into a hug.

"Would you like me to pick you up?" Owen asked. "This one here still can't drive yet."

"No, it's okay. I'll get a taxi here. Don't go to any trouble."

Owen stepped closer. "It's no trouble, Jessica. You're family now."

Tears filled her eyes. "In that case, yes, please."

"Let me take you home," Owen said.

She shook her head. "I already have a taxi waiting. But thank you."

"Oh, I have something for you," Evan said, grabbing the gift from the shelf.

"Evan, it's lovely." She shook it and frowned. "But when did you get it? You said you haven't known about me for long."

"We went away, and I saw it. I thought you might like it."

"I do." She hugged him. "Thank you."

They finished making plans for the next day, and then they saw her to the waiting taxi before waving her off. As the door closed behind them, Evan stared at nothing, trying to sort through his feelings.

"How did our parents produce me and her from them? I was expecting her to be more like them, but she's so…"

"Like you," Owen finished. Evan shook his head, but Owen continued. "She is. You look alike, you act alike. You have the same mannerisms for certain things. There would be no denying you're related if no one knew." He chuckled. "Besides, it's that whole nature versus nurture debate that no one can agree on."

Evan swallowed hard and stared at Owen, wanting to ask a question but not knowing how to. In true psychic fashion, Owen stepped closer.

"Talk to me, Ev. Tell me what's going on in that head of yours."

"This question might hurt…" Owen smiled as if he'd expected it. "Does it feel worse losing someone unexpectedly or *knowing* you're going to lose them?"

Owen blew out a breath, his eyes off to the side as he thought about his answer. Then he met Evan's gaze again. "I think they both hurt the same. Even though Amy was only missing in the beginning, I think…deep inside somewhere, I knew she wouldn't come home. I hoped, don't get me wrong, but I think I knew." He fiddled with the buttons on his shirt. "One of the worst things was the sheer helplessness I felt, and I expect you'll feel the same."

He slid his arms around Evan, pulling him to his chest. "It'll be awful. You'll feel anger, resentment, frustration, and every other emotion that you could possibly feel because you can't change a thing." He lifted Evan's chin, brushing away his tears. "But I'll be here with you—both of you—every step of the way."

Evan kissed him and then tucked his head back into Owen's neck and held on. This was going to suck, even more than the concussion, but he wouldn't change anything because at least he got to know his sister before it was too late.

26

Owen

When Owen pulled up outside Evan's parents' house the following morning, he sent a message to Jessica telling her he was there. There was no way he was knocking on the door because he could only hold back to a certain extent, and if they said anything to him...

She acknowledged the message with a thumbs up, and he waited for her to come out. As she did, her mother was behind her, helping her down the steps. Owen climbed out of the car and held out his arm for Jessica to take when she arrived at the gate. He didn't acknowledge Bernadette at all. He couldn't.

"Good morning, princess. Are you ready for your adventure today?"

Jessica's smile lit up the grim, sunless day. "Yes, I'm so excited."

He helped her into the front seat and rounded the car again, seeing Bernadette waiting at the gate with a wheelchair. Swallowing down any anger for the moment, he headed towards her.

"Please look after her," Bernadette said.

"I look after family. No matter what they did or didn't do."

Bernadette's expression crumpled, but she just sniffed and nodded. "Jessica won't always say when she needs the wheelchair, but she has a tell." As much as he didn't want to listen, he did. "She'll rub her side and rotate her shoulder as if she has an ache in it, but it usually means she's getting tired. She might fight you about the wheelchair, but please put your foot down. She needs it, despite what she thinks."

Owen nodded and put the wheelchair in the back of the car before climbing into the driver's seat again. "All ready?"

"She told you about my tell, didn't she?" Owen grinned. "Damn woman," but she said it fondly. She waved at her mother, and they headed off.

Evan had wanted to come, but he hadn't wanted to see his parents, so he'd decided to stay home. They would pick him up before heading to Windsor Castle. His concussion had eased, which was a good thing, though Owen would still keep an eye on him.

"I know I'm going to cause Evan a lot of pain, and I'm really sorry you'll have to pick up the pieces."

Owen's throat tightened. "You don't need to be sorry. Getting to know you is worth it."

"How can you say that?"

It didn't seem like she knew about Amy, so he told her what happened. "We got through that, and we'll get through this. I promise you, it's worth it despite the pain we will feel."

Jessica pulled a tissue from her bag and wiped her face. "I'm sorry you went through that. Amy sounds like a wonderful girl. I would've liked to meet her."

"You and her would've got on well. I can guarantee it." He laughed.

Evan was waiting outside the door when they pulled up, and he climbed into the backseat. "Hey, you," he said with more excitement in his voice than he'd remembered hearing for a while.

"Hey, yourself," Jessica said back, grinning at him.

"Ready to meet royalty?" Evan teased as Owen pulled back out onto the road.

"It's fine if no one's there. I know they're busy. I'm looking forward to seeing the castle."

Evan frowned at Owen, but he shook his head. He hadn't told Jessica that she was, indeed, about to meet royalty. He'd arranged for certain royals to be available as they were around. And if the entire Sexy Sixteen said they'd be there, well, who was he to say no?

The guards let them through, and he parked in the usual spot. His stomach fluttered—he was as excited about seeing her reaction as Evan was. They climbed out, and Owen stopped in front of her and put his hands on his hips.

"Now, are we going to have a problem if I bring the wheelchair with us?" He raised his eyebrows, opting for the big brother demeanour.

She glared at him, working her jaw, but sighed. "No, bring it along. I won't use it yet, but I might need it."

"Good girl," he said, and he heard her gasp.

"Good girl, indeed," she muttered, though she smiled.

He grabbed the wheelchair, meeting Evan's gaze and seeing the gratitude in his eyes. He pressed a kiss to his lips as he passed, and Evan grabbed him and held on a little longer before letting go.

"You two are far too cute," Jessica said.

They headed towards the doors Owen and the royal family usually used, and almost immediately, someone was upon them. And he might've guessed it would be Randall.

"Good morning, Randall."

Randall beamed. "Morning. I hear we have a special guest today." He held out his hand to Jessica. "Randall—"

"Metcalfe, the king's personal assistant," Jessica breathed with wide eyes.

If this was how she was with the people who surrounded the royal family, she might need the wheelchair to keep herself from fainting when she met the real deal.

"Nice to meet you, Jessica. I know you have these two *buffoons* to show you around, but would you care for one more tagalong?"

Jessica laughed, and Owen gasped. "Buffoons! I'm telling Dominic."

Randall rolled his eyes and tucked Jessica's arm through his, patting her hand. "He already knows what I call them. The three of them are like pre-school kids when they get together."

"I can imagine."

Randall answered Jessica's questions as they wandered through the halls, Evan and Owen walking silently behind them while Owen pushed the empty wheelchair. He caught Evan's hand in his own and squeezed.

"You okay?" he whispered.

Evan nodded. "I am. Thank you for doing this for her."

"It's the least I can do."

They reached their first destination, and Randall opened the door, gesturing for Jessica to go first. Silence followed, and Owen peeked around the door to see Jessica standing there with her mouth open, staring at the royal family. All of them, except for the king.

"Oh my god," she whispered.

Randall took over again. "Come on. Let's find a seat and we can introduce you." He guided her over to what Owen thought of as an old-fashioned armchair. But they were surprisingly comfortable depending which one they sat on.

"Everyone, this is Jessica. Jessica, this is everyone," Randall said.

Freddie came closer and crouched in front of her, stopping her from rising. "It's very nice to meet you, Jessica."

"T-Thank you, Your Highness. You, too."

"Please call me Freddie." He gestured to Damon. "This is my husband, Damon." Damon rose and held out his hand, and Jessica shook it.

"I can't believe you're all here," she murmured.

Freddie grinned. "We always try to meet up as a group when we can. Meeting you gave us an excuse because we've all been really busy lately. So thank you for giving us this chance."

"You're thanking me?" Jessica breathed. "This is incredible."

Evan knelt beside her, putting his hand on her arm. "If it's too much, let us know."

She shook her head. "It's not. It's just...wow." She chuckled. "I never believed I'd meet you all. So, thank *you*."

"Anyone who means something to those around us means something to us. Family is important," Christian said, "and those who risk their lives for us, we consider them to be family, too."

Owen's throat closed. He knew they felt that way, but every time one of them mentioned it, it hit harder. This family was something else. He doubted anyone else would consider their staff to be family.

They spent around an hour talking with the princes and their partners. Christian's dog, Oreo, came and sat at Jessica's feet and didn't leave until Christian and Oscar had to go. Jessica gave the dog a hug before watching them go with a smile.

Randall stood. "Are you hungry? Or tired?"

Jessica shook her head. "I'm good, thank you."

"Great, then we have another stop on our tour. Right this way." He gestured to the door.

They wandered down the hallway a little further, and Owen grinned when he saw where they were headed. Although he'd requested this tour, he'd had no input in it. Randall had taken over and told him he'd organise it all.

Nick stood as they reached the door, nodding his head at them and holding the door open.

"Okay, right through here," Randall said. "This is my office. Excuse the mess."

There was no mess at all, as far as Owen was concerned.

Dominic rose from his chair and grinned. "Right on time, as usual, my love." He leaned down to kiss Randall chastely—for a change. He held out his hand to Jessica. "Nice to meet you."

Jessica blinked. "You, too. Mr Ainsley."

Dominic grinned. "Dominic, please." He glanced at Randall and nodded.

Randall stepped forward, knocked on the door and waited for the command, at which Jessica blanched and stepped back. "No way," she whispered.

Randall grinned and opened the door. "Your Majesty, your appointment is here."

"Appointment?" Jessica breathed.

Evan gently guided her through the door, and Owen left the wheelchair in Randall's office and followed them in, clapping Dominic on the shoulder as he passed. Jessica was frozen in the centre of the room, staring at the king as he walked towards her.

"Oh my," she muttered. She swallowed and wiped her hand on her trousers before curtseying. With her balance not being solid, she wobbled, and Owen grasped her elbow to help her back up.

"Thank you, Jessica. You don't need to stand on ceremony for me," Andrew said. He gestured to the chairs. "Please have a seat. I'd love to chat for a few minutes if you have the time."

"If I have the time..." She cleared her throat. "Of course, Your Majesty. Whatever you need from me." She glanced at Evan and mouthed, "What the hell?" and Owen barely contained his chuckle.

Surprisingly, Andrew didn't shy away from her health concerns. Although, knowing Andrew as he did, he shouldn't be surprised.

"I'm sorry to hear about your health," Andrew said.

Jessica smiled. "Thank you. It is what it is, but I'm glad I've been able to meet Evan and all of you. You've been so kind."

"To be honest, I have an ulterior motive for this meeting," Andrew said, and both Owen and Evan straightened, not knowing about this.

Owen glanced at Randall, who waved him down, which reassured him a little. Randall wouldn't let anyone mess with them.

Jessica crossed her legs and faced him, hands in her lap, head cocked to the side, listening. "How can I help?"

"We've always been involved with the hospitals and providing what we can for them, but I find it increasingly difficult to get true accounts for certain things because," he sighed, "people tend to tell me what I want to hear, rather than the truth."

"And you want me to tell you the truth? About what?" she asked.

"Your treatments, your care, your appointments. Anything that you're willing to share. We want to do everything we can to help provide the best care possible, but when people...smudge the truth, it's not easy to figure out."

Jessica brightened. "I can do that. During my treatments through the years, I've spoken to many people about their experiences. Many people don't realise that some patients don't mind talking about their health. In fact, they want to. They want to be heard and not quietly put in a corner. I have plenty of things to say about it, but you might not want to hear it," she said candidly.

Andrew smiled. "I want to hear everything. I can't help if I don't know where the problems are, and I can't celebrate if I don't know what's going right."

"I'd love to help."

As Andrew and Jessica discussed her illness and Randall made notes, Owen pulled Evan against him, knowing what they heard was difficult for him. She had been dealing with this for many years, and as she spoke, they realised just how bad things had got. After half an hour, Jessica rubbed her side and rotated her shoulder, and Owen squeezed Evan before sitting forward.

"Excuse me, Your Majesty. Sorry for interrupting. Is there a chance we could continue this a little later? There's still one more stop on our tour I would like to let Jessica see."

Andrew's brow furrowed a little, and Owen met his gaze, hoping he understood the undercurrent to his words. Normally, Owen wouldn't have interrupted him for anything, but Jessica's health was important to them all.

"Of course! I let time run away with me." He leaned forward. "You are welcome to come back anytime, Jessica. And we can make more appointments to chat whenever you're free."

Jessica smiled. "I look forward to it, Your Majesty."

Andrew sighed. "Please call me Andrew."

Jessica bit her lip and winced. "Thank you...Andrew."

Andrew's grin lit the room. He'd finally got someone to call him Andrew to his face—a feat he had yet to get anyone else to do.

When they left the king's office, Owen guided Jessica to the wheelchair. She glared at him but didn't argue when he helped her to sit down. He crouched in front of her.

"You have two choices now. We can settle you into a guest room so you can have a rest and then have more energy to continue our tour, or we can keep going and only get one more stop before we take you home."

She glanced at Evan, who stood beside her, and reached for his hand. Then she looked at Owen again. "A rest sounds wonderful."

Owen grinned. "Good choice."

"May's old bedroom is ready for use," Randall told him, and Owen nodded his thanks.

Once they'd settled her in with any phone numbers she might need when she woke, they headed for Sec HQ. They'd return with Jessica later to introduce her to everyone, but for now, he wanted to check in and see how the hunt was going.

Brett was on the phone yelling at someone when they entered, so he headed for Felix instead.

"Anything new?" he asked.

Felix grinned. "Yes, but I'm not sure you're going to like it."

Owen's heart skipped a beat, expecting the worst, and exhaled. "I don't like any of this, anyway."

"Well, remember how you had a close encounter with a bullet?"

Owen punched Felix's biceps. "How could I forget?"

Felix chuckled and faced the computer, bringing up a document. "Well, we got a fingerprint from the bullet, and it—"

"Wait, you found the bullet?" Owen said.

Felix faltered. "You didn't know?" He glanced to the side, and Owen followed his gaze to Brett. "I might be in trouble for telling you that. I didn't realise they hadn't told you."

Owen waved his hand. "Keep going."

"In for a penny..." Felix muttered. "Anyway, we got a fingerprint from the bullet, and it matches the fingerprints from the gifts you'd received."

Evan stepped closer. "You're telling me he was aiming for Owen?" Evan's voice dropped to a deadly growl.

Felix stared at him but nodded, then scrunched up his face. "Well, kind of." Evan glared at him, and Felix continued. "Taking into account the weather conditions that day—little wind, clear skies—there was no way he wouldn't have hit Owen if he'd been aiming to kill him."

"He was making a point," Owen said. "Showing us how close he could get."

Evan growled, "Too fucking close."

Felix nodded. "That's my guess."

"Are we any closer to finding out who it is?" Owen asked.

"No, and it's pissing me off," Brett said, joining them. "Anika never saw her kidnapper's face because he always wore a mask, but she knows his voice, as does her father. But unless we have a voice to offer them, we have nothing. And her memory will only last so long before it's distorted by time."

"Anything from the house?" Evan asked.

Felix shook his head. "Nothing. The explosion incinerated everything useful."

"The knife?" Owen asked.

"Again, nothing more than the same fingerprints we can't identify."

"We should get Malachi involved. He's more tenacious than anyone I've met recently." Owen was only half-joking. He crossed his arms over his chest and paced away and back again several times. "It's someone we know," he said, coming to a stop again.

Brett frowned. "Why do you say that?"

"Think about it. 'New year, old enemy.' If they're calling themselves an old enemy, there must be some link or previous event that connects them to us. When Randall was kidnapped last year, it was Addams who was doing the heavy lifting. This time, it was the guy himself. The one behind Addams. At least, we think it was. It could've been someone else pretending to be the guy. But he's counting. Dominic was one; I was two. It stands to reason that there is an overarching connection."

"We've been cross-referencing everything in yours and Dominic's lives, and nothing is jumping out at us," Brett said.

"What if it's not the friendship?" he mused, following his train of thought.

"We've tried investigating the links between you two and the royal family and their events. Nothing."

Owen shook his head, the thought manifesting. He stared at Brett. "What if it's nothing to do with the royal family at all? What if it's to do with the bodyguards?"

He watched his words sink into Brett's head, and the man's eyes glazed over. Then he snapped to attention. "Felix, run a program to see if you can find any connections between the bodyguards. Anything outside of work, anything in their personal lives that we know of. They'll hate it, but we need to know." He glanced at Owen, a small smile on his face. "You're not just a pretty face."

Owen chuckled. "If I was, I wouldn't be here. Pretty doesn't save lives on its own. Oh, did anyone check out Mum's house?"

"Yes," Brett said. "She has a new security system now."

"I'm sure she loved that."

Brett returned to his desk, and Felix chuckled from behind them. "She cursed a little more than they expected."

Owen laughed again. "Sounds like her."

Felix continued. "He did mention that he loved her mug, though. He loves anything to do with Laurel and Hardy."

Owen raised his eyebrows, a weird feeling bubbling in his stomach. "How old is he? Is he single?"

Felix grinned. "Old enough and yes."

Felix returned to his new orders, so Owen turned to Evan, who wore a big smile. "What?" he asked.

"I love you."

Owen grinned. "Wowed by my brains, are you?"

Evan shook his head. "Wowed by you, in general."

27

Felix

F elix glared at his computer as he set to work on the almost impossible task Brett had set him. Cross-referencing so many possibilities was going to take a while. They had a lot of guards and a lot of criteria to cover. But he'd not let Brett down yet. And he wouldn't start now.

Letting his fingers fly over the keys, he set the parameters he wanted the search to work through, but his mind was elsewhere. Someone was going after them. The guards. The question was, why? It was a question they needed to answer quickly because, otherwise, someone was going to get hurt.

Once he set the program running, he delved back into the shooting. When he'd stood in the place Owen had been shot, it had been an eerie feeling. Even as people mulled around, conversations flowing in through the gates from the street, it still felt like someone was watching, waiting. Felix wasn't easily spooked, but that had done it. He'd figured out the potential trajectory from the wound Owen sported and tracked it to where he thought it might've ended up, and lo and behold, beside a crumbled piece of stone wall was the bullet.

Even now, knowing that if that person wanted Owen dead he'd have been dead, Felix wondered whether they were playing into their hands. Was he supposed to find the bullet? Was he supposed to link things together? Were they just riding their way through the already written story that finished with one or more of them dead?

He didn't know, but he was fed up with it. He wanted to get ahead of the plan. To find something so they were steps ahead instead of behind. He wanted to be able to give Brett something to take the strain off him because he looked close to losing it, and if Brett lost it, so would everyone else. Felix especially.

If Brett needed him to find a connection, he would do whatever it took to find one.

28

Evan

A couple of days later, before Evan started back at work, he woke cocooned in Owen's arms—cast and all. How many times had they gone to bed with Evan spooning Owen to wake up the other way around? He'd lost count. But it gave him an idea. He wanted to give Owen something he'd never given anyone. He rolled to face his lover, taking in the relaxed expression as he slept. They'd had a rough few days, weeks really, but they were getting back on an even keel now. He hoped.

Brushing his fingers across Owen's body, he teased his nipples until they beaded, then he lowered his head and flicked his tongue over the tips. Owen's breath caught, and Evan smiled, glancing up to meet his eyes.

"Mmhmm," Owen hummed, rolling to his back and giving Evan more room to play. "A nice way to wake up."

Evan straddled his waist, caging him in with his arms. "I want you," he whispered, and Owen grinned.

"You can have me."

Evan licked his lips. "What if I want you to have *me*?"

Owen's grip on his thighs tightened as he stared at him. "Are you sure?"

"Yes." He rocked back, nestling Owen's cock against his ass.

"You've never done...*anything* to do with bottoming?"

Evan shook his head. "Only want you."

"I..." Owen blew out a breath. "Yes. Okay, yes. If you're sure."

"I am."

Owen's smile grew. "Then get on your stomach while I introduce you to the joys of rimming."

Evan's stomach swooped, and he fused their mouths together rather than doing what Owen instructed. He was still very much the dominant one, but he could submit—to an extent. Topping from the bottom, wasn't that what they called it? He gentled the kiss, licking into Owen's mouth before lifting his head. Owen's eyes were glazed over, and Evan smirked.

Climbing off and laying on his stomach, he rested his head on his hands and waited. As dazed as Owen appeared, it took him a minute to react. Then he slipped in behind Evan, pushing his legs apart.

"I can't wait for this," Owen said, his breath fanning over the skin of his ass cheeks.

Evan automatically clenched, his body not used to having much play in that area, but he breathed out and relaxed. But he tightened again when Owen licked a stripe from his balls to his pucker.

"Holy..."

Owen chuckled. "It's about to feel even better."

Evan understood the mechanics of the act because he'd done it himself, but he'd never been the recipient. He wasn't sure what to expect, which was strange considering he knew men loved it.

Owen licked him again and again before focusing on his hole. He massaged his tongue on the ring, and Evan groaned as the nerves in the area fired with heat. Clenching the pillow beneath his head, he focused on his breathing. Well, at least until Owen pressed his tongue against his pucker, pushing inside a small amount and sending a sting through the area. But he knew it would take time for his body to adjust, and he wanted to give this to Owen. He wanted to give *himself* to Owen.

Evan relaxed more and more while Owen worked his hole, massaging and stretching him with his tongue until Evan was pushing back for more, sweat dripping down his forehead.

"God, I'm so hard I could come from the sounds you're making," Owen said.

He'd barely finished talking before fastening his mouth around his pucker and working on him again. Evan's body heated more, licks of heat travelling down his spine. He wouldn't be able to come from it, but he was so fucking hard.

"Jesus, Owen. Please," he groaned, grinding his hips against the bed, trying for the friction to take him higher.

"Ah, ah, ah. No cheating. I'm making you come tonight. Nothing else." Owen raked his teeth over Evan's ass. "Now onto the next level."

Evan chuckled, though it sounded strained. "This isn't a video game, you know."

Owen reached for the lube from the bedside table and laughed. "I don't know. It could catch on. 'See how high you can get your partner to progress to the next level,'" he said in an announcer's voice.

Evan rolled his eyes, but his ears picked up the click of the tube opening. His breath caught when Owen dribbled some down his crack. "Some warning would be nice."

Owen snorted. "Sorry."

Evan closed his eyes and allowed himself to relax into Owen's ministrations, the massaging of his finger against his hole. He knew Owen would press inside, but he tried not to worry. No, worry wasn't the right word. Owen would take care of him, but this was new. Evan had never had anything inside him. Nothing at all. Not even a finger. He kept breathing as Owen pressed harder, and he felt it the moment Owen slid inside. The burn was minimal, which Evan put down to the prior rim job. The finger slid in and out, in and out, before pressing against his prostate.

Evan saw stars. "Holy fuck," he breathed.

Owen chuckled darkly. "Welcome to your prostate."

"I knew…but I also…never knew," he panted.

"It's indescribable," Owen agreed. "I'm going to try two fingers. Let me know if it's too much."

Evan would hate to call an end to the fun, but he also knew if he kept quiet, Owen wouldn't ever trust him to be truthful again. So he needed to do as he was told.

The burn was instant, and he hissed, but he breathed through it, the exhaling helping to lower the pain each time. Owen slid inside, twisting his fingers but not scissoring them. Yet. He pushed against his prostate again, helping him to relax. Evan lost himself to the preparation, finally understanding what it meant when Owen said it was enjoyable, even as it was a little painful. Painful pleasure, he thought he'd said.

His cock was as hard as it had ever been, and he couldn't keep himself still, even as he tried to. "Fuck, Owen. Just fuck me already!" he ordered.

"I'm getting there, Mr Impatient."

Owen removed his fingers, and Evan pressed himself back, chasing them. Owen palmed his ass cheeks and squeezed. Then his hands disappeared, and Evan whimpered. Fucking *whimpered.*

Glancing over his shoulders, he watched Owen slick his cock, the squelch as he stroked his shaft loud—and fucking hot—in the otherwise quiet room.

Owen met his gaze and raised his eyebrows. "Ready?"

"About fucking time."

Owen grinned and positioned himself. Evan froze as he felt the blunt head of his dick resting against his pucker.

"How did I not know how sexy that felt?" he asked.

Owen pressed a little and withdrew, basically massaging his hole with the head of his cock. Evan pressed his head against the pillow and lifted his hips slightly. Owen grabbed his hips and dragged him to his knees, and Evan kept his forehead on the bed, opening himself further.

"Ready?"

Evan pressed back in answer, and Owen tightened his hold on his hips and held him still as he pushed forward. The burn was back, and Evan exhaled, fisting the covers. He gasped when he felt his ring give way, and Owen slid part way in.

"Holy fuck," Owen breathed, and Evan agreed. "This isn't going to be as slow as I wanted," he growled.

"I don't care how fast it is, just move!"

The burn was still there, but Evan could feel the potential for pleasure just outside of reach. But that potential came full force when Owen slid back and forth, gaining inches with each movement. As Owen's groin met his ass, they both sighed. Owen leaned his forehead against Evan's spine.

"Just give me a second."

Evan gritted his teeth, needing Owen to move, but also wanting him to stay in the same position forever. Why had he waited so long for this? But he knew the answer. He'd waited for Owen. The only person he could trust with that kind of intimacy.

"Ready?" Owen asked. Evan nodded. "I need your words," he teased, and Evan growled.

"Fucking move!"

Owen withdrew and thrust back in, and then he repeated it several times, and Evan found the pain ebbing away and pleasure taking point. Fire licked down his spine, pooled in his groin and sparked outwards from there.

"Holy shit. This feels amazing."

Owen tightened his hold and increased his speed, and Evan gasped as a galaxy of stars exploded behind his eyelids. He lost track of everything as Owen slammed into him, sending his careening higher and higher until he wasn't sure he would ever fall over. But then, Owen canted his hips with a final thrust, and Evan burst. Tremors wracked his body, tingles sparked all over, and he swore he floated above their bodies. When he came back to, Owen was plastered to his back, and they were collapsed on the bed, only their panting audible.

Owen was still inside him, but Evan could feel his release there, too. He didn't want to move. So he didn't.

"Jesus Christ, you wore me out," Owen grumbled as his cock slid free.

Evan winced, knowing he would be feeling that for days and loving the idea of it.

"Are you okay?" Owen asked.

"Uh-huh."

Owen moved, and Evan heard his soft footfalls pad to the bathroom before coming back. His hand touched his ass cheek, and Owen cleaned him. Then he cuddled in behind him and pulled the covers over them.

"Still okay?" Owen asked.

"Still perfect, you mean," Evan murmured. He dragged his eyelids open and glanced over his shoulder. "That was better than I could've hoped for." Owen froze behind him, and Evan squeezed the arm banding around his waist. "Was it okay for you?"

Owen was quiet for a moment, and Evan began to panic, when Owen finally spoke. "It was great. I just...don't think it's something I want to do all the time. But if you want to, that's fine. We can switch whenever you—"

Evan shut him up with his lips, a harsh smack of their mouths together. He pulled back. "I agree. Now and then only."

Owen's breath rattled from his lungs, and he smiled. "Yeah, now and then."

They settled back, and Evan could've easily fallen to sleep again, but he kept himself awake, barely.

"Matteo's coming over tonight, isn't he?" Owen asked, pressing his lips to Evan's shoulder before moving away, sending a cool draft of air over his back.

"Yeah. I think he needs to talk about what happened with Edward. Understandably, he's a little shaken." Evan pulled himself to sit against the headboard, wincing, and draped the covers over his lap.

Owen frowned. "Why?" His expression cleared. "Oh, I remember now. You said he had a thing for the doctor."

Evan nodded. "He still likes the guy, and I can see why, but after all this, he's not sure what to think. He just needs a sounding board, I think."

"And you're the one he chose?" Owen stared at him, hands on his hips.

Chuckling, Evan said, "Yeah. I explained how I have mixed feelings about the guy, but he still wants to talk."

"Do you want me to head out tonight, then? Give you two time to talk? I can visit Dominic, I'm sure. Or Mum."

Evan wasn't sure what Matteo would prefer, but he went with his instincts. "No, stay. If he wants to talk privately, we can always disappear into the bedroom or something."

"Well, if you're sure. I don't mind heading out if I need to."

Evan climbed from the bed, his ass making its presence known, and wrapped his arms around him. "I know. You got on well at your birthday party, so I'm sure he'll feel comfortable around us both." He dropped a kiss on his lips and pulled back. "I'm going for a shower."

"Why not have a bath? Soak for a while. I can bring you some breakfast."

Evan grinned. "Reminds me of not so long ago when you did the same thing."

Owen swallowed hard. "I like doing things like that for you," he murmured. "Makes me feel useful."

"You *are* useful. And not just useful, you're vital. Don't ever forget that." And Evan would try to remind him every chance he got.

Owen smiled and left the room while Evan contemplated the need to soak his muscles. The bath won. An hour later, after topping up the water several times to heat it and eating some breakfast, he headed to the living room when he heard Owen curse. The man sat on the sofa, glued to the TV screen.

"*—arrested on counts of withholding evidence, aiding a kidnapper and child endangerment. Dr Wallis has no comment at this time.*"

"*That was a report from Malachi Sanders.*"

"What's that about?" Though he had a feeling.

"Edward's been arrested for being part of the cause of the house explosion." Owen grimaced. "I can't believe the police are doing this to him, knowing what he's been through."

Evan settled beside him. "Can those hold? The withholding evidence and stuff?"

Owen shrugged. "I have no idea. Withholding evidence, possibly. Aiding a kidnapper, I wouldn't say so. As for child endangerment, that's just ridiculous. He wasn't putting his daughter in danger, he was making sure she survived." He shook his head. "They just want someone to blame so the media will stop hounding them about not having the criminal responsible."

"That's not fair."

They watched the news on and off during the day, spending their time lounging around and generally resting up before they were back to work the next day. Matteo turned up at four o'clock, and Owen shoved a bottle of beer into his hands the moment he sat down, which he proceeded to down in one go, so Owen gave him another one.

"How are you?" Evan asked.

Matteo huffed a laugh. "Well, the man I've been crushing on not only put my friends in danger, but he's been arrested for being part of it. How do you think I am?"

"He won't be charged, I'm sure of it," Owen said.

A dim flare of hope shone in Matteo's eyes. "Really?"

Owen nodded, explaining the same things they'd talked about during the day. There was only certain information they could share with him about the investigation because they knew it was about Owen and not so much Edward, but few others knew it. They couldn't take the chance until they had more information.

Owen stood. "I'm going to make dinner. Shout me if you need anything." He leaned down and kissed Evan before leaving.

"You two are so good together," Matteo said, his eyes sad again.

Evan reached for him, clasping their hands together. "If you and Edward are meant to be, you will be. I believe that with all my heart. Don't give up on him if you truly feel something for him. He made a mistake, but he's human. Don't let this one thing tarnish what might be."

Matteo gave a watery laugh. "When did you get all sentimental?"

Evan snorted and sat back. "No idea. I blame him." He nodded towards the kitchen.

"I heard that!" Owen shouted.

"You were meant to!" Evan called back.

Matteo sighed. "Can we watch something mind-numbing tonight? Something I don't have to think about."

"Sure. Anything in particular?"

Matteo shook his head. "Anything."

They flicked through the movie selection, vetoing several films and laughing at Owen's shouted comments, but eventually chose

Daybreakers, to be followed with *Queen of the Damned* and, if they had time, *Interview with the Vampire*. Matteo had to go to work at midnight, which was why they'd cut him off after the second beer. They'd have plenty of time to ply him with fluids before he had to leave.

It was during their dinner, while finishing the first film, that Matteo said something that made Evan realise just how invested he was in Edward.

"I still can't believe this happened to Anika. I helped her with her school project the other week. She wanted to interview a nurse about how their job was the same or different from a doctor's job. Edward asked me if I'd be willing to talk to her, and we spoke for about two hours while I did her nails and hair. She's such an amazing kid." Matteo stared at the screen, moving his food around the plate but not eating.

Evan made a split-second decision. "We'll help them, Matteo. They'll get through this, and we'll be there to help them. Okay?"

Matteo's tear-filled gaze met his. "Okay."

Owen disappeared and returned with ice cream—cookie dough. "Everything is better—"

"With ice cream," Evan and Matteo finished in unison, laughing.

Evan glanced at Owen, who nodded at him with a small smile. He might've been on the fence about his feelings towards Edward, but Matteo was heartbroken. If it meant he could help his friend figure out what was going on, he would push aside his feelings on the subject. He wouldn't forget what happened, but he would forgive. Because if his past had taught him anything, he didn't need to forget events that had happened, but forgiveness was the only way he could move forward. It might be different for other people, but that was how *he* worked.

During the second film, Evan curled up in Owen's arms, despite the bowl of popcorn and chocolate raisins Owen had made even after a bowl of ice cream, and Owen pressed his lips to his temple before whispering in his ear, "You are absolutely amazing, you know that? You've not only forgiven me for my crap, but you're willing to forgive Edward for putting us in danger. I doubt there is anyone in this world who is as self-sacrificing and empathetic as you are. I love you so damn much." His voice cracked on the last sentence, and Evan tightened his hold.

"I love you, too," he murmured.

29

Owen

"Get in the car, Evan," Owen ordered a week later, but Evan crossed his arms over his chest and wouldn't budge from his stance by the passenger door.

"Not until you tell me why."

Owen raked his fingers through his hair. How the hell was he supposed to give Evan a surprise when the pigheaded asshole wouldn't do as he was told? Owen exhaled.

"It's a surprise, and it can't be a surprise unless you do as you're told."

Evan narrowed his eyes but then sighed and climbed in. Owen's shoulders lowered. *Thank fuck.* He climbed into the driver's seat and started the car.

"Since when do you give me surprises after I've just finished a long ass night shift? Usually, you wait until I've at least slept."

Owen smiled at his tired grumbling. "I promise you'll be able to sleep soon. It won't take long."

Evan huffed and stared out of the window as Owen navigated the roads. He'd been planning this surprise since he realised he wanted to marry the man and keep him beside him always. Asking his mum for help made sure Owen didn't slip up and leave something where Evan could find it. She had booked everything using his credit cards. He just hoped he wasn't making a huge mistake. Not the asking him to marry him part, the destination part.

"Why are we parking at Heathrow Airport?" Evan asked fifteen minutes later.

"Because this is part of the surprise."

"Where are we going?"

Owen grinned. "You'll have to wait to find out."

"Is this like a weekend getaway?"

"Kind of. Except you're not back at work until Tuesday."

Evan's eyes widened. "How did you manage that? I've had so much time off lately, I'm surprised I still have a job, let alone taking holidays."

Owen chuckled. "It took a little persuading, but they saw it my way in the end."

Evan opened his mouth to reply, then shook his head. "I actually don't want to know."

Owen hadn't had to do much, to be honest. When he'd approached Evan's superior about him taking two extra days that week, the woman had been extremely kind and generous, saying she understood the need to recuperate after such an ordeal. Once that was squared away, everything else fell into place.

Owen led Evan into the airport and to the check-in desks, Evan's eyes widening and a grin spreading across his face when he saw their destination. After they'd dropped off their bags and headed towards security, Evan tugged him to a stop.

"We're going to Italy?" Owen nodded, and Evan threw his arms around him. "Oh my god, I love you."

Owen hugged him back. "I'm glad it's an agreeable surprise."

"We only get a few days, though. There's so much for me to show you."

"If we don't get to see everything this time, we can come back. I know this place was a big part of your life."

Evan slid his arm around Owen's shoulders as they waited for their turn through security, and Owen put his hand in Evan's back pocket. Evan told him about some places he thought they should go, but their first stop was going to be one place Evan hadn't mentioned. It was the second part of his surprise—and third, if all went well.

As expected, Evan fell asleep on the plane, and Owen spent the time researching the best way to get them to their location without Evan figuring it out until they got there. It was highly unlikely he'd be able to hide it for long, but he wanted to try.

A groggy Evan stumbled along with him as they departed the plane just over three hours later. The temperature was around the same as it had been when they left England, though the breeze was a little chillier. They found their luggage, and Owen led them to the car hire place he'd arranged for a car from. Evan said he'd drive, but with how tired he was, Owen had vetoed that.

"Sleep while I drive. You'll feel better after a bit more, I'm sure."

Evan sighed but agreed, and within seconds, he was asleep in the passenger seat. How long he would stay that way was another matter. Owen followed the directions he'd been given, and within half an hour, they had arrived at their first destination. Their hotel was a beautiful building full of architectural delights, but all Owen wanted was for Evan to sleep some more before they continued the surprises in around three hours.

While Evan slept on the comfiest bed Owen had ever remembered, he put his plan into action. He left a note for Evan in case he woke up and headed down to reception to ensure everything was in place. Then he went back to the hotel room and watched TV while waiting for Evan to wake.

"Coffee," Evan croaked when he crawled from the bed.

"Already waiting for you," Owen said, rising. "Let me grab it." He made Evan a cup and handed it to him. He jumped onto the counter of the kitchenette-style area that was part of the suite and pulled Evan between his legs. He slid his arms around Evan's back and held him while he drank.

"Hmm," Evan said, humming the noise that made Owen understand he was coming out of his sleep-deprived blur. "Thank you. That was just what the doctor ordered." He yawned, though, ruining the words.

Owen laughed. "Apparently you need more, though."

Evan put his cup aside and wrapped his arms around Owen's waist, resting his head against his chest. "I'm good for now."

Owen raked his fingers through Evan's hair, then gripped it and pulled him up to face him. "I need you to get dressed. We have somewhere to be."

Evan narrowed his eyes but sighed. "This trip is going to be full of surprises, isn't it?"

Owen grinned. "Of course."

Evan nodded slowly. "Okay. Off I go." He refilled his cup first.

Jumping from the counter, he headed for his phone, making sure he'd memorised the directions correctly. He didn't want to take the chance that Evan would peek and see their destination before they got there. He also patted his coat pocket to make sure he had what he needed. He did. Exhaling quietly, he tried to steady his nerves.

"Okay, I'm ready. Well, about as ready as I can be," Evan said.

"Awesome! Let's go!"

Owen asked Evan to talk about the places they passed as he drove, and Evan did so with a smile on his face.

"As much as I loved living here, I don't think I could do it again," he admitted. "It's beautiful, and the people are fantastic, but it's not home. Not really." He added a few more details but then went quiet.

"Are you okay?" Owen asked.

Evan exhaled shakily. "I know where you're taking me," he mumbled.

Owen frowned. "You do?"

"To see Antonio," he whispered.

"He was a big part of your life," Owen murmured. "I thought it was a good starting point." He rubbed his cheek. "Am I wrong?"

Evan shook his head, a smile curving his lips. "I'm glad. I wasn't sure I'd ever get to see him again."

Owen parked outside the cemetery, and they climbed out. He took Evan's hand and let Evan lead him to where his friend was laid to rest. They stopped in front of a stone headstone with the Italian inscribing: *Antonio Rossi, father, husband, son, friend. A man known for seeing things clearly.*

They stood in the chilly air, and Owen encouraged Evan to talk about him, which he did. He told funny stories of how their first appointment went, and how their relationship developed into friendship, and how Evan got a roasting when he finally explained about Owen.

Owen hoped he wasn't about to make a mistake. He pulled the box from his pocket and let go of Evan's hand. "I chose this place as our first destination because I wanted Antonio to witness something. I hope you don't find it morbid, though." Evan glanced at him, and Owen dropped to one knee. Despite the cold ground seeping into his jeans, he knelt, looking up at his beloved. "Evan, we've been through so many ups and down, as friends and as a couple, but I want those times to continue. I don't want to ever be without you. And I want to thank Antonio for perhaps helping to nudge you to return home so we could have this second chance. Evan, will you marry me?"

Tears were streaming down Evan's face, but his voice was strong when he replied, "Yes. Without a doubt, yes."

Owen stood and pulled the white gold ring from its bed and slipped it on Evan's finger. Then he cupped his fiancé's jaw and kissed him. "I love you."

"I love you."

Their time in Italy went quickly, but they got to experience together all the things Evan had experienced alone the first time. When they reached home in the middle of the night, they both passed out, but their phones blew up several hours later with calls and messages. It was their own fault because they'd not only forgotten to put their phones on silent, but they'd sent a message to everyone before they went to bed telling them the good news.

They had just decided to go back to sleep when the doorbell rang, and Owen groaned. "Never again do we tell people our news before we've had some sleep. Agreed?"

"Uh-huh," Evan mumbled.

Owen dragged himself from the bed and stumbled to the front door, not even looking to see who it was before he pulled it open. "What?" he barked.

The girl standing on his doorstep jerked back, the flowers in her hands trembling. "Um, Mr Morris? I have, um, a delivery?"

Owen wiped a hand over his face. "Sorry, I've not had much sleep. I apologise. Thank you for delivering them."

She thrust the bouquet at him and raced away. He didn't blame her. He hadn't had enough sleep or coffee for this day to begin. He carried the flowers to the table and reached for the note.

"Who was it?"

"A florist. We have flowers."

He glanced at the note, rubbing his eyes when they didn't want to focus.

Owen,

Congratulations on your upcoming nuptials. I'm sure you'll be wonderful together. I just hope you make every minute count because I've not finished with any one of you yet.

Ciao!

Owen froze, then grabbed the flowers and raced back to the front door. He threw them into the bin and slammed the lid before pushing it as far away from any house as he could without it being on the road. Running back to the bedroom, he grabbed his phone and dialled, his gaze meeting Evan's wide eyed one.

"Brett, we've just had another note. Delivered with flowers, which are now in the bin outside our house just in case there's a gift we don't want near us. Could you please send someone for it?" He gave him the details of the florist and the woman in case it was relevant.

"When I get hold of this guy..." Brett muttered. "Hold on."

The line went quiet, so he focused on Evan. "I've no idea who this guy is, but he not only knew we went to Italy, but he knows we're engaged, too. This fucker is pissing me off."

"Let me see." Evan held out his hand for the note, reading it with a furrowed brow. "The handwriting looks similar, but he's not done any capitals this time."

Brett came back on. "We have the bomb squad on their way. I think it's unlikely to have a bomb in it because we've confirmed the woman who delivered it works at the florists."

"He must've visited the place because Evan says the handwriting looks similar."

"We'll look into it. In the meantime, stay inside until the bomb squad has done their checks. I'll call you shortly."

"Okay." He hung up and exhaled. Then frowned and stared at the phone in his hand. "How did he know we were engaged?" he muttered. "We only sent that photo to a few people, and all of them we trust implicitly."

"Maybe he's watching us? I hate the idea, but it's possible."

Owen shook his head. "I'm too tired for this shit." He dropped onto the bed. "The flowers were nice before they became tainted. A pink and white bouquet. Very pretty."

Evan chuckled. "You and your flowers." He snuggled against Owen's side. "Think we'll get any sleep?"

A rumble of a truck sounded, followed by shouting, and Owen sighed. "I doubt it."

They received a call from Brett an hour later. The bomb squad had cleared the bin, finding no explosives, which was a good thing. The flowers were toast, though.

"Bring that note in so we can check it for fingerprints, though I'm sure we know who'll they'll belong to," Brett said. "Or rather, we *won't* know who they belong to."

Owen and Evan gave up on having a lovely relaxing last day of their brief holiday and got dressed before walking to the castle. Surprisingly, when they got there, they found Jessica chatting with Randall.

Evan leaned down and hugged her, not letting her get up from the wheelchair. "Hey, I wasn't expecting to see you today."

She grinned, though Owen could see the strain in her actions. "I was just talking through some more details for the king. It gets me out of the house."

Evan squeezed her hand. "That's great."

She tugged on him. "Let me see it, then." Evan chuckled and held out his hand, showing off the engagement ring. "Ooh, excellent choice, Owen. You definitely have good taste."

Owen slid an arm around Evan's waist. "I know I do."

Evan flushed, and they laughed. "Are you heading home now?" Evan asked.

Jessica nodded. "Yes, I need a sleep, and I have an appointment this afternoon."

Sadness flowed over Evan's face, but his smile didn't dip. "Okay. Let me know how it goes. I'll call you before work tomorrow to chat, though call me before if you need me."

"I will." She waved and Randall pushed her towards the exit. Evan watched them go, his smile finally failing.

"She's not got long," he murmured, and Owen tightened his hold, knowing there was nothing to make things easier on any of them.

When she disappeared, they continued towards Sec HQ. "I'm sure I've been in this place more than I would if I was working," Owen muttered as they entered.

The place was heaving, not only because guards were working as normal, but they had increased presence in the run up to the prince's wedding. Prince Douglas, that was. They were getting married in less than three weeks, and plans were coming together. It was a lot easier now they'd already been through three royal weddings in the last year. They kind of knew what to expect. Owen would be working that day, but Evan had been invited as a guest. He was hesitant to go on his own, but Owen was sure he'd still go to show his support.

"The note, as requested, boss," Owen said, holding it out.

"Thanks." The man sounded more stressed than usual.

"Anything I can help with?" He hadn't planned to stay, but if Brett needed him, he would.

Brett started to shake his head but then paused. "Actually, do you want to get Dr Wallis out of jail?"

Owen raised his eyebrows. "How?"

"The police officers are trying everything they can to pin something on him, but we all know he's as much a victim as you and Anika were. Someone needs to go to bat for him, and who better than the ones who got hurt?"

Owen glanced at Evan to see how he had reacted to the news, but Evan was already nodding his head. "Yeah, we'll go. Anything in particular we need to say or not say?"

Brett sighed. "The usual. Don't mention that this is in any way related to Dominic's case. That's more hassle we don't need. Just sweet talk your way through it."

"All right," Owen said. "Anything else?"

"Yeah." Brett met his gaze. "After that, relax because this is what you're coming back to tomorrow." He waved his hand around the room, and Owen groaned.

"Did I mention I had some more holidays booked…" He grinned and left the cursing boss behind.

As they headed back home to collect their car, Evan said, "You don't, do you?"

Owen frowned. "What?"

"Have any more holidays booked?"

Owen chuckled. "No. I think we've used our quotas for now. It's time to let someone else have time off. I know for a fact Edward is going to need it."

It took them three hours, but they got Edward released. They'd kept him in jail for the past week, all because they couldn't agree on what to do with him. After speaking with the police, the counts of endangering a child and aiding a kidnapper were dropped, but the count of withholding information had only been put on hold, but they had hope that would be dropped, too. They just had to wait to find out. Edward barely said a word except to express his gratitude and to apologise. When they finally dropped him off at home with his ex-wife and daughter, he was a shell of his former self. Which was understandable, considering everything he'd been through. It would take time, but he hoped he'd recover. He was sure Matteo would be around to help, too.

By the time they arrived home, they were exhausted, and both fell asleep, but not before cementing their feelings one more time with a kiss hell bent on tattooing itself on their souls.

And Owen hoped it would.

30

Evan

As much as Evan hadn't wanted to attend Prince Douglas's wedding on his own, his sister had begged for him to go. If she wasn't able to experience it, then he had to, so he could tell her all about it. She had received an invitation, but Jessica's health was failing. Fast. Doctors weren't sure how long she had left, but they were all in agreement that it could be at any moment. Whenever Evan stopped to think about it, his throat closed up.

So, he did what she asked and attended the wedding, then headed straight for her to tell her all about it. His parents had agreed to a truce with him during Jessica's last days. He hadn't wanted to miss time with her, but he didn't want to be around them, so they made it work. Someone was with her all the time, even though she hated it.

Evan received the devastating call in the middle of his night shift the day after the wedding. He leaned against the wall and slid to the floor, eyes overflowing. He wasn't sure how long he sat there before warm arms surrounded him, and he drew in Owen's scent.

"Come on, sweetheart. Up we go."

Owen helped him to stand, and they somehow made their way into a room, the lights hurting Evan's raw eyes. He dropped into a chair, and Owen pulled another closer to him, sitting and wrapping him in his arms again. There was no need for any other words.

He spent the following days in a haze as he worked through his emotions. Anger at his parents for denying him years to get to know his sister. Anger at himself for not visiting the hospital sooner to get tested. Anger at Jessica for leaving him so soon. Grief at not knowing enough about her. But then there was the love he felt whenever he thought about her laugh, her wit, her sarcasm. She went toe to toe with Matteo several times—and won. She was a light the world should not have snuffed out.

Eventually, he reached acceptance. Just like he had with Antonio and Amy. The circle of life was exactly that, but sometimes, those circles were a lot smaller than others.

Jessica had requested to be cremated, and her memorial took place three days after her passing. The royal family had wanted to attend but understood they couldn't, but their presence was felt, especially when King Andrew came onto screens the day after with an announcement.

Evan and Owen sat on the sofa, watching the TV as Andrew stepped towards the podium.

"Life can be fickle. It can be long. It can be hard. It can be joyful. It can be tiring. It can be far too short. Recently, I came to know a young woman who tirelessly helped to create something wonderful. Something I hope will bring support and hope to those who might've otherwise slipped through the cracks.

"This young woman helped create a new procedure for those undergoing long-term treatments of any kind. Jessica Montgomery spent the last weeks of her life helping us to help others, knowing

she would never benefit from it herself. She was a miracle, and we will continue the work we began together.

"This work was something I know my late wife, Louisa, would've agreed with, and as time moves forward, we will change and add things as required, but I wanted to officially proclaim the Jessica Foundation to be up and running."

Evan sobbed as the words sank in. Jessica would never be forgotten.

One year later

As the one-year anniversary of Jessica's death dawned, Evan felt optimistic. He was a little sad that his sister couldn't attend his wedding, but they had chosen this day especially to take a sad moment and breathe new life into it. It was what Jessica would've wanted.

They had chosen a small wedding, though their friends had insisted on a big celebration afterwards. They had even agreed that Nick could plan the after party, on the understanding it happened at the club they'd been to. Evan and Owen didn't have any information about it other than that it was all arranged, and they didn't have to worry about it. Evan wasn't so sure, but if it meant he got to see Owen singing karaoke drunk again, he was all for it. They'd visited the drag show a few months after everything had happened, and Owen had loved it so much, they spent many a date night there, too. It wasn't for everyone, though, which was why they'd chosen the karaoke bar.

"Stop staring out of the window and finish getting dressed," Matteo said with a huff. "Anyone would think you were happy. Ugh."

Evan chuckled, catching Matteo's grin. "I know. What a drag to have a groom-to-be happy about his impending nuptials." He did continue dressing, though, not wanting to keep Owen waiting too long.

The past year had been tumultuous to say the least and certainly wasn't for the faint of heart. But they'd made it through, and he couldn't wait to become Evan Morris. Despite his surname linking him to his late sister, he had no qualms about leaving it behind. He had other things that linked him to her.

A knock sounded, and Matteo opened the door a crack, frowned as he listened, then glanced at Evan. "Um, someone would like a quick word?"

"Who?" Matteo opened the door a little further and saw his mother. He shook his head, turning away. "Whatever you want to say, I don't want to hear. Not today."

"Please. As much as it should be, this isn't about me. It's about Jessica."

Evan glared at her, still not having forgiven her part in keeping him from his sibling. "What about her?"

"Before she..." Bernadette swallowed. "Before she passed, Jessica wrote you a letter, but she made me promise to deliver it in person on your wedding day. I couldn't say no. She was my little girl." Her voice broke.

Evan breathed. As much as they hadn't wanted him when he came out as gay, they had worshipped the ground Jessica had walked upon, and he could give her that leniency. He stepped closer and held out his hand. She put the letter in his palm.

"You've done your duty. Now you can leave."

"Can I..." She stared at him, licking her lips. "Can I stay to watch?"

Evan laughed, a sharp bark of noise. "No. Not even if Jessica was here begging me. I do not want you here. You are not *my* mother." He turned away, hoping Matteo would see her out. He stared out of the window, watching the clouds billowing across the blue sky.

"She's gone," Matteo said.

"Was I too harsh?" he asked when he turned to face him, fingering the envelope.

"Not at all."

Evan stared at the envelope and then at his watch. "I'll have to read it afterwards."

Matteo rested his hand on Evan's arm. "I think they won't mind waiting a few minutes." He tilted his head. "Do you want me to get Owen?"

Evan bit his lip, flipped the envelope over and paused. Bringing it closer to his eyes, he chuckled. "No. It's okay. I'll read it after." He held it up for Matteo to see.

Yes, it can wait until after the wedding, buffoon. X

They laughed, and Evan put it in his jacket pocket. As much as he would've liked to read Jessica's words before his wedding, if she said it could wait, then it could wait. And he would be able to read it with Owen, too.

He took a deep breath. "Let's do this."

They exited the room and headed down the corridor of the hotel, but not before Matteo messed with Evan's "look" some more. After careful discussion, he and Owen had chosen to have their small wedding at a hotel in Brighton. It was near the beachfront, and they had a small room with double doors that opened to the view. Despite it being a little chillier than they would've liked, the doors would be opened and an arch of flowers standing in front of it where he and Owen would be married.

With only a dozen guests, the small room was more than adequate, and they were pleased with the result when they'd been to see it the previous day. After agreeing that Owen would wait for Evan at the front and Evan would walk down the—very small—aisle, they had separated this morning, going to different rooms to get ready. He hadn't seen his fiancé since then.

He and Matteo stopped by the entrance door, and Matteo turned to him. "Are you ready?"

"Never been more ready in my life."

Matteo hugged him and slipped into the room while Evan waited for his cue to enter. A second later, Sally exited, and Evan frowned.

"Is everything okay?" he asked.

Sally smiled. "Yes, don't worry." She clasped her hands in front of her. "I wondered if you would like me to walk you down the aisle." She seemed so nervous, but Evan couldn't be more excited.

He dragged her in for a hug, earning a squeak from her. "I would love you to." He kissed her cheek.

"Come on then. Let's get you married."

She opened the door and gestured for him to join her at the threshold. Instead of having her arm through his, she swapped them so he was holding her arm and escorted him down the aisle. The moment his eyes met Owen's gaze, he was lost. The man was so handsome in his dark grey suit with light grey shirt, offering the opposite of what Evan wore—a light grey suit with a dark grey shirt. So similar yet so different, just like they themselves were.

When they stopped at the front, Evan kissed Sally's cheek again and joined hands with Owen, stepping in front of him, their sides to their guests. He couldn't have told anyone who was there because he only had eyes for his soon-to-be husband. And he wasn't even slightly nervous about his vows.

"Welcome, friends and family. We are here today to join these two people in marriage." The officiant paused. "Owen, can you repeat after me?"

"I, Owen Morris, take Evan Montgomery to be my husband. To trust and to care for. To honour and to cherish. To love and to support. As I stand before these witnesses, I vow to you, Evan, that I will be wholly yours."

"I, Evan Montgomery, take Owen Morris to be my husband. To trust and to care for. To honour and to cherish. To love and to support. As I stand before these witnesses, I vow to you, Owen, that I will be wholly yours."

The officiant took over again. "With the witnesses present, I ask you for your final answer. Owen, do you take Evan to be your husband?"

Owen smiled, reached for the ring and slid it on Evan's finger. "I do."

"Evan, do you take Owen to be your husband?"

"I finally do," Evan said, reaching for a ring and slipping it onto Owen's finger as their guests chuckled.

"With those vows, I now pronounce you husbands. Congratulations. You may kiss."

Owen cradled Evan's face and kissed him. Chastely and properly, but with a hint of heat to remind them of what was to come that night. Cheers sounded, and they pulled away.

Evan slid his arm around Owen's shoulders and faced their guests. Sally had tears in her eyes, as did Randall. Dominic, not so much, but his smile was so wide. Matteo fist-bumped the air and hooted. Dominic's parents, Tom and Chance, and his sister, May, were also present, having been a huge part of their childhood. The two men he hadn't expected to come were Brett and Felix, who Owen had become a lot closer to over the years. Marie, who they'd finally managed to have a proper get to know them chat instead of the three hospital visits Owen had done, had been overwhelmed at her invitation. And their final guests had been something of a last-minute addition when he and Owen realised they'd become a lot closer to them since their ordeal the previous year: Edward and Anika.

Anika reminded them so much of Amy, and they had still kept in contact since everything that had happened. Owen and Anika were as thick as thieves—and often got into as much trouble.

They greeted, hugged and kissed their friends and family, receiving congratulations until Evan thought his cheeks might never move again. They ached that much. When someone had asked Evan what to buy them for a wedding gift, Evan had brought an idea to Owen, who had made it known exactly how much he appreciated the idea. Any guest who wanted to, instead of providing a gift for them, would donate to the LGBT+ homeless youth charity that Freddie and Damon were supporting.

"I think it's time for photos," Sally said, pointing to the photographer who stood quietly by the flower arch.

The pictures took about half an hour, and then everyone dispersed. Their night of debauchery was getting started. Despite having to travel back home after their amazing wedding, they wanted to get back for the party Nick had organised. Originally, Nick had said he would do it for a few nights later to let them have the chance as newlyweds before their night out, but both had agreed that they wanted their wedding night to be full of friends and family, and if that meant heading home so they could visit the karaoke bar again, they would.

As they settled into the back of the car they'd hired to drive them home, Evan pulled Owen against him, holding him tightly.

"Is it everything you thought it'd be so far?" Owen asked, snuggling up to his chest.

"Everything and more," Evan said. "Evan Morris. I love it."

Owen gripped his suit, crinkling paper, and paused. "What's that?"

Evan's heart skipped. "Oh, I forgot for a second." He pulled the envelope from his pocket. "My mother turned up before the wedding."

Owen sat up so fast, he nearly clocked Evan's chin. "She what?"

Evan waved him down. "I sent her away, but she was doing Jessica's bidding." He held up the envelope. "Apparently, she'd tasked her mother with bringing this to me on my wedding day."

"What does it say?"

Evan shrugged. "I waited for you so I could open it."

Owen leaned against him. "Open it, then. Let's see what little sis has to say."

Evan's throat closed, but he tore open the envelope and unfolded the thick paper.

Dear Evan,

This is going to sound really bad, but I hope Owen, and no one else, is reading this next to you. If, for whatever reason, you've ended up marrying someone else, they better be worthy of you.

Anyway, I know you weren't expecting to hear from a dead girl, but surprise!

(Bet you thought you'd got rid of my sarcasm, eh?)

Evan, I love you. I know we didn't get as much time together as we deserved, but I'm so glad I got to know you. You are an amazing man. You deserve all the happiness in the world, so I have one last gift for you.

As this is your wedding day, I arranged a surprise for you. Yes, even from the grave. I'm clever like that. At your earliest convenience, please visit King Andrew (or, god forbid, his successor if he's no longer around).

Don't be sad. This is only ciao, not goodbye.

All my love.

Jessica.

Tears ran down his cheeks unchecked, but he smiled.

"I can hear her voice in my head." Owen chuckled, though he sounded as choked as Evan felt.

"Me, too." He folded it back up again and put it back into the envelope. "I wonder what surprise she has in store for us."

"And what the king has to do with it," Owen said.

"Those two were almost as bad as you and Anika are." Evan laughed and wrapped his arms around his husband. "I love you."

"And I love you."

Owen lifted his head and found Evan's mouth. It was unhurried and gentle but had every ounce of love poured into it. They rested their foreheads together and closed their eyes. Evan soaked in the moment of stillness, being thankful for so many things, but especially for Antonio, Jessica and, of course, Owen.

When they arrived home, they didn't bother to stop. They went straight to Windsor Castle. As if anticipating they wouldn't be able to wait, Andrew met them in the corridor when they were heading towards his suite. He grinned.

"Congratulations on your wedding," he said, hugging them both. "I'm assuming you're here for the gift your sister left you?"

Evan nodded. "I have no idea what it could be."

Andrew huffed a laugh and gestured towards his office. They followed him down as he explained. "She came to me not long after I met her for the first time and asked for my help. With everything she had been doing to help me, I couldn't turn her down."

"I doubt anyone could," Owen said.

They entered his office, going straight into his domain. They waited while he went to a cupboard and returned with a box. He gave it to Evan.

"I'll leave you to look. Let yourself out when you're done."

Andrew clasped their shoulders and left, closing his office door behind him.

They sat on the sofa, and Evan stared at the box. "I'm a little scared," he admitted.

Owen gripped his biceps, keeping his arms around him, and Evan opened the box. Inside was a book and the snow globe he'd bought her from Brighton. He pulled it out and set the box aside. Opening the front cover, the inscription read: *To the best big brother anyone could ever ask for.* He swallowed hard and turned the page, his chest aching, his throat closing, and his eyes filling with every page.

Between the pages of that book were pictures of him and Jessica. Somehow, she had found pictures of him at the age he would've been as she aged through her life. A picture of her as a baby opposite a picture of him as a sixteen-year-old. A picture of her at five opposite a picture of him at twenty-one. And so on.

"How...?"

Owen exhaled. "She must've had help from Mum or Dominic, maybe. Tom and Chance, possibly. It's the only way she could've got some of these photos of you."

On the last pages, she had put pictures of all their family and friends.

The final page held another inscription:

You are my brother.
You are loved.
You are worthy.

Want to know what happened when Brett finally caught up with Owen about his "best in the business" comment? Read Brett vs Owen: https://bookhip.com/TBVGDKJ

Or if you want something with a little more steam, how about when Owen disobeys Evan in Daring to Disobey? https://bookhip.com/JRSKBLS

Read on for a teaser of Protecting his Secrets.

Would you like to read my books before anyone else? You can sign up to Steamy Delights, a membership subscription service, and gain early access to chapters from my work-in-progresses, exclusive bonus content and more. I have four tiers available: Contemporary, Kink & Daddy, Taboo & Dark and Club Royal Bonus. See which one grabs your fancy: https://reamstories.com/elouiseeastkink

And for a taste of the free short story you get if you sign up to my newsletter...

Protecting Jason

Jason doesn't have the strength to fight his stepfather for a happy life, so, to stop the man from turning his fists and words to his younger siblings, he takes the brunt of his anger himself. He vows to get those children away from him as soon as possible. Then, when there is one bruise too many for his best friend's eyes, they come up with a plan for a fake boyfriend for Jason—someone who's really a bodyguard.

Darius doesn't get asked to the royal family's domain often, but he doesn't say no when he is. Being asked to be a fake boyfriend is far from usual, but he's happy to do it if it means he gets to spend time—and protect—the man he can't stop staring at. When things don't quite go the way Jason hopes, Darius offers another option. One that might backfire. But with Darius at his side, Jason finds more strength than he ever thought possible.

And maybe, he might've found the one person who could give him his happily ever after.

This is an MM bodyguard romance that spans both the Club Royal and Guarding Royalty series.

Get this book FREE here: https://elouiseeast.com/newsletter

Protecting his Secrets

How close is too close when it comes to who he's willing to die for?

Nick wants what every person wants - someone by his side through thick and thin. But why does he always pick the duds? Providing levity and protection for his friends and family is his way of loving them, but there's still someone out there determined to bring them down. While everyone is working hard to find those responsible, someone else is taken as a pawn in their game. And it's Nick's turn to fight.

Malachi has worked his whole life to get where he was. His obsession with the royal family stems from a chance meeting when he had been six years old. Despite hating to air their dirty laundry to the world, he eases his conscience by secretly working to show them in a better light. No one knows his alter-ego, but it's getting harder to hide.

When Nick protects Malachi from becoming another statistic, the reporter is given the chance of a lifetime - but it's not without its dangers. And they're soon fighting for their lives.

Protecting his Secrets is a kinky, forced proximity romance with a serious yet funny bodyguard and a reporter who thinks he's got the inside scoop.

Grab it here: https://books2read.com/protectinghissecrets

Books by Elouise East

Guarding Royalty
Protecting his Past
Protecting his Heart
Protecting his Secrets
Protecting his Life

Club Royal
Royal Firsts
Rogue Royal
Secretive Royal
Grieving Royal
Disowned Royal
Trained Royal
Awakened Royal
Commanding Royal

Illuminate Matchmaking
Ignite
Blaze

Just A Little Crush
First Kiss
He's Behind You
A Special Love

Standalone
Treehouse Whispers
Star-Crossed
Protecting the Thief
Sizzling Chauffeur
A Home for Barney
Mattie

<u>**Elouise R East (taboo)**</u>
Dark & Divergent
Forbidden Temptation
Too Many Secrets: A Life of Secrets
Too Many Secrets: The Lake House
Secrets in his Eyes

Collide
When Fantasies Collide
When Dreams Collide
When Pleasures Collide
When Cravings Collide
When Hungers Collide

Dark
Defying Sanity
Stronger Together

About Elouise East

Elouise East writes sweet and steamy connections in gay romance. She also touches on taboo stories under the name Elouise R East.

Books that tell the stories where friendship and family are the focal point - be it blood family or chosen - are very important to her. That's why she includes a variety of personalities, talents, ages, situations and abilities as she believes a story or character needs. She wants her characters to be real, to be relatable, to be free to have whatever views they tell her they have. And trust her, most of the time, she does not have *any* say in the matter!

Her characters come to life on the page for her as well as her readers. Their stories unfold in front of her as she writes, and she has very little input into how they want to be shown. Just like real life, the lives of her characters change with every choice, every interaction and every conversation. And she wouldn't have it any other way.

She writes books that are emotionally realistic, even if liberties are taken with other aspects of the stories. She doesn't know any other way to write. It comes from deep inside.

Who is she? A single parent to two children living in the UK. An avid reader who still tries to devour every book she can get her hands on. A student of learning about any subject that takes her fancy. An author of books she would read herself. And a romantic at heart who loves anything cheesy.

Who's joining her on her journey?

Stalk her here... ;-)

Website : https://elouiseeast.com

Newsletter : https://elouiseeast.com/newsletter

All links : https://elouiseeast.com/links